Little Nothings

Little Nothings

JULIE MAYHEW

RAVEN BOOKS

LONDON · OXFORD · NEW YORK · NEW DELHI · SYDNEY

RAVEN BOOKS
Bloomsbury Publishing Plc
50 Bedford Square, London, WC1B 3DP, UK
29 Earlsfort Terrace, Dublin 2, Ireland

BLOOMSBURY, RAVEN BOOKS and the Raven Books logo are
trademarks of Bloomsbury Publishing Plc

First published in Great Britain 2022

A catalogue record for this book is available from the British Library

ISBN: HB: 978-1-5266-0634-1; TPB: 978-1-5266-0635-8;
eBook: 978-1-5266-0631-0; ePDF: 978-1-5266-5208-9

2 4 6 8 10 9 7 5 3 1

Typeset by Integra Software Services Pvt. Ltd.
Printed and bound in Great Britain by CPI Group (UK) Ltd, Croydon CR0 4YY

To find out more about our authors and books visit www.bloomsbury.com
and sign up for our newsletters

À Françoise,
avec admiration

'He who knows neither self nor enemy will fail in every battle'

– Sun Tzu, The Art of War

On the pale, slim road that winds down from the foothills of the mountain, there is a bright white figure of Jesus with his arms outstretched.

When I think of that summer, this is the image that first comes to mind: a bright white Jesus standing on the dry grass verge, too large to be part of a roadside shrine, too small to call a statue. Its strange size is unsettling, and intentionally so. The cliff edge is right there, beyond the car window, falling away to nothing but tree trunks that might break your back, and rocks to crush your skull. The figure is a warning to go carefully around the hairpin bends, to be sensible, judicious.

Yet, when I caught sight of it, the day we drove away from the ruins of the old town, it told me the exact opposite. You see, I had, moments before, been conspiring in the cool shade of an ancient fig tree and I was looking for reassurance, for encouragement. Then, there it was, with its arms aloft, as if ready to catch me.

I dare you, the figure seemed to say, *I dare you to fall.*

1.

We were on the slow minibus – Pete, Ivy and I – the one with the broken air-conditioning.

Airport transfers were allocated according to family surname, so the others, being at the front of the alphabet (Addison-Connors, Ebury, Gamage) took the first bus. We, the Travers family, were assigned to the second.

'We should negotiate a swap with some of the other passengers,' I told Pete, as we rolled our luggage along the shaded loading bays, 'keep the group together.'

Pete – hot, bothered, his pale shirt already darkening at the armpits – said, 'It's a forty-five-minute journey, Liv, don't make a scene.'

I took one of the single seats. Pete and Ivy occupied the double seat across the aisle. We crawled away from Corfu's Kapodistrias airport, gazing out of our respective windows, past car-hire depots and supermarkets shimmering in the heat, past strip outlets selling, of all things, fur coats.

When the driver made his third, unscheduled stop early in the ride to fire rat-a-tat Greek at yet another someone he knew at a pavement bar, one of the passengers spoke up, a woman. She lacked the boldness to demand that the man stop yakking and get a fucking move on; instead, she meekly requested that the air-conditioning be turned up, just a little bit. This was when we were informed, in broken, unapologetic English, that the air-conditioning was out of order. We were all aboard a slow-rolling greenhouse.

I spread the pages of my passport and used it to fan my throat. Ivy – a small, aggrieved princess in a Minnie Mouse t-shirt – grumbled, already tired from the early flight. She refused Pete's offerings of water, shrinking back from the bottle, digging in her chin, just like she had as a baby in her highchair when offered a spoonful of puree she didn't like the look of.

'Hey, Spud, come on,' Pete coaxed, 'just a sip.'

The water was too warm, Ivy complained, pouting, sliding down in her seat, the bare skin of her thighs farting against the pleather. Her friends all had fridges with built-in water dispensers, she told him, not entirely apropos of nothing. That way, the water is always perfectly cold whenever you're ready to drink it.

'That must be nice,' Pete replied, patience incarnate. Ivy was the smart kind of nine-year-old; she knew what she was saying. I shot Pete an exasperated look, expecting a brief moment of collusion, but instead he pulled Ivy towards the questionable comfort of his hot, damp chest, and cocked his head at me. Wordlessly, Pete said it again: *Don't make a scene, Liv.*

I left him to his pandering and returned to the view – ordered rows of olive trees arcing across the brow of scrubby hills. We dropped down onto a coast road where cheap resorts spilt into the sea, littering the water with inflatables. Ahead of us, there were mountains.

When we finally stepped free from the bus, not the scheduled forty-five minutes later, but ninety, Pete's shirt was soaked through, stuck to his back. Ivy and I stood aside as he hefted and grunted, liberating our luggage from the back of the minibus. A brace of porters – local men, young, in crisp, white shorts and polo shirts, their skin conker-brown – dashed across the gravel to physically restrain Pete from this task.

'No, sir, absolutely not!'

They were to do the heavy lifting, they said, keep our suitcases safe; we were to go for a welcome drink, immediately.

A lush lawn sloped away from reception towards a poolside bar. The sweaty crotch of my jeans chafed as we headed over. I'd planned to change my clothes the moment we landed, but the queue for passport control had quickly become the bunfight of luggage reclaim and, before I knew it, we were being ushered onto a minibus. I might have excused myself then, found a hotel bathroom, but I had them in my sights – my girls, my gang, my oasis in the desert.

They were standing beneath the canopy shading the bar, drinks to their lips, the skirts of their dresses rippling in the lightest breeze. It took everything I had not to break into a run to be beside them.

'You're here!' shrieked Beth on our approach.

The husbands clapped Pete on the shoulder.

'All right, Speedy Gonzales!'

'Got a bit of a sweat on there, have you, mate!'

They swallowed him up, steering him in the direction of cold, Greek beer. I reached down to push aside the gluey vines of hair that had stuck to Ivy's cheeks and forehead, but she wrestled free. Showing none of my restraint, she ran full sprint to the others' kids, her friends, sitting at the pool edge, their shoes off, feet dangling in the water. Ivy splashed and giggled, her minibus sulk vanishing instantly.

'We were worried!' Beth said, thrusting a glass of champagne into my hand. 'We've been texting you!'

My phone was in my rucksack, switched off, nothing but a black block that occasionally took pictures since I'd gone pay-as-you-go and rarely paid-as-I-went.

Gulping at the drink, I shrugged. 'I've got no signal.'

'Just make sure you don't join an Albanian network,' Binnie said, champagne flute clutched close to her neck. She struck a forbidding note with the word 'Albanian', and I tensed at the prospect of where this might be going. 'It's only a couple of miles across the sea that way' – she gestured vaguely – 'but you'll get stung for roaming charges.'

Binnie's face had the kind of angles that meant she looked striking with little effort, but those same angles could also make her seem stiff, severe even, if you didn't know her like we did. It was an effect she compounded by unfailingly wearing her hair scraped back in a ponytail, the finish on each side of her head mirror shiny. Beth and I, meanwhile, fussed about with fringes and bob cuts – anything to distract from the meagreness of our own facial features. Ange had taken this a step further and had extensions put in, beautiful, bouncy strands of honey-blonde, which swung across her shoulders onto mine as she clamped an arm around me, squeezing me tight to her bosom.

'Just like you, Liv!' she said, landing a gooey, lip-balm kiss on my cheek. 'Always making a grand entrance!'

This wasn't true, but I appreciated the comment, the suggested notoriety. The soothing effects of Beth and Binnie's initial clucking and pecking, familiar as it was, had reached my nervous system – the alcohol too – and I felt my body loosen joint by joint within Ange's embrace. I belched up my gulped-down bubbles.

'Classy,' said Ange.

'I'll fetch more drinks,' said Beth, scuttling off, apologising her way to the bar.

'So, where's your dress?' asked Binnie.

I winced in defeat. 'Still in my rucksack.'

How smug I'd felt at Heathrow at six a.m. wearing English-weather clothes for the English leg of the trip, while the girls scuffed and shivered through Terminal 5 in flipflops and long kaftan dresses. Now I was basting myself in damp jeans and clammy trainers.

'That reminds me,' Ange said coyly, a finger poised at the corner of her mouth, 'I have a little something in my bag for you for later.'

It knew what it was – t-shirts. I was sure of it. At Heathrow, airside, I saw Ange lean in to whisper to Beth when a group of hens passed by wearing matching pink tops bearing the slogan *Team Bride*. Pointedly, Ange and Beth had turned to me and grinned, complicit. She's actually gone and done it, I thought, had t-shirts made – *The Only Way Is Up* across the front, *The Liv and Pete Comeback Tour* across the back. When Ange brought them out, I'd be obliged to put one on, pose for a group selfie, acknowledge the sweetness of the gesture, even though the printed slogan was a lie.

'Cryptic,' I replied before deflecting. 'Ugh, let's just get in that pool, shall we?'

Binnie's hand twitched protectively to her sleek ponytail.

'We can't,' Ange complained, with a teenage roll of the eyes. 'We have to stay here for a welcome talk from the rep.'

'Oh, man!' I played along. 'Really?'

'You know, it might actually be useful,' Binnie offered.

Ange pulled a face. 'Okay, Mum.'

'No, come on,' said Binnie, embarking on a list of every useful thing we could learn from the rep – best restaurants, supermarket locations, kids' club arrangements. But it was too late. Ange and I were nod-nod-nodding along, stroking our jaws, pantomiming our deep interest. It was a proper ganging-up.

'Oh, piss off, you two,' said Binnie, trying not to laugh.

Beth returned, thrusting a silver tray of drinks between us.

'We made it,' I said, raising a glass. 'We're here. Thank fuck.'

'Thank fuck!' the others chimed by way of a toast, saying it loud, drawing sideways glances from those around us. We sniggered, went quiet.

I looked down at our circle of feet on the patchwork paving. The girls' colourful toenails were expertly manicured; mine were home-painted, still encased in bashed-up New Balance. As if sensing this small up-swell of despondency, Ange's arm reached across to squeeze me tight again.

'You are going to enjoy yourself, aren't you?' she said.

'Of course!' I replied. 'Just look at this place!'

We were surrounded by luxury – absolute luxury, a virtual parody of it: neat white buildings, pineapple palms, striped parasols, fawning staff in monogrammed aprons. Modern jazz throbbed from the poolside speakers. Glasses clinked; laughter pealed. The lush lawn gave way to a raised sun deck where alliums craned their sparkler heads from flowerbeds that managed to appear wild, though were surely meticulously planned. Beneath the deck lay a private, pebbled cove, with a wooden jetty stretching out into the water, the planks just the right amount of crooked to feel characterful *and* safe. Beyond the boundaries of the hotel complex stretched the wide mouth of the bay, curtained by green hills, the ocean so still and vast it forced you to exhale. I had three weeks in this paradise, three weeks in the company of my girls, my gang, my oasis in the desert.

'I'm going to enjoy it because I fucking well deserve to,' I said, finishing my second drink with an emphatic swig, Ange nodding her righteous agreement.

It was as if both of us truly did believe it.

When I fell pregnant with Ivy, we moved out of London.

Pete's parents had divorced as soon as he left home for university, his dad settling down south, away from the family home in the Midlands. To be nearer his 'fancy piece' according to Pete's mum, though we never caught sight of this other woman, not in those early years. We did, on our weekend visits, get to know the leafy little commuter town Pete's dad had chosen as his new home. It was all clean cars and coffee shops, boutiques and bunting. The place had the artificial veneer of a living history museum or a preserved frontier town. It was ridiculous. But it was also the kind of place you envisaged bringing up your children.

Our friends were horrified. Why would we swap the fast-beating heart of London for the drowsy suburbs? The practical answer: with a baby on the way, we needed to move to a place where we could afford a second bedroom. The deeper truth: living at a Zone 2 address did not mean you were at the centre of things. Our friends were sneery about our decision because it implicated them too. They weren't ready to own it, the fact that none of us were cool anymore.

And when I say 'our friends', I should clarify that I mean *Pete*'s friends. Another deeper truth that I had accepted long ago: I just wasn't friend material.

On my first day of school, I was shoved through the door of reception class by a mother who didn't want to hear anymore of my nonsense because of course the other children would be nice to me. I exited that same door at three-fifteen p.m. as anxious and friendless as I'd arrived. My parents suggested it wasn't in my DNA to be popular. Their intention was, I suppose, to make me

11

feel somehow better about my social failings, less responsible, but I do wonder if their saying that to me at such an impressionable age was what made it so.

And then, there was the invitation to Melissa Graveney's birthday party.

I was nine. Melissa lived in one of the proper houses across the road from our estate and she went to a different school (because her family had ideas about themselves, according to my parents). I wouldn't know anyone at the party – not even Melissa, not really – but my mother was insistent that I go. Invitations like that did not come along every day, especially for someone like me.

It was excruciating from the moment I walked in. Melissa's front room was alive with the expressionistic dance of wild-haired sprites, dressed in velvet waistcoats and bishop sleeves, speaking in vowels as round as the whole wide earth. I hid in a corner, charging a balloon with static on the cheap polyester of my Little Miss Chatterbox socks until the organised games began.

The first of these was Squeak, Piggy, Squeak, which I had never played before. I concentrated hard during the early rounds in order to grasp the rules – so hard that when it was my turn to stand in the middle of the circle, blindfolded, fumbling for a lap to sit on, demanding of my piggy victim that they squeak attempting to guess who they were from the timbre of their voice, I realised I had not memorised anybody's name.

At my school there was an abundance of Claires and Emmas. Here, the kids were called things like Skye and... I could only remember the name Skye. I offered it as my guess. Wrong. Lost for anything else to say, I offered it again.

'It's a boy, stupid,' Melissa informed me, and I leapt from my chosen lap, ripping away the blindfold, abandoning my turn because everyone knew you caught fleas from touching boys.

At the birthday tea, a goofy-toothed girl in a frilly blouse teased me for the way I had said Skye's name over and over. Then she tried to shove cake in my face. So, I bit her on the arm, hard enough to draw blood. My mother was summoned to collect me immediately.

'I didn't know the rules!' I protested, trying to explain how my poor show in Squeak, Piggy, Squeak was at the root of this expulsion.

'Next time,' my mother fumed, dragging me back across the road, 'just eat the fucking cake.'

At secondary school, I filled the time I should have spent hanging out in girl gangs in shopping centres by studying for an extra A-level – Spanish. Teamed with German and (my favourite) French, I believed this would equip me for a gap-year odyssey where I would meet outliers from every continent, people who would become my tried-and-true friends. But gap-year odysseys cost money, I discovered later, the kind that demands your parents have savings not terrifying debts. I went straight to university on a full maintenance grant, with maxed-out loans, loitering at the edges of various groups, invited along to this bar and that club, occasionally, but never as standard. I'd sit in the tiered seats of the lecture halls, watching the huddles of girls below me whispering to one another, writing in the margins of each other's notepads, suffocating with laughter at what had passed between them, and I would think, *I wonder how that feels?*

I'd taunt myself by asking, *Is there still a chance to find it?*

Pete's friends predicted that, once we crossed the M25 Rubicon, and as soon as Ivy was born (or 'Spud' as she was known in utero, a nickname that stuck and which Ivy hates, except when used by Pete), I would be instantly initiated into a band of clannish suburban mums. Pete's friends also predicted for us a rambling mansion with a grand sweep of garden that would require a ride-on lawnmower, such were the house-buying spoils once you left Zone 6.

We bought a two-up-two-down off the high street, the front door opening directly into a living room not quite big enough to hold a full-sized sofa. The paved square of yard was overtaken by the numerous bins required for the complex recycling system. The instant friendship group I was forecast – another myth, based on the faulty assumption that every woman who grows another being inside of themselves is alike, that all their pre-existing interests fall away after childbirth, so they can focus on one, unifying passion: babies.

I tried to join in. I ate every piece of fucking cake I was offered – metaphorically and literally. At coffee mornings, I jogged Ivy on my knee, smiling along to interminable conversations about sleeping patterns, feeding patterns, shitting patterns. I offered a woman a tissue at the end of a tearful monologue about how Mothercare had cruelly discontinued the nursery curtains that would have perfectly matched her baby's cot bumper. One time, I asked a gathering of mothers at a playgroup if they had read the book that I was working through in hallucinatory chunks during night feeds – nothing grand, just some bookshop-table thriller. They met my question with violent stares. What was I trying to do, make them feel bad, these women who were too exhausted and overwhelmed to read anything more than the dosage on the back of a bottle of Calpol? I was, they informed me, just showing off.

Fuck them, I thought, and I started taking that book to playgroup, reading it ostentatiously, steering well clear of all the inane, one-note baby chatter. As Ivy clambered over the massive, plastic toys, the sort we had no room for in our two-up-two-down, I watched the tribes cluster – the blondes already back in their twenty-four-inch jeans; the earth-huggers in harem pants, newborns bandaged to their chests; the late-starter mums with the expensive handbags, intolerably fierce with everyone except their own terrorist children. And I saw this as confirmation of what I had always known – I would never ever find it.

On Tuesdays, I took Ivy to a singalong music class. For my sanity, every day required a timetabled reason to get dressed and leave the house. The location was an enormous church hall, of which we occupied one small corner, sitting cross-legged on the dusty floor. The surrounding unused space was intoxicating to Ivy, and no amount of cajoling or tambourine-banging would convince her to stay within the confines of our circle. She crawled, she rolled, she basked in that expanse of parquet, like a dog in a field full of fox droppings. And I – understanding how she felt – let her.

This enraged the class leader.

'Can you please bring her back?' she snapped, transforming from Truly Scrumptious to head of the Gestapo between the bars of each song. I did as I was told – clambered to my feet, scooped up Ivy, dumped her back in position, only for her to squirm free again, giggling at this brilliant game of fetch.

Rage leached into the class leader's singing, into the ditties about bus wheels and bobbin-winding, and the mother beside me, to my left, tipped her head forward and began gently shaking. Knowing this crowd well, I presumed she was crying; music, however inane, had the knack of triggering a new mother's persistent undercurrent of depression.

But no, the woman was, beneath her mess of hair, sniggering – at Ivy, at me, at our absurd battle with the nursery rhyme *führer*.

From my right came another snort, from a woman with a scraped-back ponytail.

I looked to each of them in turn, and as soon as we made eye contact, that was it, we were done for. All three of us were suffocating with laughter.

And, at last, I knew how it felt. Fucking wonderful, that's how.

I woke knotted in the sheets, naked but for a pair of knickers, my dry tongue fused to my teeth, the pillow bearing my portrait done in yesterday's make-up. I could hear Pete moving around next-door in the small lounge and kitchenette, where there was a fold-out sofa, big enough for a child. He was ushering Ivy into her jelly shoes.

'Where are you going?' I called, my voice emerging in splinters.

'Breakfast.'

'Wait!' I swung my legs off the bed and the room tilted, forcing me to grasp for the firm, horizontal reassurance of the nightstand. I blinked the cool, square floor tiles into focus. Pete was in the doorway, watching, quiet, stony-faced. I waited for the teasing. *Ahh, did poor ickle Livvie get attacked by the nasty wine monster?* It amused him to see me like this; it wasn't often that I let myself go.

'Was I a mess last night?' I asked.

This was usually where he comforted me. Our routine went like so: I would replay everything said and done the evening before, all the slights delivered unintentionally, all the secrets shared that I shouldn't have, all the people I had offended with my too-much behaviour, then Pete, as counsel for the defence, would dismiss the lot. I'd been fun, he'd confirm, everyone still liked me, and, really, had I actually been that drunk?

'Just sleep it off,' he said. The stony face remained. 'You can give me a lie-in tomorrow.'

'No, wait!' A moth of panic was fluttering in my throat. 'What did I do?'

'Not now,' he replied.

'Oh, god, are the girls cross with me?'

He sighed. 'I'm sure the girls think you're absolutely marvellous.'

'What's that supposed to mean?'

Ivy came to the door, threading her arm around Pete's thigh and slotting her thumb into her mouth, a thing she only did in our company, lest anyone accuse her of being a baby.

'Let's go, Spud,' said Pete, making a game of walking away with Ivy still hanging from his leg.

The door slammed shut behind them. I flopped back onto the bed. Beginning the first day of a holiday with a hangover was the worst kind of carelessness – like crashing your new car on the way home from the dealership. I was squandering luxury. The sun would feel like a punishment. Every request from Ivy – to tie back her hair, to get an ice cream, to blow up an inflatable – would come like a knife to the brain. I'd wallow if I wasn't too careful, give in to morbid thoughts of our life back home, boxed up in the back bedroom of Pete's dad's house.

I had to get up. I pulled on yesterday's t-shirt, which was right there on the floor, and seized the bottle of complimentary mineral water from the dresser. Cracking the seal on the patio doors, I stepped from our air-conditioned bedroom into the soft punch of early-morning heat.

The family in the adjacent apartment were out on their balcony – rough forms visible through the woven screen. A small child bobbed to a song playing tinnily from a handheld device. A male voice carried across, one half of a phone conversation: 'Yeah, we need to look at the business justification for a subscription model... Yeah... Yeah...' His wife flicked through a magazine and sighed, each turn of the page a snap, a protest against her husband making work calls on their holiday.

I slunk into the shade to slug my water. The view from two tiers up was quite something – the calm sea gently glimmering, paddleboarders dotting the expanse; it was thin consolation for being separated from the others. Apartments had, it seemed, like minibuses, been allocated according to surname. Beth, Binnie and Ange were all on the ground level, overlooking the lawns, their patios connecting. As a group, we'd migrated to that shared patio after the welcome talk, the evening before.

Our rep, a fifty-something Brit with a pebble-dash tan, delivered her well-rehearsed speech, and Ange and I muttered jokes throughout, finding innuendo in everything the woman said.

If water sports are your thing, you'll love it here.

This is a restaurant for those of you who like a bit of meat.

Binnie shushed us but we did not shush, and as a result, I remembered nothing of substance from the talk. Except for the bit about the snakes.

There are lots on the island, the rep had said, including one species of deadly viper. Not that we were to worry unduly; the viper was predominantly nocturnal, reclusive, and lived up in the hills. That said, earlier in the week, a hotel resident had reported seeing one by the rocks in the private cove.

Beth had yelped in response, a somewhat extreme reaction that had Ange and me snorting champagne out of our noses.

'Did you know about this?!' Beth demanded. 'Did you guys know that there were snakes here?!'

Collectively, we shrugged. Our unwillingness to join Beth in her state of terror was infuriating to her – and hilarious to us.

The rep sensed her audience's need for calm. These guests had surely seen a harmless snake, she said by way of reassurance, and mistaken it for a dangerous one. Still, a snake was a snake, and most of them would bite if stepped on, so she advised us not to go down to the cove in the dark when you couldn't see what was beneath your feet.

'But these creatures are much more frightened of us than we are of them,' she added. 'I've lived on the island for eight years now and I've not had a single snake in my garden.'

'Poor woman!' whispered Ange.

And that set us off again.

With the talk done, the free bar ended. Beth tasked Kenny with buying the first round of paid-for drinks, Kenny needing no encouragement. Beth's garrulous, loud-shirted husband was the lush of our group, the pusher. He bought a frightening amount of booze, lining it up on a table on the connecting patio, inviting us to admire his haul, this abstract sculpture he'd fashioned from liquid and glass. We swore we'd never get through it all, but I'm pretty sure we did.

Ange sent Jason to the supermarket in the bay for food, and Jason leapt on this hunter-gatherer mission, hamming it up, beating his chest, putting on a caveman voice and saying he would do anything for his 'darling wifey'. He was being ironic; they were not married. Ange had turned down every one of his proposals. Marriage was outdated, she said, unnecessary, plus it was a total waste of money. Why, she wanted to know, did women invest so much time and emotion into a single day when the relationship was the thing?

Dev joined Jason on this trip to the supermarket – Binnie's husband, a lean, poetical-looking chap, though he was nothing of the sort unless you got him onto the subject of cycling, which I was always careful not to – and the pair returned with packets of sausages, white bread rolls and Heinz tomato ketchup. I assumed they had tossed Ange's shopping list into the sea and gone rogue, but no, the boys had done good. The food was chosen with the kids in mind apparently. After a long day of travelling, Ange reasoned, there was no way we'd get *taramasalata* and stuffed peppers past them without tantrums. It was a convenient piece of chicanery. Ange wanted the comfort of hot dogs for herself. This was what had stunned me and Pete the most when we'd been initiated into this moneyed little corner of the middle classes – their reliance on fish fingers, frozen pizzas and ready meals, the premium sort, but the kind of fodder us lower types were supposed to subsist on. The other thing that had surprised us: the distinct lack of book-shelves in their houses.

I looked at Pete and we had our brief moment of collusion at last.

'Wall's fucking sausages?' he mouthed at me.

'I know!' I mouthed back, wide-eyed.

The boys had also bought, as per Ange's instructions, a dispos-able barbecue for cooking the sausages, and Jason set about making fire with the help of eldest son, Duff. This was the kid's genuine name, the one on his birth certificate. Jason laid claim to some distant Celtic heritage, which Ange had pounced upon when naming her three boys – Brady, Beacon and Duff. She was inordinately pleased with her name choices, but this boastfulness often conveyed an edge of doubt, of defensiveness maybe.

Jason and son created some impressive flames. Smoke plumed and we cheered their efforts, and this was what brought a flurry of chirruping hotel staff to our patio. The owner of the complex was soon on the scene too – a tall Greek man in expensive sports gear and sliders. He came marching across the lawn, swiping his arm through the air like an axe, issuing curses we didn't understand.

Those of us who were seated, rose to our feet. Ange stepped forward, fork raised.

'No!' yelled the owner. 'No barbecue!'

'Yes barbecue!' retaliated Ange, immediately on the front foot. How else were we supposed to cook enough sausages for eight adults and eight children? Surely not on the small hob in the apartment?

'Because, I mean,' Beth chipped in meekly, 'just think of the smell.'

The owner was appalled. Of course, the sausages (a word that seemed to contain infinitely more Ss in a Greek accent) should be cooked on the hob in the apartment – if, he added, disparagingly, sausages were what we felt we must eat right now. (Another exchange of looks between me and Pete.) What did we think the hob was there for in the first place? the owner persisted. And what did we think this place was, an exclusive aparthotel or a dirty campsite?

'We know it's an exclusive aparthotel,' Ange returned, 'because we are paying your exclusive prices.'

The owner was done with words. A waiter arrived at his side with a bucket of water and – translation not needed – was instructed to throw, whether Ange got out of the way or not.

'You just dare!' she cried, refusing to step aside.

That was when Jason took over, cranking up his estuary accent a few notches (an accent that sat well on him, though it was surely affected, he being the son of a wealthy Kent landowner). He grasped Ange by the shoulders and forcibly moved her away, before employing his geezerish, *alwight-alwight* patter to soothe the situation. He sympathised with the owner, admitting that we had, in hindsight, been thoughtless, starting a fire with dry shrubbery so close by. And, yes, we had not considered the feelings of other residents and how the smoke might upset them. Jason poured the remainder of his bottle of Mythos beer onto the barbecue and the coals hissed to nothing.

The owner retreated, placated. Duff sighed, disappointed. Then Ange let loose, hollering her unspent anger into Jason's face. It was the kind of display we were used to. Ange and Jason were out and out fighters, never sulkers, no matter the company. In a sense, they were an unlikely couple – Jason so laidback, Ange such a woman of action – something I'd tried to explain to her directly, though I hadn't quite got across my meaning. Which was, that their differences were a good thing, they balanced each other out. Ange and Jason's arguing, the freedom and passion of it, was something I'd come to see as healthy in a relationship.

Their spat led to a division of the sexes – a 'boys' table' formed on one side of the patio, a 'girls' table' on the other. We sent the kids to bed on full stomachs of hot dogs cooked in the kitchenette in Binnie's room, neither Ange nor Beth being willing to put up with the after-smell of fried food. Ivy bedded down with Beth's eldest, Amelia, her closest friend in the gang, and we carried her up to our apartment later. Rather, Pete did. I presume.

The boys instantly forgot the barbecue drama. Their end of the patio was filled with laughter, mock-arguments, noisy posturing. A game started up that involved balancing an empty beer bottle on the bridge of the nose. Us girls, meanwhile, were compelled to keep returning to the altercation with the hotel owner, like cats drawn to the twitching of a dying bird.

'I'm sorry but I still can't get over how he spoke to me,' was Ange's refrain. The guy had no right, she said, he had disrespected her. Who did he think he was?

We agreed – he'd been rude. And we reassured – of course Ange would have extinguished the barbecue straightaway if only the owner had asked nicely. As the night darkened, as the drink flowed, our speeches of support grew more and more emphatic.

Close to midnight, the citronella candles lit, Binnie gave a sermon on Ange's courage under fire: 'I'm sorry but…' (This is how all our sentences began, though we weren't sorry, not in the least.) 'I'm sorry but you were so brave tonight, Ange.' She had stood up to the man, Binnie said, slurring a little, her usual poise still there in the pauses. Because wasn't this one Greek man just like *all* men, with their intolerable need to order women around? Binnie raised a thin finger, signalling that she would delve into her legal training to deliver the final blow. And he was a particularly stupid man in this instance, because he had not realised, should he have gone through with his threat of throwing water over Ange, that it could technically have constituted assault.

Pete tuned into our conversation then. There was no need for me to look over; I could feel his attention.

Beth spoke next. 'I'm sorry but that man should be grateful we're here at all, at his *exclusive aparthotel*.' She looked to each of us in turn to receive a nod of agreement. 'Because isn't Greece actually fucked right now? I mean, don't they, like, need us? British people, I mean, British money. Far more than we need them, anyway. We could just go on holiday somewhere else, like Spain or wherever, somewhere more welcoming, if they're going to treat us like that.'

Pete, I knew, would be bristling at her words – *us* and *them*, the whiff of Brexit posturing. I was bristling too, but I understood that Beth was just shooting from the hip. Politics wasn't her thing, nor reading newspapers, none of that. Her opinions were all second-hand and roughly sketched; quickly retracted and apologised for, if challenged. I didn't challenge her because the content of her speech wasn't the point. This was what Pete could not grasp. He wasn't around our table. He wasn't close to the girls like I was. The moment was about supporting Ange. Binnie had said her piece, Beth too, then came my turn to prove myself. We were the daughters in *King Lear*, if you like, except 'love, and be silent' wasn't an option. I needed to offer something audacious.

'I'm sorry', I said, 'but why are we still talking about that fucking greaseball?'

The girls howled. *Greaseball!*

It was the perfect coda.

I turned to Pete, finding him exactly as I knew I would – staring, incredulous. *Greaseball?*

I picked up a discarded hot dog bun, tore off a chunk and forced the dryness of it down my throat. I called to Kenny over Pete's head.

'Hey, you're slacking here! Us ladies need more wine!'

But Pete's disapproving gaze didn't wane.

So, I got up to dance. '*C'est si bon*' was drifting across from the pool-bar speakers. Climbing barefoot onto the low wall that divided the shared patio from the sloping lawn, I stumbled a cha-cha-cha along the bricks, curling my arms through the air, singing tunelessly in the original French about the sweet nothings we exchange with the ones we love.

What? I shrugged when Pete refused to return my smile.

He gave a sorry shake of his head as if to ask, *Who* are *you?*

I stopped dancing, stood tall, hands on my hips. It was a good question; one I'd been scared to ask for months. If I had been close to his ear, maybe I would have, fortified by all that wine, put it to him. *And who the fuck are you, Pete Travers?*

After that momentous music class it was easy. So easy that I couldn't understand why it had always been so hard.

I'd imagined that friendship required an awkward plucking-up of courage, a formal proposal of some kind. *Please will you be my friend?* It was a revelation to discover that it can just happen.

We exchanged numbers, Beth, Binnie and I, vowing never to return to those singalong sessions again. We met for coffee instead, and not just on a Tuesday, on Wednesdays too, Thursdays, whenever we felt the claustrophobia of motherhood closing in. A vast church hall wasn't what we needed in order to expand and breathe; we needed new walls around us, grown-up voices, genuine laughter.

We hung out in each other's living rooms, taking it in turns to fill the kettle, battling one another at *Pointless*. We covered our faces with Binnie's expensive Clarins masks, dyed chunks of Beth's hair crazy colours and cut me an ill-advised fringe, meeting the following day to repair the damage. We were teenagers on a sleepover – the teenagers I had seen in films at least, my only reference point.

The kids played peaceably on the living-room floor as we talked – Beth's daughter Amelia, Binnie's son Henry, and Ivy. Occasionally they were curious about one another, occasionally possessive of a toy, but generally they played happily alone, side by side, as babies do when they're small. It was a huge leap forward when, one afternoon at our house, Amelia took a Stickle Brick and added it to a construction started by Henry. When he did not object, Amelia did it again, and they began taking turns, delighting in each other's additions. Ivy paused in her sorting of wooden shapes to observe this new alliance, her lips puckered, blowing accidental bubbles. Silently, I willed her to pick up a Stickle Brick, to join in, but she just watched, eventually returning to her shapes.

That night, after Pete had cracked open his first beer of the evening and relayed his fresh list of work frustrations across the kitchen table, I shared the moment when Ivy had chosen not to play with Amelia and Henry.

'Do you think it's genetic?' I asked him. 'Do you think she'll turn out like me, with no friends?'

'But you do have friends.' He listed all the people we'd left behind in London.

I shook my head. 'They were your friends.'

'And you have Beth, you have Binnie.'

I did. Of course. I still needed reminding.

'You're a different person now,' Pete told me, the implication being that this was a good thing, me being different since meeting those women.

My friendship with Beth and Binnie stretched effortlessly into the evenings. We'd dress up for drinks at a bar on the high street or drive to the leisure park to catch a film we all wanted to see. Binnie and I joined a midweek book club, which Beth briefly attended, hopelessly hopeful that it would turn her into a reader.

We found babysitters and began a monthly rotation of dinners at each other's houses, folding our husbands into the mix. Hosting involved scrabbling together enough IKEA crockery to serve six, then making a massive lasagne, or a big pot of chicken curry, something that could be forked into your mouth while you sat on the sofa, or on the living-room rug, none of us having a kitchen table big enough to accommodate the whole group.

Sometimes we'd all go out to a local pub, and when we did, I would stall on my way back from the bathroom so that I could observe the group from a distance: Pete and Kenny in intense conversation, Dev trying to explain the wonders of cricket to Beth, Beth misunderstanding everything on purpose, Binnie laughing along, physically nudging Dev towards a different subject. I just needed to stand there and take it all in, truly believe it – that these people were my actual friends, my brilliant gang.

And the gang grew. Beth had another girl, Paige, and Binnie gave birth to a second son, George, soon afterwards. Their pregnancies overlapped in a staggered sequence of wilting, blooming and popping. I was there for it all, ever-enthusiastic when Beth demanded someone place a hand on her swollen belly to feel the kicks, sympathetic to Binnie's detailed accounts of her morning sickness. I cradled both of their tiny babies in those first, private, animal days, when all you want to do is hide away. I brought congratulations cards and meals for their freezers, and I buried my envy. Pete and I had been trying for a second baby for a while but with no luck. The girls knew and they were kind. It would happen soon enough, Binnie said, I just needed to not want it so much.

But I did want it, desperately, more than ever. I wanted to be like the others. I wanted Ivy to have a little brother or sister. Amelia and Henry's bond had continued to flourish. He prepared food for Amelia's cuddly toys; Amelia brought jigsaws to playdates specifically so Henry could help her complete them. Ivy continued to watch from the sidelines.

I tried to help. The next time Amelia and Henry joined forces on a Stickle Brick construction, I broke off from conversation with Beth and Binnie, picked up Ivy and planted her in the centre of the game. I pushed a brick into her hand.

'Take it,' I said. 'Just take it.'

Ivy, who was already distressed that I had yanked her away from her colouring book, began to wail. I stopped dead, suddenly able to hear myself:

Take the Stickle Brick, Ivy.

Just eat the fucking cake, Ivy.

I burst into tears.

Crying was nothing strange. All three of us, perpetually tired and overwhelmed, were prone to it as we shared our daily, micro exasperations. Even Binnie, who had a tough, legal-eagle persona that she slipped on as easily as a jacket. But as I soothed Ivy, I apologised for this outburst. I was stressed, I said, about not getting pregnant, about feeling left out, about how we wouldn't qualify for IVF or have the money to pay for it, about depriving Ivy of a sibling, Ivy who just didn't seem to be able to join in. She would likely turn out like me, I said, in this flood of self-justification, 'me, who had zero friends until I met you two'. I came to a halt, ashamed. I hadn't meant to share that – how I had been unwanted all those years.

Binnie assumed this was a cue for one of them to object. 'Of course you had friends!' she said. 'Of course people liked you.'

I lacked the energy to pretend. 'Until you guys, I thought I'd missed the boat,' I said.

Beth pulled back. 'What, like, no friends at all?'

'Well, there was Gabi...' I said. I had to offer them something.

Gabi. I'd met her while working a part-time job at uni, in a café in the Winter Gardens. Gabi was British-born with a German father and had taken up her history of art degree late. This, combined with her sophisticated, androgynous way of dressing, gave her the air of an exotic grand dame – though she was probably only twenty-six. Gabi taught me the foibles of the café's temperamental espresso machine and on breaks, out back by the bins, regaled me with her many opinions: the beatification of Lady Diana had come too late, pop culture was inherently misogynistic, and those swishy-haired rich girls who were studying for vocational degrees, they could just fuck off.

After a shift, we'd go to my digs and smoke roll-ups that always contained a little something-something. We'd climb out of my bedroom window and lie back on the flat roof, which Gabi generously called my 'balcony'. It had never occurred to me to venture out onto that flat roof until Gabi came along. I'd taken my landlady's warnings as gospel – it wasn't safe, the roof wouldn't hold the weight. With Gabi, I was more carefree, more fun. Through her, I believed, I had found my true self. So when she asked if I fancied spending the Easter holidays with her in Berlin, my answer was a-thousand-times-yes.

Gabi missed the last week of lectures and headed out to Germany early to see her dad. She would meet me there, she said, at Tegel airport, but she didn't turn up. I found a payphone and called the plus-four-nine number she'd given me in case of an emergency.

'You need to get a bus,' she said, like this was obvious, like it was irritating to her to have to spell it out. She told me the name of a bar I should head for.

When I arrived, Gabi was drinking beer with friends – a white boy with dreads and a shaven-headed girl in combats. Word had just landed where the party was going to be that night so there was no time for me to drop my rucksack at the place where we were staying. (At her dad's? At a mate's? Gabi had been vague.) The party wouldn't wait. The shaven-headed girl led us on the chase, past silent shops and towers of concrete, through court-yard mazes, their walls speckled by wartime bullets. It was a stark and broken part of the city, but I loved it. I felt like I fitted right in.

We joined a queue outside a pulsing warehouse. The make-shift sign read *Sex im Weltraum* – Sex in Space. All around us were crop-haired boys, long-haired boys, pink-haired boys and a herbal fug. Our group of four became eight, twelve, more, and by the time we'd reached the entrance, though I only grasped every other word of what was said, a deal had been struck: that night we would all stick together. Moving as one on the dancefloor, climbing the crescendos, our hands reached for the twitching lasers as sweat trickled down our spines and down the graffitied walls. I let go because I knew the room, the music, would hold me.

The place we were staying, it turned out, was an abandoned building, lit by industrial torches coiling from a noisy generator. Gabi pulled me up a seemingly endless staircase, into a room with a mattress on the ground. She pushed me down onto it, crashing on top of me, her elbow smashing against my lip.

'Don't worry,' she said, 'I'll kiss it better.'

Her mouth was on mine, her hand working at the front of my jeans. I shoved her away, laughing, assuming she was high.

'Come on, Gabs,' I said, 'we're friends.'

Her reply was entirely sober. 'You think,' she spat, 'that I would waste my time bringing a *friend* all the way to Berlin?'

The fairy-tale quality of that torchlit room fell away.

But I'd paid for my own flight, I argued, and wasn't this just a squat? I was trying to prove that I was no freeloader, but it came out sounding rude. Gabi told me to leave. I took a breath to protest, but what could I say? How could we come back from this? I knew we were done. I left, and walked the river, dog-tired and stunned, my rucksack heavy on my back. I followed a long section of the Wall then trailed through the dark alleys of Mitte. All the while I tried to work out where it had gone wrong, where *I* had got it wrong. The pain was too much – to have been given a small taste of friendship, to have experienced the intoxicating feeling, only to have it snatched away again. I didn't want to go back to my uni digs alone, couldn't contemplate sitting out on that flat roof by myself, but what choice did I have? Morning came and I caught the bus to Tegel airport.

I finished my story by telling Beth and Binnie how much I wanted to go back. I knew that version of Berlin didn't exist anymore; it had been cleaned up since the turn of the century. It wouldn't be the same, but that was okay. I could go back, and this time it would all be different.

Beth and Binnie were silent.

'I mean, it wasn't a total disaster!' I countered, suddenly aware of how miserable I sounded. 'I met Pete for the first time as I waited on the platform for the Gatwick Express. He was heading back to uni too, my uni. How about that! He was just standing there, as tall and shaggy as he is now, wearing an awful Smashing Pumpkins t-shirt that he still won't throw away. It was from the *Infinite Sadness* tour, and I told him, that's what I'd just been on.' I shut my mouth.

Still, the girls were quiet.

Beth turned to Binnie. 'We should go,' she said.

I thought she meant leave. I expected them to quietly collect their things and their children, and head for the door.

'Yes!' said Binnie. 'That's a great idea. The three of us. A girls' weekend. We could walk the Wall, find that club. Make some new memories for you, Liv.'

I was dumbfounded, that I could open myself up like that, expose the rawness within and still be accepted, be held closer even.

Berlin immediately went onto the list of things we were going to do once Beth and Binnie stopped breastfeeding. We put that trip right at the top. And I was excited. Not least to discover, through our friendship, how much more of my true self I'd let bubble to the surface.

The initial days of the holiday were lazy and pool-bound. We fell wordlessly into a routine.

Breakfast was taken as late as possible, with the family up earliest responsible for claiming a long table in the restaurant, big enough to accommodate us all. Pete and I took it in turns to accompany Ivy, maintaining the fiction he had cooked up that first morning when I'd stayed in our room, hungover.

'Is Liv okay?' the others had wanted to know. 'Is something wrong?'

'She's fine!' Pete told them. 'We've just agreed to give each other alternating lie-ins.'

He was so pleased with himself when he relayed this exchange, so proud of his ingenious cover-up. Instinctively, he'd known, without me having to ask, that we must present a united, happy front to the girls. I could anticipate Ivy's wants and needs the same way. I felt like a coddled child.

'You are much better at lie-ins than the other mums,' Ivy informed me, back in our room, snapping the elastic of her Mickey Mouse swimsuit onto her shoulders. 'Once you've had two children you just can't do it anymore.'

'Is that so?' I replied.

This was a recent habit of Ivy's – parroting the adults, with no concept of discretion. She had cultivated a grown-up tone of voice but lacked her own vocabulary to match it. On the second morning, when it was my turn to take Ivy to breakfast, she steered me around the buffet in the manner of a world-weary tour guide, advising me to avoid the 'yukky' eggs because they had tomatoes mixed in with them. The mini chocolate croissants were 'much betterer' than the ones that we ate at home, but were small, so I was to take two to ensure I felt 'all full up'.

After breakfast, our routine was to return to our rooms and get ready for the pool. The boys stayed behind and bagsied loungers, guarding them, cups of coffee in hand. That first week we harboured hopes of securing a spot on the raised sun deck with its craning alliums and uninterrupted view of the bay, but soon learnt those places were the preserve of the *super* early risers.

'I'm going to get up at six tomorrow,' Dev would say in all confidence the night before, taking a generous swig of beer, anointing himself a hero before the fact. 'I'll throw some towels down, then get out on a paddleboard while the conditions are still calm.' He never did.

So, we occupied two rows of poolside loungers beneath the largest of the pineapple palms. From that choice spot, we kept an eye on the kids in the water as they attacked their assault course of rainbow Lilos and blow-up donuts while remaining far enough away to avoid getting splashed.

That first morning when Pete and Ivy returned to the room after breakfast, they changed quickly, leaving me to nurse my hangover a little while longer. Morbid thoughts descended, just as I'd anticipated, but it wasn't the miseries of our boxed-up life back home that plagued me as I took the stone steps down from our apartment. Robbed of my layers of English-weather clothing and wearing only a bikini, I was filled with dread about my body, and how the others would perceive it.

I was thin. The baby weight we'd all retained and added to with our boozy nights together – mine had gone. You could see my ribs, my collarbones, the crests of my pelvis. Disaster was the cause, so who could possibly begrudge me this meagre silver lining of weight loss with no effort whatsoever? The girls could. I was a traitor. Our party line was that we didn't care about our thickening middles and the newfound chafing of our thighs; they were the payoff for having children, for living life with gusto. My thinness was an assault on our group bravado.

On the night of the thwarted barbecue, the men had shed their t-shirts in the pressure-cooker heat of the early evening and had poked one another, verbally and literally, for being too chubby, too puny, too hairy, not hairy enough.

'What can I say?' Kenny had declared, clutching two great handfuls of his own belly. 'It's hard to be this successful *and* slim.'

They'd laughed about it. No one seemed especially wounded. I wanted that for us women – to be able to slap each other's backsides, voice quick, brutal assessments of cellulite and stretch-marks, make bad jokes of our flagging breasts, then move on. But this wouldn't happen. Our bodies, our self-esteem, they were a zero-sum game.

I wore a light, mannish shirt over my bikini to deaden the blow. Though this Greek trip had been christened *The Liv and Pete Comeback Tour*, during which I was supposed to rise phoenix-like from the ashes of the last few months, there was an unspoken quota on how many grand entrances a woman could make. No one said a word as I spread my towel over a lounger. Not Beth, not Binnie, not even Ange, who could usually find the right playful jibe for these kinds of situations. *Someone around here needs to eat a few more pies!* Their silence hung heavy and I kept the mannish shirt buttoned up as much as possible. I didn't want to burn, I said, which wasn't exactly a lie.

Those early lazy days were punctuated with sallies down to the cove to snorkel, with thrown-together lunches of bread, crisps and cold cuts, taken on the shared patio. I lay beside Binnie mostly, both of us content to be silent, monosyllabic at most, our rhythms slowing in the heat. Ange was the one to organise trips to the bar for cool drinks, to the supermarket for food supplies, delegating confidently. Beth flitted between Kenny and her daughters, topping up their sun cream, spraying them with mosquito repellent, generating a great chemical cloud that caught in the throats of the guests in our immediate surroundings. Beth would go over to these strangers, ostensibly to apologise, sliding seamlessly into conversation, becoming their trusted confidant in minutes, such was her knack.

'See that woman over there,' she said after a twenty-minute exchange with a couple in their sixties. 'She's twelve months cancer-free. Her son paid for their entire holiday because he felt so guilty about not being around during her chemotherapy, what with him living abroad.'

Ange's three boys provided the days' intermittent drama. One sibling would shove another, making him fall hard on the slippery edge of the pool or, in a particularly harrowing incident, into the spikes of a prickly pear cactus. Threats would be made to withhold ice creams and screen-time, but rarely upheld. When Brady deliberately snapped a hotel ping-pong bat after losing a match, Jason strong-armed his youngest son to the pool bar to confess. We sat up on our loungers to watch it play out, the small boy gentle-seeming in that moment, his face tear-stained beneath his mop of brown hair.

Binnie sighed. 'Jesus, those boys!' she said for my ears only, and I almost laughed, stopping myself when I saw that Ange was looking our way and had potentially heard.

The Connors boys were a nightmare – this was a truth universally accepted – but only Ange was permitted to say so. She deserved a medal, she told us, for simply keeping them alive. We SMOGs, as Beth and I were called, an acronym for Smug Mothers Of Girls, had no idea. With daughters, Ange said, you were always just 'parenting-lite'.

We didn't argue back. We let Ange be right. The same way we nodded along to her sermons on how old school it was to get married these days, to want to be owned (that's how she put it) by a man. We smiled and kept quiet in part because she had a point; Beth, Binnie and I had been suckered by all those rescued princess narratives we were fed as little girls. But I also knew, in a way hard to articulate, that marriage was more nuanced than that. I didn't feel owned. I felt like I belonged. Or I had when things were good. Sometimes Beth would softly counter Ange's anti-marriage swaggering with reminiscences of my wedding, Binnie and I joyfully chipping in. That wedding, Ange knew, had been more than a bowing-down to outdated tradition.

During those early days by the pool, Ivy proved the accuracy of Ange's SMOG theory by diligently working on an independent project. She'd packed notebook and pens, anticipating that obsession would strike, and in this behaviour, I recognised my own, young, only-child self. I too would become possessed by a subject – capybaras, say, or the lives of Native American women – and draw pictures, write stories, make models, create museums. I had thought it a survival technique peculiar to me, a way to manage the many hours I spent on my own as a kid, escaping my parents' fighting, no siblings or friends for company. But Ivy had strong, comfortable bonds with the other children, participating gleefully in their recreations of Wipeout in the pool. Yet still she retained the need for distance and would every so often take herself off to be alone.

The subject Ivy had landed upon for this project was snakes, specifically the dangerous species alleged to lurk in the hotel cove at night. Sitting at the end of my lounger, squinting into the sun-bleached screen of Amelia's iPad, she pronounced its Latin name aloud – *Vipera ammodytes* – followed by the English translation – Nose-horned viper. It was the only deadly species to live on the island, she informed me, adopting the tone of a jaded lecturer who'd had to teach this shit for twenty years.

'The Latin name means "sand diver",' she went on, 'but actually it's tricking you because it doesn't like sand at all. It likes things rocky.'

It pleased Ivy to stumble on an inconsistency like this, an error she could correct – something she must record in her notebook, then illustrate.

'Stay and do it here,' I urged, but she politely refused, wandering away from the pool to a shaded spot on the other side of the lawn.

'She's so funny,' I said, shaking my head, watching her spread papers and pens across a stone step.

'But she's just like you,' Binnie replied.

'Do you think?'

I was surprised, pleased. Lately, I'd feared there was a disconnect forming between me and my daughter. Ivy had developed a confidence in her opinions and was noisy with them. When in the company of Amelia and Paige, she often took the lead. This was the kind of girl I'd never been and never could be, or so I thought. Binnie attributing Ivy's qualities to my influence gave me a warm surge of pride.

'Oh, yeah!' Binnie said with a grin. 'Both of you just keep disappearing.'

My pride shrivelled as swiftly as it had bloomed. I couldn't fathom what Binnie meant. I was right there, wasn't I, sunbathing with everyone? Except for my lie-ins, I was there all the time. Then I found myself making my second trip of the morning to our room – to fetch a scrunchie for my hair and a hat for Ivy – where I dawdled on the balcony a while, listening in on my neighbour's daily business calls, willing his wife to take out her fury on its true object, her husband, rather than the pages of her magazine. I picked up a book and read a small section, one of the French novels I was too self-conscious to take to the pool, and as I replaced the bookmark, ready to head back downstairs, I thought, oh, yes, here I am, disappearing.

It was the hotel complex – that was the problem – the dazzling, bright white perfection of it, the way it demanded your happiness at all times. Everything we could possibly need was contained within its grounds, or else within the half-mile of the bay. There was no reason to venture any further for the whole three weeks. Three weeks. An alarm had started ringing through the circuits of my brain – *oh god oh god oh god oh god*. But it was only Pete that I wanted to escape. He'd cornered me in the bathroom as we got ready for dinner, the evening after our speeches in support of Ange and her argument with the angry hotel owner.

'You go too far,' he'd said, 'when you're with those girls.'

Trapped, I'd retaliated. 'Well, if you don't like my group of friends, Pete, feel free to find your own.' Which was rich, after all those years in London when I'd relied upon his social whirl.

'I'm not saying I don't like them,' he said, 'I'm saying I don't like who you become sometimes when you're with them.'

I hadn't meant it, I told him. That word. *Greaseball.* I hadn't meant it like *that*.

'You're misinterpreting me,' I said, 'making it seem worse than it was.'

He pulled a face in the bathroom mirror.

'Look, okay, I'm sorry. Just let it go, will you?'

'That's not who you are, Liv,' he said, kissing the top of my head, a gesture so generous in the circumstances, so tender, that it threatened to destroy me.

Distraction arrived on the Friday of that first week when a blacked-out minibus pulled up on the hotel driveway, disgorging a large, loud, well-heeled family. Beth alerted us to them and we flipped onto our bellies on our loungers for a better view, becoming immediately absorbed in the task of working out who in the group was related to whom. A mahogany-skinned patriarch in his seventies led the party, striding across the lawn, dressed in the kind of long-sleeved shirt and cotton slacks that put you in mind of an Englishman in Colonial India. In his wake came a matriarch of similar age, her silver hair cropped just so, her sunglasses stylish, huge. This was his wife, possibly, though from the way they were interacting, and from the similarity of their noses, Binnie was sure they were brother and sister. A wild litter of young grandchildren followed, four boys and a girl, the little ones pudgy, born of the cabbage patch. The girl, the blondest of the lot, resembled a character from a German fairy-tale. They immediately laid hands on swimming-pool noodles, this gang of kids, and began whipping one another, yelping like puppies.

Five travel-weary adults in their thirties and forties made up the rest of the party – three women, two men – a mixture of siblings, or cousins perhaps, plus partners. Like fishermen to the siren, they were drawn, as we were on our arrival, to the offerings of the poolside bar.

'Oh my god, how rich are they?' said Beth with hushed glee.

About as rich as you, was the logical answer, since they were holidaying in the same place, but I understood what she meant. There was rich, and there was *rich*. These people had the kind of money that allows generation after generation to attend boarding school with royalty and future prime ministers. This was estates-on-Dartmoor money, winter-breaks-spent-on-Uncle-Gustav's-yacht money. It was in the way they held themselves, in the expensive simplicity of their clothes. Pedigree shone through, as it does in dogs and horses, in the lustre of their hair, the symmetry of their faces, the soundness of their teeth. It was audible in their clipped consonants.

'Euripides!' called one of the adults from the shade of the bar, a well-built blonde in wide-legged trousers, her voice several octaves lower than any of ours. She waved her arms at the mob of fighting children on the lawn. The smallest of the bunch, one of the cabbage-patchers, lifted his head briefly before deciding his mother should be ignored, returning to his business of thwacking a swimming-pool noodle against the grass, hard enough to create a divot.

'Rippy, darling!' she persisted. 'Please come and get some water.'

'Her kid is called Euripides!' Ange hissed in delight.

I knew that Ange, mother to her own unusually named children, was throwing stones from a glass house with that comment, but it didn't need saying. Pete, by coming and looming over my sun lounger at that exact moment, seemed to be suggesting that it did.

We watched the tired adult arrivals sip their drinks, soaking in the new surroundings, oblivious to the dismay of the residents caught in the crossfire of their children's violent noodle-whipping. The youngest of these grown-ups removed herself from the huddle at the bar and took her highball to a table with a view of the sea. She had the air of someone unattached – no partner in the group, no responsibility to any of the shrieking grandchildren. Her focus was her own. She sat and removed her crumpled Panama hat, placing it on the table with the kind of deliberateness you would expect of an actress on stage, someone who knows they are being watched but mustn't acknowledge it, only make their behaviours interesting, significant. Beneath the hat, she was distinctly attractive, in a clean, plain, boyish kind of way.

'That's how I said you should have had your hair cut,' said Ange.

'Liv's hair *is* cut like that,' said Binnie.

'Not really,' I replied. Ange was right. This woman's bob had the kind of natural, easy shape that suggested no cut had happened at all.

The woman slid down into her chair, kicking off her white, beat-up plimsolls, offering her naked toes to the sun – more deliberate, emphatic actions designed to impart great meaning, if only you paid close attention. And I was paying attention. I was struck by the oddest sensation: that I was watching myself.

She was younger than me, more beautiful, more refined, but she was separate, other; this was where we aligned. She was the person I might have been if my life had been different – the fortunes of my birth, my decisions, everything, I suppose.

'She's too thin,' said Ange, her words coming like a snap of the fingers releasing us from this woman's spell.

Beth and Binnie shared the briefest glance before chiming in their agreement.

Yes, yes, they said, *much too thin*.

Pete shifted his stance and cleared his throat. I thought he was readying himself to speak in my defence. He'd made the connection too – I was that woman; Ange was criticising me. But he didn't speak. And really, there was no need. It was a relief to hear it out loud at last, to be given the freedom to be what I was – *too thin*. This beautiful stranger would bear the brunt of my friends' resentment now, so I unbuttoned my mannish shirt and offered my whole, insufficient self to the sun.

Correction: my trip to Berlin was not at the very top of the list of things we'd do once Beth and Binnie stopped breastfeeding. Above that – above the spa days and London lunches – was our wish to pull off another big celebration. This, we'd learnt by experience, was the true cement of our friendship.

Binnie and I had been godmothers to Paige at her christening and had thoroughly embraced our roles. We spent an inordinate amount of time online seeking chic, elaborate hats to wear, then we threw ourselves into the task of decorating the function room for the family party afterwards: collecting jam jars for weeks then tying them with ribbon and filling them with wildflowers; sourcing vintage tablecloths and silver confetti in the shape of old-style prams. Beth knew nothing of our efforts, so when she walked into that transformed room, met by a forest of helium balloons on strings, standing tall from the back of every chair, she burst into tears. It gave us a taste for it, for pushing the boat out.

There wouldn't be another christening – my family had never been churchgoers, Binnie's neither – and no one in our gang had a big birthday on the horizon. We were at a loss, until Beth and Binnie discovered that Pete and I weren't married.

There had never been a right time for us. Pete's parents' divorce had rumbled on and on, as had my dad's gambling jags and my mother's distraught phone calls relaying his behaviour. The idea of bringing together our two sets of parents for something joyful was the unfunniest of jokes. For a while, Pete and I talked of eloping somewhere beautiful and hot, but it was pure fantasy; there wasn't the money to make it real. Before we knew it, I was pregnant with Ivy.

'So, you should do it now!' Beth said.

We were at Binnie's house for our monthly dinner. We were drunk and Beth was convincing. Planning a wedding 'as proper grown-ups' – Beth's words – meant we could do it on our own terms, forget family and make it a friend thing. Pete and I had been boyfriend and girlfriend for almost fifteen years by then. Our parents had given up asking whether we were ever going to tie the knot. If we did, they need never know.

A chant started: '*Do it! Do it! Do it!*' The boys rounded on Pete, goading him to propose and, laughingly, he sank onto one knee on the kitchen tiles. He took my hands in his and the room hushed. When he asked, there was a crack in his voice. When I said 'yes', I was ambushed by ecstatic tears. On paper, that moment should not have been romantic, but it absolutely was. The others erupted into wild cheers of congratulation, causing Henry to appear on the stairs in his Thomas the Tank Engine pyjamas, demanding that we keep the noise down.

And we were off. We spent inordinate amounts of time online choosing chic, elaborate hats for Beth and Binnie, and a suitable outfit for me. Beth pushed me towards a traditional white gown. Binnie said I should shun convention and wear a tux. I split the difference, and chose a red, sleeveless dress with a mermaid spill of a skirt that I had to hitch above my knees to get up the steps of the town hall for the ceremony. I looked like a bottle of wine, Beth said, in a good way.

Binnie did the reading using that beautiful, legal voice of hers – my own translation of Georges Perec's lines written for the wedding of Alix Cléo Blanchette and Jacques Roubaud, the names and places swapped, tenses tweaked. I'd always liked the humour of that poem, the idea contained within it that Pete and I just happened to be getting married on the same day in a piece of wonderful serendipity. Beth coached Ivy and Amelia in the performance of a song, the girls still tiny then and so determinedly out of tune that Pete and I had to stifle laughter.

For the reception, we took over the upstairs room of a local restaurant. Just the six of us, plus kids. Beth and Binnie papered the walls in hundreds and hundreds of pink and red cut-out paper hearts – a simple plan but the effect was jaw-dropping. At the end of the room was an impressive pyramid of champagne saucers. After cutting the cake, Pete and I held a magnum of champagne above the uppermost glass and poured and – the pyramid gave way with a dramatic crash. There was glass everywhere. We stood staring at the glittering carpet, hands to our mouths. Then we started laughing, so hard I thought we'd never stop. Beth got so hysterical that she literally wet her pants, which made us laugh even more.

'Well, what do you expect after two vaginal births!' Binnie called out indignantly in defence of Beth's bladder – a phrase that fell into common usage, a payoff line to almost anything we said, the more incongruent the better.

'I just can't get into the second series of *Mad Men*.'

'Well, what do you expect after two vaginal births!'

'Jumpsuits look great on everyone except me.'

'Well, what do you expect after two vaginal births!'

The wedding became part of our mythology. I had married Pete that day, but also it had been a marriage between me and those girls, an elaborate gesture that demonstrated the lengths we were willing to go to make one another happy. I would walk down the aisle for them, and they would show their affection with hundreds and hundreds of pink and red hearts.

We kept the memory alive with stock phrases.

'Your wine-bottle dress, Liv!'

'Oh, the song!'

'But those cut-out hearts!'

'The pyramid! I nearly died!'

Saying them became a ritual, an instant means to lift our mood, a reminder of the brilliance of our friendship, and a deeply personal longhand for *I love you*.

The remaining items on our list – the spa days, the London lunches, my trip to Berlin – they fell by the wayside. I told myself this was because we had peaked with our wedding planning. How could we ever do anything to match that? But the truth was, when we made those plans, we had no real understanding of how our lives would change once Beth and Binnie stopped breastfeeding, and once the kids started school. Our horizons opened, far beyond those living-room rugs scattered with toys.

Binnie returned to law, like she always said she would. Beth and I were keen to earn our own money, but doing what? Both of us had decent degrees (mine, in languages, was perhaps more decent than Beth's combination of psychology and a random something else) but neither of us had put our education to good use, nor discovered our groove. I'd gone straight into the library service after graduating, found little satisfaction, then left it behind when we moved out of London. Beth had flitted from one hospitality job to another, finally abandoning the late hours to raise Amelia. We both envisaged a glorious renaissance in our mid-lives but had no concept of how these new starts should take shape. In lieu of any better ideas, Beth became a part-time viewings assistant at a local estate agent, and I began applying for library jobs again.

It was Pete who pushed me towards the college course in literary translation. I'd been doing small freelance projects on the side – French instruction manuals, guidebook blurbs, that kind of thing – but poems and stories were my passion. Any part-time job that I found to fit within Ivy's school hours would be a compromise, earning me pin money at best. This was my moment to pivot. But with Beth and Binnie working most days, with me catching the train into London a couple of evenings a week for college lectures, the opportunities dwindled for the three of us to get together for coffee or for wine. Our home-hosted dinners became sporadic. We'd thought ourselves time-poor and tired while raising babies, but juggling work and study alongside parenting was a whole new level of exhaustion. A fortnight could go by and I would realise that I hadn't spoken to Beth or Binnie at all.

Then, just when we needed her, along came Ange.

Angela Addison was also a part-time viewings assistant at the estate agency where Beth worked.

'Oh my god, she is so funny,' Beth told us on a rare Friday night out. 'Really ballsy! You have to meet her, you'll adore her.'

Beth made it happen one bright day in September after school pick-up. Binnie was working and couldn't be there, but I headed down to the café in the woods for my introduction. The three of us huddled around an outside table, the kids making a balance beam of a nearby fallen tree. Beth had hyped up Ange so much that I admit I was initially underwhelmed. I was expecting an imposing titan of a woman, a regal Teutonic blonde maybe, but Ange was perfectly average, just like us, short, mousy-haired. The only indication of superiority came via her dog Saint, who sat panting at her side, a huge, wolf-like beast with piercing blue eyes.

Beth was desperate for me and Ange to like one another, and she gabbled fast, selling me hard.

'Liv can speak two other languages fluently!'

'Amelia just loves Liv's daughter Ivy!'

'Kenny just loves Liv's husband Pete!'

'Liv is so smart that she's going back to college.'

I liked this person that Beth was describing; a more impressive version of me.

'And did I tell you about Liv's wedding?' Beth asked.

Ange nodded, but Beth barrelled on regardless.

'Your wine-bottle dress, Liv!' she exclaimed.

'Oh, the song!' I said, understanding that Beth wanted me to perform our ritual for Ange's benefit.

'But those cut-out hearts!'

'The pyramid! I nearly died!'

The scene done, we grinned at one another.

I waited for Ange's acclaimed ballsiness to surface. *What the hell was that all about?* she might, quite rightly, have asked. But she just smiled, rubbing at the fur around Saint's neck.

Beth leapt into the silence. 'Liv is so brave,' she said, 'she's thinking of getting her hair chopped off!'

As she paused for breath, I clarified. 'A short bob, maybe. With a heavy fringe.'

Beth turned to Ange and (hallelujah) gave the woman a chance to speak: 'What do you think? Should she do it?'

Ange took her time. This was it, I realised, this was where her strength lay, in her ability to listen and wait, to make what she said count. Ange looked me in the eye, broadened her smile and told me, 'I think that would *really* suit you.'

Such was the conviction of her response, the warmth she invested in it, that I chopped all my hair off the very next day.

Ballsiness didn't have be aggressive, it didn't need to be loud. It came across in the quality of Ange's attention, in her honesty and the truth of her emotions. She wrote open letters to her loved ones and posted them on Facebook:

Dearest Jason, I never thought I would find myself in a partnership as perfect as ours...

My darling baby Duff, it makes me proud every day to watch you grow into the most beautiful boy...

Mum, the sacrifices you have made so I can flourish in this world are too great to number...

I had never met anyone so unashamed of voicing their feelings.

'How bold is that?' I said, showing Pete one of her letters on my iPad.

He snorted at it. 'Why doesn't she just turn to the person sitting next to her on the sofa and say that to their face?'

'Why don't *you*?' I replied. 'You haven't even noticed my new haircut.'

'I noticed,' he said, rubbing his bristly chin against my cheek, nestling close.

'And!' I demanded.

'I'd adore you whatever your hair looked like.'

I pushed him over on the sofa.

'Your turn,' he said, as I loomed over him, threatening a playful slap. 'Tell me how you really feel.'

'I think you're a dickhead,' I said, 'and I love you.'

Ange became the impetus to restart our monthly dinners. I reclaimed our coffee table from beneath piles of college texts, found a recipe for an impressive paella that required four kinds of seafood and much skinning of fresh tomatoes, and scrabbled together enough IKEA crockery to serve eight. I made some purchases too – a sparkly top, cloth napkins, fresh flowers, various perfumed candles.

'Jesus, what's all this?' said Binnie as she walked into our low-lit, fig-scented living room, a bottle of wine in each of her fists.

Our monthly dinners were supposed to be easy-going, thrown together. Beth pointed out each of my new, extravagant touches to Ange and Jason the moment they arrived.

'She never makes this much effort for us,' said Beth, mock offended.

I'd been right to go the extra mile though. While Beth and Binnie turned up in jeans, Ange wore a long silk skirt, her arms jangling with bracelets, her face iridescent with make-up. To her, this was what an invitation to dinner required.

I reserved Ange a space on the sofa – she couldn't possibly sit on the floor in that delicate skirt – and I made sure that she drank from a proper wine glass, not a tumbler. Still, she seemed awkward, poised there in her finery, shoulder to shoulder with Binnie and Kenny, forking up paella from a plate on her lap.

'We should have done a pub lunch first,' I said, acknowledging the shortcomings of my hospitality, 'you'd have had a bit more space then, been able to move around and get to know everyone.'

'Oh, no! This is lovely,' Ange protested, speaking as always with conviction, with warmth. She took a pause, smiled knowingly and added, 'It couldn't have been better, even if you'd decorated every wall with cut-out paper hearts.'

Her comment landed clumsily, but it was sweet; I understood the intention. She was just trying to speak our language.

The next day Ange sent a text to thank me for dinner, then a second saying she would be happy to organise that pub lunch I had suggested.

I began typing my reply – *Did I suggest a* – but was interrupted by a notification. Ange had added me to a message group called *The Girls* along with Beth and Binnie. Then came a link to a shared online calendar with a request to mark which Saturdays and Sundays we were free.

Ange had three sons, that enormous dog, a part-time job, but seemingly none of our exhaustion. She was a born organiser. Through her, I could see how our horizons might broaden yet again, how we would, after all, go on those longed-for spa trips and London lunches, even pull off my trip to Berlin. Her joining of our ranks was seamless, and it was executed with humour too. When Ange got around to adding a profile picture to our message group, she chose an image of a cut-out paper heart.

Around five each day, we'd leave the poolside, return to our rooms and get dressed up for dinner.

In this we demonstrated absolute commitment. It was important to us girls to make an effort; to take a good dress and accessorise it well, to select the perfect heel to bring out the glamour in a pair of jeans, to execute a tick of eyeliner with gold-medal precision. Our outfits were chosen to beg admiration from the others, and I knew my participation in this game of impress and praise was going to be a challenge that holiday.

In the run up to departure, Beth, Binnie and Ange talked of the new playsuits they'd bought, the co-ord sets, the strappy sandals. I, meanwhile, had found a bargain designer sundress on eBay and some charity-shop shorts that I could potentially reframe as a 'vintage find'. This wasn't good enough. Then it occurred to me – back when Pete and I were still liquid, I'd ordered a big delivery of clothes from a fast-fashion site and in the package there had been a dress with foundation on the neckline and a drink spill on the hem. It had clearly been worn for a night out, then sent back, with no one noticing its faults. This would be my trick for keeping up with the girls. Most of the contents of my suitcase had been bought last minute, so I could adhere to the returns window and get refunded. I'd tuck in swing tags, go careful when eating and drinking, then run an iron over everything as soon as we got home. With no access to credit, I'd not been able to buy much, but if I mixed and matched carefully, I was sure my haul would get me through.

Primped and perfumed that first Friday night, we met beneath the canopy of the pool bar to sip drinks and exchange compliments.

'How did you get your hair to go like that, it's amazing!'

'Oh my god, your earrings!'

'Where are those trousers from? I need a pair!'

Ange homed in on me. My lipstick was a great shade, and how was I possibly so tanned already?

'You look relaxed,' she said, linking her arm through mine as we wandered into the bay, the first time most of us (except those running supermarket errands) had left the confines of the hotel grounds in the last twenty-four hours. 'Do you feel relaxed?' she asked.

The question seemed loaded, teasing, the beginning of something. Would it be tonight that Ange whipped out those *Liv and Pete Comeback Tour* t-shirts?

'How relaxed do you need me to be?' I countered, playing along. 'Should I mix a bit of the kids' Benadryl with my white wine this evening for whatever you've got planned?'

Ange feigned shock. 'You are awful!' she cried, giving me a quick dig in the ribs with her elbow. 'I was actually being genuine.'

'Of course you were,' I said, pecking her on the cheek, leaving a print of my coveted lipstick on her powdered skin.

We spent that first week working our way along the pretty tavernas of the seafront, a new one each night. We skipped the sports bar with its huge screens playing MTV on silent, and La Liga highlights at full volume. Their menus offered burgers and chips and neon cocktails by the jug, little else. We were after checked tablecloths, bowls of olives, a blackboard listing fresh fish, the full cliché – plus a kids' menu featuring pizza, if that wasn't too much to ask. That night, we had booked the priciest of the bay's restaurants, which boasted the best views of the sunset. Our table was set beneath one of the fairy-lit trees on the tiered patio and we cooed, delighted, changing our tune as soon as we'd taken our seats. The tree was alive with bugs. Mosquitoes hummed at the peeling trunk. Wasps swarmed the ashtrays of burning coffee grounds placed at the tree's base precisely to deter them.

The maître d' arrived, a determined-looking woman with an explosion of hair and a low-cut top, and began distributing menus and describing the specials.

'Could we please move?' Ange asked.

The woman frowned as she made a performance of looking around her for a spare, unreserved table. We were a group of sixteen. The restaurant was busy. There was no other space on the terrace – unless of course we wanted to eat inside? We didn't want that. We wanted to hear the waves lapping against the stones and see the sun do its dramatic daily swansong, turning the sky and sea a candy pink.

So we sucked it up. The dads took seats in the middle of the table, nearest the tree, at the centre of the insect warzone. The kids sat together at one end, us girls at the other. Binnie's two boys took time to settle, shrieking at the approach of every wasp. Ivy instructed them not to flail about. Wasps were just like Nose-horned vipers, she told them, they rarely attacked unless provoked. She seized this opportunity to educate the table on 'caudal luring', a technique used by snakes to attract small prey.

'They keep their body very still and hidden,' she explained, in that jaded lecturer voice of hers, 'then they waggle the end of their tail so it looks like a tasty worm.'

The moral of this story, in Ivy's telling of it at least, was that small prey only had themselves to blame for their own stupid deaths. Binnie's boys were wide-eyed, even more spooked. Pete pulled Ivy close for a rough hug – a gesture that said, Well done for being so clever, but please shut up. Henry asked to sit on Dev's knee; George sat on Binnie's. He stuck a soothing finger into his mouth and began thumbing the front of his hair. Binnie wore a rare expression of motherly enchantment.

'I love it when he does this,' she mouthed to us.

'Ah, to be a SMOG,' sighed Ange, dropping her focus onto the menu.

Binnie cocked her head.

Ange looked up – feigning surprise that she had not been understood. She spoke sweetly. 'I'm sorry, Binnie, but your boys aren't really like proper boys, are they?'

Here was proof that Ange had definitely heard Binnie's withering comment about her nightmare sons after the incident with Brady and the ping-pong bat. Earlier at the pool bar, I'd sensed an edge when Ange said of Binnie's flippy little skirt: 'Wow, I'd never have the nerve to wear something as short as that!'

Beth rescued the moment. 'Look out,' she announced. 'Poshos at two o'clock.'

Ange and Binnie immediately turned in their seats, Beth hissing at them not to be so obvious.

The wealthy new arrivals had stepped onto the terrace and a waiter was guiding them towards a table set back against the restaurant building.

'Oh, here we go,' said Beth.

'What's happening?' asked Binnie, reliant on Beth and me to narrate the action playing out behind her.

The group were refusing to sit down. A tall, fine-featured man in his forties was voicing their complaint. He was the eldest of the adult siblings, we had decided while observing them at the pool bar – eldest son to the mahogany-skinned patriarch. The sturdy blonde in the wide-legged trousers was this eldest son's wife, a fact we'd established from the way he occasionally rested his hand on her not insignificant backside. That made Euripides (aka Rippy) their child, along with the other blond, cherubic boy and the little girl from a German fairy-tale. The latter two children had yet to have their names yelled across the lawn for us to gut and fillet.

The fine-featured eldest son explained loudly to the waiter that this was not the table they had asked for. They wanted, he said, an 'unencumbered' view of the sea.

We sank behind our menus to mimic his pronunciation of this word, dropping the *uh* deep into our throats, dragging out the *er*: 'UHHn-em-cUHHm-berrrrred!'

'Ladies!' Dev delivered the playful warning shot. 'Play nice, yeah?' He gestured for George to return to the children's end of the table, away from us harpies,

The waiter shrugged at his unhappy customers; his tourist English did not extend to the word *unencumbered*.

'We want to sit somewhere else,' the eldest son enunciated, teetering on the brink of condescension. He pointed to the sea. 'Near the water.'

The waiter, understanding now, gave the same performance we had received from the maître d'. He looked about helplessly at the lack of other tables.

'Ach, give it a rest, Hugo!' murmured Beth.

We shrieked at this placeholder name – *Hugo! Perfect!* – attracting affectionate head-shaking from the boys, even Pete.

Ange and Binnie gave up on discreet glances then; they swivelled in their seats to watch the drama play out. Everyone else on that restaurant terrace was doing the same. The maître d' joined the fray, and this prompted the elderly matriarch to step forward, expensive handbag nestling in the crook of her elbow as she attempted to settle the matter woman-to-woman.

'I mean this really isn't the table you promised,' the matriarch drawled.

We parodied this too, of course: '*I mean I'm ruuuurlly just too rich for this kind of shit.*'

'Honestly, who do they think they are?' said Ange.

'People who are used to getting exactly what they want,' replied Binnie.

She spoke prophetically. The family held strong; they would not sit. The maître d' sighed, clicking her fingers at a trio of loitering waiters who disappeared into the restaurant, returning swiftly, carrying a small table each, upside down, above their heads. They wound their hips dancer-like between the already seated diners on a journey to the front of the terrace.

'I'm sorry but... what the actual fuck?' said Beth.

The tables were set at the edge of the stone beach. With military speed, tablecloths, cutlery, glasses were brought. The family sat down – in the best seats in the house for the imminent sunset.

We all gasped. *Unbelievable!*

As we tucked into baked feta, *sofrito* and *pastitsada*, washed down with too much wine, we continued our dissection of the family. It felt good, joining forces for this trash-talk, after the sour exchange between Ange and Binnie. Nothing unites women more than a common enemy.

For Beth, the family's main offence was that they had not, like us, dressed for dinner. The elderly matriarch and patriarch wore the same clothes they had arrived in. The sturdy blonde's top was different, but she'd kept on the wide-legged trousers. The other mother of the group, a harassed-looking brunette (younger sister to 'Hugo', we speculated) had done the same. Her harem pants were the ones she'd travelled in; only her vest was new. This lack of effort, Beth argued, spoilt the ambience for everyone else.

'I suppose, for people like that,' she said, 'this is basically Pret a Manger. But for people like us, this place is really special.' We were back there again, in a them and us situation, but on more agreeable terrain this time, because we were the underdogs. 'For people like us, a holiday is a once-a-year thing,' Beth went on, 'it's a real event, so we like to make an effort.'

This was conveniently disregarding the trip she, Kenny and the kids had taken to Dubai during February half-term. Binnie, Ange and I conveniently let this go. Why let the truth get in the way of a good argument?

I looked across at the wealthy family, searching out the younger woman, the thin one, the actress. During the earlier disagreement about their table, she had stood at a distance, arms crossed, head down. Uninterested perhaps, embarrassed probably, accustomed to her relatives making these kinds of demands. She had taken a seat at the very end of their seafront table, her chair angled towards the stones of the beach, away from the chatter of the group. Her bearing was regal as she looked out across the pinkening water, as if somewhere, unseen, a photographer might be capturing her in this moment. She poured water, tore bread, all in that deliberate way of hers – a quiet performance for no one. Except me, I suppose. I wondered if she had noticed us girls in return but dismissed the idea straightaway. We were surely beneath her consideration.

The actress *had* changed for dinner – another detail we conveniently excluded from our wholesale takedown of her family. She wore a red linen shift dress, suitcase-creased, paired with simple Havaianas. It was the sort of outfit I might have put on to do the school run in summer, but there was an elegance to her take on it, a show of confidence in her lack of effort. By comparison, Beth,

Binnie, Ange and I, with our hair-teasing and accessorising, our flippy skirts and bold lipsticks, we were too much.

'So, what are you going to wear, Liv?' This was Beth.

'Huh?' I had not been aware of the new turn in our conversation. 'Wear for what?'

Binnie gave me a friendly eye-roll. 'Keep up, Liv.'

Beth wanted to know what I was going to wear for our lunch the next day. Ange had made the reservations before leaving home after seeing the restaurant on a TV food programme. This lunch was on the schedule – as were the days ring-fenced for being lazy by the pool. Group holidays were too often paralysed by indecision and disagreement, Ange said. This schedule, drawn up in advance of our trip, was her gift to us; so we could relax, no difficult choices to make.

The lunch would mark Jason's birthday – the elder statesman of our group. He was turning forty-five. Taxis were booked, the children had been signed up with the hotel kids' club for the day. We could dawdle over our food and drink long into the afternoon.

'I guess I'll wear... I dunno... Something fancy, right?'

'Fancy-ish,' Beth clarified.

I mentally sorted through my limited options, as Ange described a white broderie anglaise playsuit she'd purchased specifically with this lunch date in mind.

'I thought I'd wear my green maxi,' said Beth.

She looked to me for approval. I was blank.

'You know! The one with the bird print and the, wait...' She picked up her phone, opening her photos. I leant in. But Beth halted suddenly in her scrolling, smacking the phone face down onto the table.

I laughed. 'What was that about?'

'Nothing! I just didn't think...' She fluttered a hand through the air, then lurched for her wine. 'Nothing! It just... It doesn't matter!'

Binnie stood abruptly. 'I need the loo,' she said, strutting away. She was escaping something and I watched her go, bemused, catching Beth's pleading look to Ange as I turned back.

'What's going on?' I said.

Ange pulled herself up tall, took a breath.

Beth shook her head urgently. *No.*

But Ange always knew when it was the right moment to look someone in the eye and speak honestly. 'Beth means the green maxi dress she wore for the last-night dinner in Berlin.'

From somewhere, I found a bright smile. 'Berlin?' I enquired.

Beth was silent, her eyes fixed on the oil-stained tablecloth.

The boys had sensed the temperature drop at our end of the table. Jason arched back in his chair to attract the attention of his darling wifey. Ange dismissed him with a flick of her wrist.

'Show me then,' I said, nodding at Beth's phone. I was sure to match my voice to my smile; I made it bright.

'Just the maxi dress?' asked Beth quietly. 'Or...'

'Show me Berlin,' I said.

I leant in again. Beth gave a long, reedy sigh of submission before scrolling to a date in May, to a picture of herself sitting cosy with Binnie and Ange on a red banquette in an expensive-looking restaurant, champagne glasses raised to the camera. A golden chandelier broke the top of the frame.

'Can I?' I said.

Beth surrendered her phone. I swiped back from there.

Beth, Binnie and Ange pouting through the holes of large baked pretzels held close to their faces.

Beth, Binnie and Ange flirting with an actor in a GI uniform at Checkpoint Charlie.

Beth, Binnie and Ange linking arms in front of a section of the Berlin Wall – the mural of the kiss between Brezhnev and Honecker, its title painted in German. *My god, Help Me to Survive This Deadly Love.* The girls' clustered bodies obscured the final verb. *Überleben.* To survive.

I couldn't breathe. I put down the phone. For a moment, there was nothing. No sound of the waves lapping. The chatter of the other diners disappeared.

I pushed back my chair.

'Where are you going?' asked Beth.

I couldn't answer her. I started walking, making for the dark of the beach. The wild pink sunset was long gone by then.

'What about the snakes?' Beth called after me.

I didn't turn back. I just kept going. I had no idea what to do with the feeling inside of me. If I'd stayed at the table, I knew it would have spilled out. I would have wept, raged, something worse. In my rush to get away, I caught my foot on the back of a chair – the one at the end of that table nearest to the stones. The actress jerked forward with an affronted gasp. When she twisted in her seat to look at me, I saw that her face was covered in freckles.

'God, I'm so, so sorry,' I managed, avoiding her eye.

Her annoyance shifted immediately to sympathy; tears were spilling down my cheeks.

'Oh, gosh,' she said, 'there's really no need.' She looked back at where I'd come from, to Beth and Ange leaning across the table in urgent conference. Briefly, the actress clasped my hand then let go.

'You're running away,' she added, her words as deliberate as her actions. 'Good for you,' she said.

2.

Ange not only brought organisation to our group; she brought ambition, energy.

We attacked that long-ignored list. Our spa day was a luxurious one. Our meal in London was at a restaurant with champagne buttons in the booths; if you needed your glass topping up, just buzz. The boys joined us for that excursion, and it was such a success that it became a monthly habit – catching an early-evening train into the capital, dressed in our finery, to dine somewhere Ange had scouted for its Instagram-able food, its Instagram-able views, or sometimes even for its Instagram-able loos. Then we'd treat ourselves to taxis all the way home, to avoid the drunken cattle-pen of the last late train.

Under Ange's guiding force, we became interested in our homes again, after years of ignoring sick stains on the carpets and crayon on the walls. Ange bought a new house, a doer-upper, and we gathered for regular weeknight drinks in her shell of a kitchen, cables coiling from the ceiling, a fine layer of dust settling onto everything as soon as you set it down. We pored over architect's drawings and leafed through glossy kitchen brochures, discussing the benefits of a separate utility room, debating the virtues of one shade of green over another. The final build was astounding, but I loved it more in its almost-finished state. I fantasised about how I would tile that naked floor, what colours I'd splash across the freshly plastered walls. The space was mesmerising – you could turn three successive cartwheels across Ange's knocked-through kitchen and never risk striking a foot. The thing I envied most, though, was her soft-closing cutlery drawer. It was twice the usual width so had room for spatulas and whisks, for keys and matches, as well as knives and forks. I would watch Ange open that drawer, find exactly what she needed straightaway, then casually bump it shut with her hip, the action evoking such a strange rush of feeling in me. How different I would be, I imagined – how easy-going, how at peace – if only I had a drawer like that.

It sounds ridiculous, I know, but Beth and Binnie were similarly seduced. Binnie sold up first, Beth next.

'When are you going to move house, Liv?' Binnie asked, her presumptive phrasing in absolute earnest, and I understood the subtext: *When are you going to join in, Liv? Like, really join in.*

Pete and I just about managed to keep up with the monthly meals in London, never missing an outing and always paying our way. We'd found a credit card with nought-per-cent interest on purchases for two years, and this was our saviour.

'Let me cover your share this time,' Kenny said to Pete one night, catching the stricken glances we'd exchanged as yet another bill came in at one-hundred-and-fifty pounds a head. Pete didn't accept of course, couldn't possibly.

'Don't be daft, mate!' he said, his voice chummy, like it was nothing, both the offer and the bill.

There were no more home-dyed hair disasters for Beth. She was frogmarched to the salon where Ange had started getting her hair done (expertly, expensively), a place that also offered elaborate manicures, involving hand massages and tea rituals. Ange booked us in, a regular fortnightly slot, and I attended at the start, echoing the girls' replies of 'Yes, please' when the woman came round offering an upsell of a gin cocktail instead of the usual green tea. But I was engrossed in my translation course by then and I really needed to buy more of the texts on the reading list. To afford that *and* the necessary new outfits for our London dinners, the manicures had to go. It wasn't that I didn't want to be there, I told the girls.

'I just need to put books before beauty for a while!' I quipped.

Binnie considered me darkly. 'Way to make us sound frivolous,' she said.

And that was when the horrifying realisation hit me: in more than just manicures, I had fallen completely out of sync with my friends.

When we got together in Ange's half-finished kitchen, after blind swatches had been compared, the new lighting sconces unwrapped and admired, Ange would nudge the conversation towards education. She was unhappy with her boys' state school – and with all the other various state-school options in the town. A glowing Ofsted report meant nothing, Ange said, slugging rosé, her pitch rising in anger.

'Take Ivy,' she said, 'who is, like you say, "super bright".' (Had I said that? Was it a phrase I would use?) 'I'm sorry but it means nothing,' Ange went on, 'because she will always be a whole year behind the kids at private school.'

Ange was highlighting the injustice, I assumed, wondering aloud how we might work together to fix the leaky boat that is our government-funded education system. It hadn't occurred to me that she was instructing us to jump ship. Ange moved her three boys across to a fee-paying school the autumn after her renovations were complete. Beth and Binnie moved their kids across in the spring.

What I had assumed to be a harmless drip, drip, drip (of manicures, expensive schools, costly London dinners, bigger and better houses), had become, without me realising, an unmanageable flood.

Pete blamed his job. His inventory of work frustrations stretched well beyond the first beer of the evening by then, lingering through dinner, interrupting whatever we chose to watch on TV. He wasn't being paid enough, he said, not like Kenny, Jason and Dev. But that alone didn't explain our falling behind. Nor did our lack of a second income; Beth's and Ange's part-time job earnings were negligible, and Pete was wrong about Dev, his pay cheque was distinctly average without Binnie's salary propping it up. Besides, the kind of money the others were spending went well beyond good wages. It was more than the spoils of a few healthy share options cashed in. I couldn't get my head around where it was all coming from. Were my friends maxing-out their credit cards like us? Had they remortgaged? Did they know the whereabouts of a magic beanstalk that led to a goose that laid golden eggs?

I was desperate to ask. But how? Ange had made her kitchen the regular venue for our midweek drinks, in part so we could talk about her construction-in-progress, but also because it was cheaper than drinking in a bar on the high street. Weight-bearing steel joists were expensive, she said, she and Jason needed to watch the pennies. Yet when I pointed out how many academic texts could be bought with fifty pounds-worth of manicure, I had been branded vulgar, wallet-shaming. So, I didn't ask, and the gnawing sensation that Pete and I were doing something very wrong grew into a mounting terror, until I was convinced that membership of the group would be revoked if we failed to pinpoint our mistakes. I would not be that lonely figure once more, peering down from the upper tiers of the university lecture hall, desperate to belong. I did belong, I had found my soulmates, and I would not be a stupid fucking idiot and throw it all away.

I addressed our spending habits first. My monthly high-street shopping sprees ended; in their place, I purchased one or two impressive items of designer clothing, pieces that could be worn again and again. It was more economical, and also in keeping with the new ambitious ethos of our group. I invested in a black silk shirt that I could dress up for a London dinner, then dress down, tucked into jeans, for a Wednesday night in Ange's kitchen. Binnie was particularly admiring of it. She fingered the fabric of the sleeve, demanding to know where I'd got it from. When I told them, Ange yelped in horror. Good god, she said, she could never afford to shop at a place like that! I was dumbfounded, felt absurd. I wanted to rip the shirt off there and then. But more than anything, I just wanted to know the rules. I was standing blindfolded in the centre of the circle, with no idea how to tell a piggy by its squeak, scared to death that I would be told to leave the party yet again.

So, I turned to a resource that, unlike our savings, was limit-less – my ability to be a good friend. I went the extra mile. When Binnie's after-school childcare fell through, I took over. Ivy walked herself home at three-fifteen and let herself in, while I drove to the private school on the edge of town to fetch George and Henry. Beth was asked to leaflet-drop all the houses on my side of town for the estate agency – *We have numerous clients looking for a property in your neighbourhood!* – but was struggling to find the time. I offered to do it, for no payment other than the additional Fitbit steps. When Ange needed a dog-walker two mornings a week, I nominated myself again, tramping through fields in the rain with that great, shark-eyed beast until both of us were tired enough for a nap.

'I swear you bring him back muddy on purpose!' Ange exclaimed on our return one particularly miserable morning. 'Is it because you're envious of my pale pink sofa?'

It was a joke. She meant it as a joke. I needed to learn how to take a joke. This was Pete's advice, a man who had grown up with two elder siblings, so had been the punchline to every gag from the youngest age. His initial sneeriness about Ange and her open letters on Facebook had faded as soon as he met her. He found her singular, hilarious. He didn't understand why I behaved a certain way in her presence, didn't see her actions and comments as evidence that I had slipped out of favour.

'You know Ange,' he said, 'always ready with a cutting one-liner. She does it to everyone.'

Did she though?

Ange texted an invitation: *Let's go out-out for after work drinks one night this week, ladies Ax.* I bristled at her inclusion of the word 'work'. That was something the others did, and I didn't, because I was lazy, or fantastically privileged to be bankrolled by Pete, or a show-off for wanting a second education. I was guilty of at least one of those things in Ange's eyes, I was sure.

'Now you really are over-thinking it,' said Pete. 'She's just making clear it's early-evening drinks, not late drinks.'

'Then why not just say "early-evening drinks"?'

He shrugged. 'Isn't "after-work drinks" less characters?'

'It's fewer,' I replied.

My texted response was as fulsome as the others' – *Lovely! Count me in!* – and I was prompt with my dates, entering them straightaway into the shared online diary. But there was no evening when all four of us were free, so Ange went with a night when I was at lectures. The previous month she'd booked cinema tickets on the same night as book club. Binnie shrugged it off.

'It won't hurt to miss it once, will it, Liv?' she said. 'The books have been pretty rubbish lately anyway.'

So, we went to see Ange's film instead. *Fifty Shades Darker*. And, at least, when the girls sniggered for weeks about putting silver balls on their Christmas lists, I was in on the joke, part of the gang. That was, until Pete threw a surprise party to celebrate my passing the first year of my course. His dad, Nigel, came over to raise a beer with his new girlfriend Sheila, a fellow divorcee, queen to a retinue of misshapen rescue dogs. A couple of our London friends travelled up on the train, and a neighbour we liked dropped by as well. But there was no Beth, no Binnie, no Ange.

'Didn't you ask them?' I said to Pete, as we cleared away after everyone had gone.

He was reluctant to answer, but yes, he admitted, an invite had been sent to all three.

This was around the same period Ivy was having night terrors, waking bug-eyed and screaming in the early hours. She was asleep, our GP assured us, unaware of her own outbursts. The phase would pass. We'd have to endure until then. Also, at that time, my mum got in the habit of phoning me late in the evening to deliver exhaustive and exhausting condemnations of my dad. She'd had to sell the washing machine to settle one of his debts, she told me, what on earth was she supposed to do now? You could leave, I suggested, and she turned on me. She had meant her laundry, how was she supposed to get her clothes clean? And what kind of daughter tells their parents to get divorced? I knew the right answer to that one – a terrible daughter, the worst.

I was tired when I met Beth for a coffee that lunchtime. The conversation came around to my completing the first year of my college course and I couldn't help it, I began weeping like a child. I had so wanted them to be at my house for my surprise party, I wailed, I had so wanted them to be pleased for me.

Beth was confused. 'Ange said that we weren't to go.'

I went cold. 'What?'

Beth was sure of it. 'Ange spoke to Pete, and he said the party was a family thing.'

'Ange spoke to Pete?' I said. 'What, on the phone? He never told me.'

Beth shrugged; that part wasn't her business. 'I dunno, but Ange absolutely got the vibe that Pete was only inviting us out of politeness. Because his dad was there, right?'

'Yes,' I said, 'but—'

'Yeah, so she felt we shouldn't turn up and intrude. You know Ange, she always wants the best for everyone.'

I took a breath. 'Does she?'

Beth's coffee stalled halfway to her mouth. 'What do you mean?'

'I mean, like, the way she keeps organising things on the nights when I can't make it.'

'But...' Beth placed her cup down. She was bewildered. 'But you were at the dinner last month and you came to Ange's place for drinks a couple of weeks ago and—'

'Yes, I'm not saying that I... I'm not saying...' My tears returned. 'Oh, Beth, I just can't get rid of the feeling that I've done something to upset her or said something. Was it because I was slow in accepting her friend request on Facebook at the start? Or was it when I said that Ange and Jason were an unlikely couple? Because I know it sounded like a criticism, but really, truly, it wasn't. I think they're great together and...' I tailed off.

Beth was staring at me, startled by this unfiltered stream of insecurity and doubt. I hung my head. What was I doing? I was digging myself a hole, fast forwarding to the finish, because the suspense about how my brilliant friendships were going to end was killing me.

'I'm tired,' I said by way of an apology, 'I've got a lot going on.'

I filled Beth in on Ivy's night terrors. That would be enough to justify my show of emotion, I thought. Beth nodded, compassionate as always, but the mood remained soured by my accusations, claims that might, quite rightly, make their way back to Ange. I knew that couldn't happen. It mustn't.

'And my mum keeps calling late at night,' I said.

69

I had never told Beth or Binnie about my dad's compulsive gambling, the pain it caused, the things he'd stolen, the things we'd had to sell, and the way my mum directed all her resulting fury onto me. I'd been vague: my mum is domineering, I told them, my father difficult. I made them sound like everyone else's mildly irritating parents. I didn't want to be cast in the shadow of their bad behaviour, but in that moment, I could see how their bad behaviour might serve me. Save me, even. I told Beth everything.

My tale done, she stretched across the table for my hand.

'Oh, poor Liv,' she murmured, 'poor, poor Liv!'

Her sympathy was what I'd been seeking so I didn't reject it, but it was misplaced. I'd won. I'd been absolved. Of course, there was the queasy aftertaste from trading in family secrets, but that was superseded by the much bigger hit of relief. I felt emboldened by what I'd done to convince Beth. It proved I was a fighter, capable of holding onto my place in the group no matter what. I would do anything, it seemed, to keep them close. Nothing was out of bounds.

I did a quick sweep of the hotel restaurant before crossing the threshold: a housekeeper mopped rhythmic figures of eight across the cream tiles, a plantation fan swirling above. The serving staff were still arranging the breakfast buffet. One lowered a steaming vat of hot food into a chafing dish; another made a still-life arrangement of oranges, apples and plums. It was all clear. I made for the silver urns that held fresh coffee.

From there, I browsed the multitude of cereals, the small glass bowls of nuts – walnuts, pecans, almonds – the deep pot of honey, yet to be invaded with its wooden dipper, the white tablecloth still clean, no golden trails. There was a painted bowl of stiff Greek yoghurt so huge I had the urge to thrust a fist into it.

Without Ivy at my elbow, telling me what to choose, I raised the lids of the chafing dishes in turn until I found the 'yukky' eggs, serving myself a whole pile of them. On the edge of the loaded plate, thinking of my absent daughter, I added four 'much betterer' chocolate croissants.

I sat at a table for two, eating alone with gusto, washing down mouthfuls of sweet, herby egg with slurps of dark, black coffee, enjoying the clash of the two flavours, luxuriating in the quiet, with no one there to watch me, to check how much I was eating.

Until Beth sat down in the chair opposite.

'I knew you'd do this,' she said.

It was just a few minutes past seven and Beth was no early riser, yet her hair was straightened, her make-up applied. She wore a pair of neat peach-coloured shorts and a grey vest that I had not seen so far that holiday. My hair was pulled back in a scrunchie, uncombed. I'd put on the sweaty t-shirt, the one from the plane journey and our first drunken night, because I needed my puny selection of clothes to stretch across three weeks. And because I hadn't expected to see anyone.

I wiped grease from my chin. 'You knew I'd do what?'

'This.' Beth nodded at my half-eaten eggs. 'Come down early for breakfast to avoid us.'

'I'm not avoiding you.' I would have tried a smile, but I could feel flakes of oregano between my teeth.

Beth gave me a look that said I wasn't fooling anyone.

We'd been here before, I realised, across the table from one another while I explained the pain of being left out. Not metaphorical pain, not imagined pain, but real, eviscerating pain, the brain lighting up exactly as if my insides were being gently removed like a string of bloody handkerchiefs. But this time it was different. I wouldn't weep, point the finger, make bids for sympathy. Because Beth had come to me. She knew she was in the wrong. I had something she needed – forgiveness.

'Seriously,' I said, 'I'm not avoiding you. I went to bed early, so I woke up early.' I gestured to my half-eaten eggs. 'And I was hungry.'

'Stay there,' Beth said, unconvinced. 'I'm going to get myself a tea.'

I watched her flick through the little envelopes in the tea chest at the buffet, past Earl Grey, jasmine, mint, in search of a basic Breakfast Blend, before fumbling with the hot-water urn, as if she hadn't dealt with its peculiarities every morning this week. While her back was turned, I retied my hair and picked at my teeth with a nail. I had embarrassed myself at the restaurant the night before, losing control and disappearing like that. I needed to hold it together then, in the breakfast room. My friends went to Berlin without me. So what? They're grown-ups. They're allowed. We'd signed no contract to say we must do everything together, that we must tell each other our every secret.

'So, did you meet any snakes last night?' Beth asked, slipping back into her seat. Her playfulness barely hid the genuine enquiry.

'Of course not! That snake story is bullshit.'

In truth, the snake story had unnerved me. After the coral glow of the sunset came sudden blackness. I'd slipped off my heels to get across the stones of the bay, but beyond the fairy lights of the restaurant, could see nothing of what I was stepping on. At the cove in front of the hotel, I leapt up the wooden stairs two at a time, then ran across the lawn, the tough Greek grass sharp against my soles. Once in our apartment, I dove straight into bed, sobbing. When Pete came in, not long after, searching for me, I buried my face and feigned sleep. Nonetheless, he relayed his plans aloud.

'I'm going back to the restaurant, so Ivy isn't alone.' Pause. 'I'm glad I've found you.' Pause. 'If you want to tell me what happened, then…' Pause. 'You know what? It's okay. I'll ask Beth.' He left.

And I thought, Yeah, you do that, you ask Beth, make her squirm all over again.

I was still awake when he arrived back with Ivy. She wanted to know what was wrong with me, why I'd left early, and Pete said, 'Mummy isn't feeling well, that's all.' I wanted to shout out, correct him: *Mummy isn't ill! Mummy is quite rightly really fucking upset!* But I didn't want Ivy thinking that either.

'You're upset,' said Beth, sipping her tea.

'I'm not upset.'

'But we went to Berlin without you.'

'Which you have every right to do.'

'Yeah, but Berlin is your special place.'

I winced. Had I ever called it that? My 'special place'. Was that a phrase I would use?

'It's fine,' I said. 'Let's move on, forget about it.'

'But I just can't.' Beth's eyes shone wet, and my chest tightened at the prospect of her bursting into tears. I didn't have enough good grace left to comfort her. 'I feel terrible,' she continued. 'It was never our intention to leave you out, it's just that there weren't enough seats for you to come.'

If I had really, truly wanted to move on, I should have nodded, acted as if I understood, but my need to punish Beth, just a little, won out.

'Not enough seats?' I said. 'What, on all the aeroplanes that fly to Germany?'

Beth deflected my barb with a loud laugh. The staff behind the buffet looked up as it echoed through the empty room.

'You see, they were Jason's flights,' Beth said, 'a freebie from a client, and Jason said Ange could use them instead of him, and the free hotel too, but it was only for three people and—'

'A work gift? For three?'

'Yeah, I know! That's weird, isn't it?' Beth stalled. 'But I think it was meant for Jason and Ange and maybe Duff too? Because Duff had been doing World War Two at school. Or something…' Her hand went to her neck, her eyes to the floor. 'Yes, that's probably it. Ask Ange.' She returned to full speed. 'Anyway, that's how it was, and Ange should have got us to club together to pay the extra, you know, so all four of us could go – I was really cross with her that we didn't do that – but Ange said that Jason couldn't add extra passengers because it was a perk that he hadn't paid for, and it would look bad if the client found out he wasn't on the trip himself, and anyway, Ange said we weren't to put you under any more financial pressure because of everything to do with this trip, and how up till then it had been so…'

I knew what my adjective would be. I waited to see if it would match Beth's, but she left the sentence hanging.

'It's fine,' I said.

'Ange was only thinking of you.'

'Of course,' I replied. 'She went out of her way to make sure I could be on this trip.' This was true. Something to hold onto.

Beth kept going. 'And I didn't want to mention anything to you about Berlin because I knew you'd feel left out, I knew you'd be upset, because of what happened with Abi…'

'Gabi.'

'Right. Ange knew nothing about that, by the way. Binnie and me would never have told her, unless you said to, because it's private.'

'Beth,' I said, 'please stop.'

She dropped her head into her hands. 'god, I feel so terrible!'

Into this pause came a resident, entering the restaurant through the patio doors. It was the actress, padding slowly, barefoot, wearing a loose, blue smock that was surely a nightie, her hair artfully dishevelled. She resembled a beautiful ghost from a play.

Beth lifted her head, sensing the shift in my focus. She followed my gaze, turning in her seat, but was too late. The actress had selected a handful of plums from the buffet, testing the flesh of each one with her thumb, then was gone. Exit the ghost. Beth turned back to me, wearing a mournful expression.

'I would totally understand if you decided to hate me forever,' she said.

Her self-pity was threatening to irritate me. I didn't want to hate Beth. I could never hate her. I loved her. Yet I couldn't quite bring myself to absolve her completely, to say I held no grudge. That seemed unreasonable. I did the best I could.

'Beth,' I said, stretching across the table for her hand. 'We've been friends for nearly nine years. You don't just throw that away over one little thing.'

She smiled. 'It's like a marriage, right?'

'Right.'

I sensed she was about to begin our ritual to-and-fro of phrases about my wedding – 'Your wine-bottle dress, Liv!' – but something pulled her up. Maybe it was for the best. Maybe it wasn't the right moment.

'Are you going to eat all of those?' she said, gesturing to my stack of chocolate croissants.

I shook my head. 'They're for Ivy too. It's my turn to give Pete a lie-in, so I'm taking her on a snake hunt.'

Before heading into the dining room, I'd wandered across the lawn – empty, quiet except for the hum of the pool filter – and put a towel on a lounger on the raised deck with its prime view of the cove. This would be our base. At reception, they loaned out binoculars. When Ivy woke up, I would tell her that Daddy had got it wrong. Mummy wasn't ill. Mummy wasn't upset. I'd left the dinner early and walked back across the beach because I wanted to do a recce in preparation for our mission today. If snakes liked the cooler evenings, they probably liked the early mornings too. We'd eat chocolate croissants as we kept lookout, and Ivy could record what she saw in her project book – a good memory to blot away the tense night before.

'But I thought the snake story was bullshit?' Beth said uneasily, opening a napkin so I could place the chocolate croissants within.

'Let's see, shall we?' I said, gathering up the spoils and heading out.

There would be no more playing the victim, no more slumping over the kitchen table and peeling labels from bottles of beer as we listed all the ways our life sucked.

'For fuck's sake,' I snapped one evening as Pete commenced his post-work wallowing. 'Just leave your fucking job then!'

He stared at me – amazement tinged with shame. Cautiously, he asked: 'And do what?'

'Get another job! A better one! At a place that fucking appreciates you!'

It was so obvious.

We had been playing small, focusing on what we lacked, not giving ourselves permission to have anything more, not recognising our strengths. Money wasn't the reason we'd fallen out of sync with the others, it was attitude. Binnie was right to ask, in her indirect way, when we were going to start joining in.

Pete responded to my show of anger with a quiet admission: a friend of Mikey's – one of the old London crowd – had asked for Pete's contact details. There was a senior consultant post going. Pete was reluctant to pass on his number. It was a big role, he said, high-profile, the kind of job he'd want to do *after* the next job. He wasn't ready.

'I'm sorry but… why the fuck not?' I countered.

He shrugged. 'Probably the same reasons you give your tutor when he suggests you apply for an MRes.'

At my next seminar, I asked for an admissions interview.

Pete told Mikey to pass on his details.

My research project was accepted.

Pete got the job.

Overnight, despite a fresh bill of course fees, our income doubled.

The old us, the small us, would have talked about chickens and how you mustn't count them too soon. We'd have pictured the worst possible rainy day and set aside money for that. The new us, the ambitious us, got busy spending.

We ditched our ancient Honda and drove a brand-new BMW sports saloon off the forecourt, whooping like joyriders. Pete took a picture of me reclining on the bonnet and I sent it to the girls with the message: *Fancy a spin?* The four of us drove to a neighbouring town for lunch and shopping, and on the way back, Ange called shotgun. Cars were her thing. She wanted to check out the features we'd chosen, prod the stereo, play with the Satnav. I braced for her verdict.

If you'd stumped up the extra for a leather interior, the investment would totally have paid off.

When you have brand-new BMW money, you should always go for second-hand Audi.

There was none of that. Ange ran an appreciative hand along the dash and said, 'I love it, it's such a smooth ride.' I looked across at her, to make sure she was being genuine, and it was like the very first time we met, when she told me I should cut my hair off because it would really suit me, or when she praised my extra touches at the dinner party – there was warmth to what she said, investment. It was as if those qualities had never gone away. And maybe they never had. I was looking for the good in people now, in life in general. It was all a matter of perception.

Pete and I took a tour of the private school and paid serious lip service to enrolling Ivy in September. At the same time, we registered with local estate agents, in search of a bigger house. We couldn't afford both – the school fees and the increased mortgage – and Ange more than anyone was sympathetic to our quandary. She was keen to help. Her solution was that we should extend what we had, lose a chunk of that ugly patio courtyard, lengthen the footprint of the kitchen, then convert our loft, bring in some skylights. We'd be amazed at the space we'd find, she said, it would feel like a brand-new home. She made a Biro sketch of our floor plan, marking in her suggested improvements, sliding the drawing across the varnished wood of her kitchen island for my inspection, punctuating the movement with a confident swish of her hair. I could imagine her doing this with the young house-hunters she took to view the tiny Victorian properties at our end of town. How could anyone resist?

When Ange wasn't working, I'd hang at her house, drinking coffee from her sleek De'Longhi bean-to-cup machine, poring over her stash of interiors magazines and kitchen brochures, paint cards and fabric swatches. She'd take me on a tour of her three bathrooms, so I could compare tile finishes and flooring options. I ran an envious hand along the rolltop of the bath in her master suite, in much the same way she had stroked the dashboard of our car. The bond between us was strengthened by my extension project; our talk became more intimate. Binnie looked tired, we noted aloud; was she genuinely happy working full-time like she said she was? Were Beth and Kenny okay? The last time we'd all gone out their usual banter had turned quickly to bickering.

'What on earth do you say about me when I'm not here?' I asked Ange, a throwaway line to which she was supposed to answer, *Nice things, of course!*

'Beth tells me about your dad,' Ange replied, not pausing for breath, 'about his gambling problem, and how you and Pete sometimes have to find the money to bail him out.'

'Oh,' I said, swallowing my mouthful of coffee too fast, feeling the hot painful bubble of it slide down my gullet.

'Oh,' Ange echoed. 'Should Beth not have told me that?'

'No, no!' I shook it off. 'It's fine!'

'I'm sorry but that's terrible,' Ange persisted. 'I would be furious with Beth if I'd divulged my secrets and she'd just passed them on.'

'It's not a secret,' I parried. 'It shouldn't be a secret. That only makes things worse.' I was justifying this to myself more than anything – to make up for telling all to Beth in the first place. 'If we cover up for him, then that's enabling. And so is giving him

79

money really, but it's difficult, because Mum gets caught up in it, and we have to help, or else, you know...'

I didn't want to say anymore. It felt wrong to be discussing something so wretched in such a beautiful space. Light was spilling in from the church-like windows above Ange's copper kitchen sink. Saint dozed in a ray of sun that stretched across the natural stone floor. Instead, I praised Beth, said how grateful I was to have her to confide in. Binnie too. Those girls had been my saviours during the baby years, I explained, laying it on thick, trying to wash away the nasty aftertaste of our gossip. Though we'd dressed it up as concern, our discussion of Beth's and Binnie's lives had been tattle, chewing gum, something to work the jaw. And also, it had been a trust exercise between Ange and me. Though I couldn't help feeling that I had got carried away and disclosed far more. Maybe I'd not been nice. I continued to backtrack.

'We go on about it all the time, I know, but the wedding Beth and Binnie planned for Pete and me was out of this world. So special. I swear, I married those girls that day as well – that's how it felt.'

Ange's expression curdled.

'Sorry, I forget.' I waved the story away. 'You're really not into all that stuff.'

'To *me*, marriage is a superficial display, a waste of money. Love is what's real.'

'Absolutely,' I said. 'I get it.'

Something playful danced across her face. 'Your wine-bottle dress, Liv!' she squeaked, in a parody of Beth.

It was a joke. She meant it as a joke.

'Yes!' I laughed.

Ange carried on. 'The song! Those cut-out hearts! The pyramid! I nearly died!'

The joke had shifted. Ange looked at me expectantly. This was where I was supposed to say what I was *really* thinking, something exposing, disparaging – like, I wasn't into marriage either and I only pretended to be for Beth's and Binnie's sake, that I thought they overplayed the memory of my wedding. Ange looked hungry for it, this tasty morsel that would confirm I loved her just a little bit more than I did the other two.

'I was so lucky to find those women,' I said, gentle with my words, but clear, loyal. 'Before I knew Beth and Binnie, I thought friendship was something that didn't happen to people like me.'

Ange covered her disappointment well.

'T'aww,' she cooed, 'that's lovely.' Then she briskly changed the subject.

I left Ange's house with a list written in her wild, looping cursive – all the items that needed to be considered when doing a house renovation, and the order in which to consider them. At the top of the paper was her architect's number, something she hadn't offered to Beth or Binnie for their extensions.

'You're an amazing friend,' I told her because after our awkward exchange about my wedding, I felt she needed to hear that. 'There's no way I'd be able to do all this without you.'

And I meant it. As Pete and I sat at our kitchen table, drinking tea with Ange's architect, a delicate, well-spoken man who listened intently to our ideas for the house, turning our words, there and then, into rough drawings, I had never felt so capable. When we'd first bought the house, my overriding sensation had been fear – of the financial commitment, of what we might miss by leaving London behind. I was out of my depth making such a grown-up move, unqualified. I'd experienced the same doubts when pregnant with Ivy. How could I be trusted to raise another human being, having had no decent upbringing of my own? When it came to the house extension, though, I felt like an adult at last. Armed with Ange's list, with phrases borrowed from her, I talked confidently about where to reposition the back door, and how the master suite with its roll-top bath should take shape in our loft.

It was around this time, when we were finalising drawings with the architect, that Ange brought up the idea of the holiday. We were having dinner at Beth's, where there were cloth napkins and various perfumed candles. Our hostess wore a pretty cocktail dress bought especially for the evening and no one teased her for it, because this was what we did now – we put on a show, we tried to impress. Beth had chosen a New York theme for her three courses and there was a typed-up menu with Statue of Liberty clip art on each place setting. Dessert was an American baked cheesecake, delivered from a patisserie in London. As we demolished it with coffee, Ange made her pitch.

Everyone around that table had, at some point, talked up the idea of going away for three whole weeks in the summer, instead of the usual fortnight. The boys were the main culprits, Ange said, eyeing each one of them in turn, like they were schoolboys who must answer to her disappointed headmistress. But had any of them actually gone and done it – told their boss they were taking all of their holiday in one go, then packed that extra-large suitcase?

'So, I think we should do it,' she said. 'Together.'

A large volume of wine had been drunk by that point, but still the group's response was cautious – *Whoa, okay. Are you serious? But how would that work?* Ange brought order with an authoritative, 'Come on, guys! Tell me something I've organised that hasn't been fun?'

She'd already found us the perfect place in a Sunday supplement – a complex of little apartments with views of the sea, a huge pool, a kids' club, restaurants nearby. There was even paddleboarding, and yoga classes for the keen. Beth nodded along, as if she could personally vouch for the place. Binnie sat back, arms folded, smiling and shaking her head at the audacity of Ange's suggestion.

In no time we were tossing around potential dates, Ange cutting though this chatter with a 'Wait, wait, wait!' She levelled the air with her hands. 'We need to start with Liv,' she said, 'because the trip absolutely mustn't clash with her university course.'

I froze, panic seizing me by the throat. If the 'secret' of my dad's gambling had been passed on, then Beth had likely reported back the accusations preceding it – that I thought Ange was deliberately scheduling get-togethers to clash with my lectures. Was this reference to my university course pointed? Did I need to apologise there and then? Both Ange and Beth looked at me eagerly. Binnie was silently leafing backwards and forwards through her exquisitely annotated Smythson diary, waiting for me to say when I was free.

The ball really was in my court. Ange was genuinely putting me first.

I beamed, said, 'Any time in July or August. Count us in.'

We claimed our reserved lounger on the bleached wood sun deck overlooking the sea. A waiter from the poolside bar delivered our drinks – iced coffee for me, milkshake for Ivy – and we made short work of the chocolate croissants, their melting middles painting our lips brown.

Ivy briefed me. We'd be lucky if we spotted anything; I was not to build up my hopes. Vipers liked the sun, but in July and August, as the temperatures rose, they became increasingly nocturnal. Ever-optimistic, we trained our binoculars on the cove's higher ledges. If we spied a particularly big snake, it was likely to be female, Ivy explained; their bodies had lighter patterns too, allowing them to blend in.

'But how will I know if it's a good snake or a bad one?' I asked.

'Just look for the horns,' Ivy instructed. She pulled my binoculars away from my face so she could show me the green snake she'd drawn in coloured pencil in her project book, the horn curling up from the centre of its face like a flipped middle finger – nature's way of saying, *Fuck off, bitches, I'm poisonous.*

We settled into a dedicated and contented silence as the sun lifted itself above the green hills, simmering gently, going easy on us for now. Ivy shifted to her belly, elbows dipping down over the end of the lounger, a more comfortable pose for holding her binoculars. I sat back against the propped head of the lounger, allowing myself a skim of the rest of the bay in magnified view.

A swimmer idled in the rocky shallows of the cove, surfacing every so often to adjust their mask and snorkel. The sea lick-slapped against the hulls of the small boats tethered to the jetty. On the road running along the bay, a delivery driver unloaded fruit from a flatbed Ape truck, bantering in staccato Greek with the owner of the supermarket. I panned further, my view suddenly obstructed by something too close, moving alongside us on the deck. I lowered my binoculars.

The actress had entered stage left, still barefoot, still in that loose blue smock. For a while she paced slowly, peeling her soles from the wood, working through all the bones of her feet, as if the action were a meditation, or a test perhaps. She stopped to look out across the water, one arm pressed against her forehead to shield her eyes, then she bent balletically at the waist to place a towel and a laptop onto a lounger already reserved by someone else. This stranger's placeholder towel she picked up, folded, then discarded on the edge of the lawn. Returning, she met my eye and smiled. I jumped at this breaking of the fourth wall, as if I had been caught in the act, not her.

'So selfish,' said the actress, her voice ringing like the note you get by running a wet finger along the rim of a glass. 'Death to the lounger-hoggers!' she added, arching an eyebrow.

'Yeah!' I replied, just that, no whip-smart remark ready on the tip of my tongue. I darted my gaze away, downwards, noticing then the great brown smear across my belly – chocolate from the croissants. I rubbed at it, needing to stand to be rid of the stuff that had sunk into the creases.

'Very nice,' said the actress, loud enough for me to hear.

'Huh?' I said, seemingly unable to progress beyond cavewoman grunts.

She brushed a hand up and down her own body, from ribs to groin, nodding in my direction, her gaze appreciative. My bare midriff appeared to be the topic of our conversation, though I was sure something had fallen through the gaps. Women didn't praise each other's bodies, not like that, not unless the other woman was big, and then the praise was really a display of something else, charity maybe, covert superiority.

'You have a daughter?' she said, gesturing to Ivy who was engrossed in the writing-down of something seen through her binoculars.

'Yeah,' I replied and, feeling I must offer an answer that contained more than one syllable, added gratuitously, 'she's really into snakes.'

The actress gave a sure, tight tilt of her chin. 'Well,' she said, going back to her original observation, brushing her hand up and down her body once more, 'if you've had a baby, then yes, *very* nice.'

'Thank you,' I replied, unsure what else to say.

Was this a continuation of our brief exchange from the night before? I wanted to know. Did she even remember me? My heart quickened at the thought of asking her what she'd meant by her words, *You're running away, good for you.* But I was too late. The actress had turned her attention to positioning her parasol. A half-hearted display of wrestling with its concrete base brought a bartender jogging eagerly across the lawn.

'No! Let me!' he cried.

Her bidding done, he asked, a little desperately, if there was anything else he could help her with. She shook her head and his disappointment was tangible. I understood how he felt.

'So, what's happening with you guys?'

A shadow fell over our lounger; it was Binnie, wearing a pair of peach-coloured shorts almost identical to Beth's. I wondered if they had purposely coordinated, or if Binnie would be cross when she discovered they were dressed alike.

'We're going over for breakfast,' said Binnie, keen and cheerful, a voice that acknowledged something bad had gone down the night before but showed she was willing to act like it hadn't. She pointed to the opposite side of the lawn; Dev, George and Henry were standing waiting.

'We've already eaten,' I replied.

'Chocolate croissants and milkshake,' offered Ivy abruptly, not lifting her head from her writing.

'Good, well...' Binnie loitered. She was testing the water, making sure things were okay between us. It didn't seem reasonable, in the circumstances, that I should make it easy for her. I picked up my book.

'Oh, what are you reading?' she asked. Binnie had ditched our book club months ago and, though I'd said it was fine for her not to come anymore, she knew I was sore about it.

'Wow, it's in French,' she said.

'*Oui*,' I replied.

'*Zut alors*!' she batted back. '*Vous êtes le grand* show-off!'

I smiled but I didn't laugh. It was one of the novels I would have translated as part of my MRes if I'd not been forced to quit. It wasn't something I felt like being silly about.

'Cool. Well...' Still she loitered.

'I'll see you later,' I said, giving her permission to go. 'We'll come and join you for a swim when we're done here.'

She left, and as she did, I swear I caught the actress dipping her head back down into her laptop, a bird-like twitch of a movement that suggested she'd been listening in. That was the moment she chose to remove the blue smock, pulling it up and over her head. Underneath, she wore tiny, white bikini briefs – and nothing else. Her breasts were small, upright, quietly impressive, in a way that mine never were, even before they'd fed a baby. The tired dads by the pool with their wide-awake toddlers shook themselves alert at this startling development on the sun deck.

'Put your eyes back in your head, Liv!'

Pete arrived, he and Binnie seemingly operating as a tag team.

'Bit punchy for a family resort, isn't it?' he went on. 'Going topless before nine a.m.'

'Shush!' I hissed as he sat on the edge of our lounger. 'Keep your voice down!'

His hand went to my thigh, an action designed as punctuation – time for business. I tensed.

'So,' he said, 'everything's sorted now, is it?'

'Sorted with what?' I replied, being deliberately obtuse. I didn't doubt that he was in cahoots with the girls, that he'd helped plan that early ambush by Beth. He criticised me for being too pally with my friends, then didn't like it when we stopped playing nice; I couldn't win.

'Come on, Liv. You stormed off from the restaurant last night.'

I glared at him, tipping my head at Ivy, who was absorbed in her project book but always listening. 'Stormed off' was not the version of events either of us had given to her.

'I just didn't know where you were,' he said, 'and what was going on.'

'Not a pleasant feeling, is it?' I replied. It was a day for holding everyone to account for their betrayals.

'What's that supposed to mean?'

'I'm just saying it doesn't feel good when you know something is going on and you're completely in the dark.'

Pete's hold on my thigh became an anxious, rhythmic squeezing.

'Liv, you're talking in riddles.'

I was. Riddles that Ivy would tune into soon, the mood of them if not the sense, so I lapsed into silence. I wished for the temerity of Ange, to be able to roar my grievances at Pete the way she roared at Jason, regardless of who was listening.

'So, no visit from Ange then?' I said, turning to look back across the lawn. 'Or is she playing Marley, sending you, Beth and Binnie as the three ghosts?'

Pete looked askance.

'Doesn't matter,' I said. And it didn't. I'd made my point about Berlin, had my sulk. I wanted us to get back to how we were now. Reconciliation was down to me.

'So, how was snake-watch, Spud?' asked Pete.

Ivy sighed. 'We need to go up into the hills to find one.'

'I think I heard the girls mention something about doing that,' said Pete.

Ivy raised her head, delighted at the possibility.

'Going up into the hills?' That didn't sound like the girls to me. There were no hiking boots in their suitcases.

'There's an old town worth seeing, or something,' Pete said, before backtracking. 'Or maybe I misheard.'

Our daughter gave another sigh – a noble one – returning to her drawing of a pair of binoculars, part of her documentation of the day.

Over at the actress's lounger, she had a visitor too – the harassed-looking brunette, who we supposed was a younger sister to 'Hugo'. She stood with her hands on her hips, talking down, the actress not self-conscious at all about her bare chest. If anything, she seemed bolder, sitting upright, supported by arms stretched back behind her, her body in the shape of an M, breasts lifted to the sky. The two women traded words, unsmiling, the resemblance between them obvious then, though the elder was not as striking as the younger. If they were sisters, the harangued brunette was an early prototype, I thought unkindly.

'Well, I'm glad you're okay,' said Pete, his thigh-squeezing evolving into a reassuring pat. 'And that we're good for Jason's birthday lunch today.'

'Of course!' I replied. 'The Liv and Pete Comeback Tour is go!'

Pete winced at my sarcasm. I avoided his eye. I wanted him to leave. The fabric of the lounger was stretched too taut with all three of us sitting on it. He was stopping me from listening in on the exchange between the actress and her sister. Pete followed my gaze just as a child – the little blonde girl from a German fairy-tale – joined the scene on the opposite side of the sun deck. The two women brightened on her arrival, knowing they must be cordial in front of the girl.

'Jesus, cover yourself up,' Pete murmured, his eyes on the actress's bare breasts. He was marking himself out as separate from the sex-starved, poolside dads; he was on the side of the critical mums. It was a hollow display of solidarity, wasted on me. I like to think the actress heard Pete's comment and that was why, at that moment, she pulled the little blonde girl into a wholesome, familial cuddle against her naked chest.

'Why should she cover up?' I said, a comeback for the sake of it, a petty bit of point scoring, the only kind of retaliation I thought myself capable of. 'She's not hurting anybody, is she?'

Then Pete lost his job.

I realise there should be some preamble to that – a period, say, when Pete returns to his wretched monologues at the kitchen table. Maybe a first appraisal goes badly and that brings about an anxious probationary period. Or unease rumbles though the company because times are tight and cuts are coming, causing him to fear that he will be sacrificed, last in, first out. But there was none of that.

It was only when I opened a letter from our mortgage provider informing us that our direct debit had failed that Pete was forced to confess – he'd been let go.

But it was just a blip, he said, countering quickly. Another job would come up. His old place would likely take him back; he'd give them a call. Whatever happened, we had breathing space, he'd get a pay-off. Unease *had* been rumbling through the company after all. Pete just hadn't said anything because he didn't want me to worry, not when everything else in our lives was going so well.

I suggested quitting my MRes to find a job. Pete wouldn't hear of it. I was overreacting, he said, and besides, the course fees were paid, we wouldn't get that back. This had been my dream for a long time, he reminded me, something I'd been putting off for years while raising Ivy.

'Think of the effort you've put in already!'

So, I carried on studying, taking him at his word.

Regardless, the private-school prospectus had to go in the bin. All talk of hiring a marquee for Pete and Dev's joint fortieth birthday fizzled out. The dates we'd agreed for the start of our house renovations got pushed back. The architect called me saying he still needed to be paid for his drawings, even though the build was delayed, and could he please check that he had the right number for Pete because he'd left several messages on his phone and received no reply.

We continued with the expensive London dinners, putting them on the credit card, even though the interest-free period had ended and the balance was growing fast.

'It's fine,' I told the girls, swigging wine we could in no way afford, mimicking Pete's casual optimism, 'something will turn up.'

At that same dinner table, Kenny launched into a story about a fella he knew who had travelled the world on the spoils of his redundancy package. 'So, come on, tell us, how much are you getting?'

I squealed at the directness of the question. 'You can't ask that!'

'Oh, I see!' said Kenny, grinning, assuming from my deflection that we'd hit the jackpot. 'Just think of the adventures you'll have!'

Pete played along. Yes, it was exciting. Yes, we were, when you thought about it, really lucky. But I saw it – the panic beneath. He was a kid who had broken a window and was running out of ways to maintain his innocence. As soon as we got home, the babysitter sent on her way with fifty precious notes, I repeated Kenny's question.

'So, come on, tell me, how much money are we getting?'

Pete pretended to be dozier from the drink than he was.

'I don't know.' He shrugged, making for the stairs, for bed. 'I don't know, I don't know, I don't know,' he repeated as he climbed.

It was all lies.

There was, I believe, a good couple of months, maybe even three, when Pete, already fired from his post, continued to get up at six a.m., put on his suit and leave the house, whiling away his usual work hours in a café (or god knows where, doing god knows what), returning to Ivy and me at eight p.m., pretending that everything was normal. And I also believe that without those months of subterfuge and obfuscation, we might have been able to save ourselves.

They repossessed the car first. It had been bought on hire purchase and Pete had missed five payments, ignoring all letters from the credit company. I began selling my clothes, thankful that I'd invested in designer labels to impress the others, because at least they had decent resale value on eBay. That covered our weekly food shop for a while. My clothes proceeds spent, I brought Ivy's baby stuff down from the loft and started selling that too. Pete watched pale-faced as I laid each item on the living-room rug to photograph it – a Moses basket, a musical mobile with a starfish and an octopus, a baby carrier, bundles and bundles of tiny, patterned sleepsuits.

'I thought we were saving all that,' Pete said, 'just in case.'

'Just in case what?' I demanded to know, daring him to say it, tears streaking my cheeks.

I quit my course and started applying for jobs, but it was too late. So many letters had gone unopened. We'd missed court dates where we could have at least rescued our house – our house as it was. All dreams of that repositioned back door and a skylit master suite with a roll-top bath had evaporated months ago. The last shreds of my denial fell away. I became one of those people with haunted eyes you see on the evening news whenever there are flash floods or bush fires, people unable to convey to everyone watching from the safety and comfort of their own lives how fast everything can just disappear.

I didn't tell the girls anything until we started selling our furniture and making arrangements to move in with Pete's dad. Nigel had a spare room with a double bed, but we needed to find a camping mattress for Ivy to sleep on beside us. Did Beth, Binnie or Ange have anything we could use? Almost as an aside, I confessed our dire financial situation. I was like Pete, at the start, frightened to say it aloud, to admit that it was real. Because would these women still want to be my friends if I were no longer able to join in, like, really join in? They were the only thing I had left that was all mine.

The girls swept me up, receiving my terrible news with hushed *oh my god*s. There was no grand outpouring of sympathy, no furious takedowns of our grab-happy creditors, and for that I was grateful. My pride was delicate. I didn't want to cry. For Ivy's benefit I had been cultivating a suit of armour, a way to be dignified in the face of crisis. *Difficult things happen sometimes, Ivy, but you stay strong and you work together!* Perhaps I should have been honest with the girls and detailed all the unforgivable things Pete had done to lead us to disaster. We'd have had a common enemy then, someone to enjoy tearing apart. But my anger was mainly reserved for myself, for trusting him, for being so Victorian about our financial affairs – I hadn't bothered my pretty little head with any of it. Also, beneath Pete's lies there was a sleeping beast I had no wish to prod. How terrifying the truth must be if he thought it better for us to hit rock bottom and lose everything rather than tell me what was really going on. My mind ran wild – and it returned endlessly to a text I'd seen on the lockscreen of his phone: *babes r u okay?* It was from someone called Becky.

'I'm sorry but why don't you just ask your parents for the money?'

Both Beth and Binnie asked me iterations of this question in the wake of our ruin, as if I'd never told them about my dad and his propensity for risking it all on a sure-thing in the two-forty at Chepstow. They were transposing their own circumstances onto mine. The Bank of Mum and Dad would always save them, I realised, and at last I understood how they afforded their huge houses and their fancy extensions and their twofold school fees. There was money behind the money. The girls were only trying to help. And they were fearful, I think: if it could happen to me, could it happen to them? Was disaster contagious? Or maybe it was embarrassment that made them clumsy with their kindness; they had so much when we had so little.

The remaining elephant in the room was our three-week holiday in the summer. I kept promising myself that I would bring it up, always losing my nerve at the last moment. In the end it was Ange – of course – who looked me in the eye and said the thing that needed to be said: 'So, what's happening about Corfu in July?'

We were having Saturday lunch on the high street, girls only. As soon as the date had gone into the diary (*We'll shout your meal, Liv*), I'd had the looming sense that it would be a summit meeting about the trip and had prepared myself for the outcome. I'd behave graciously when the girls delivered the devastating news that they had found another family to replace us. At least Pete and I might get our deposit back and we wouldn't – thank the lord – be liable for the full payment.

The pasta sat heavy in my stomach as Ange explained how the booking was in her name and she needed to know where she stood.

'I would never want you and Jason to be out of pocket,' I said, making it easy for her, signalling that we would step aside without a fight. I bit back tears. This was it: I was about to lose my friends. Now I would be bankrupt in every sense.

Ange responded with a strange peal of laughter. 'god, Liv! It's not about the money!'

Obviously, it *was* about the money, because if Pete and I still had any, there wouldn't be a problem, no need for this lunch, no rearrangements to make. I looked to Beth and Binnie who were both disconcertingly silent.

'We can't come,' I said, feeling I must spell it out. 'It's impossible. We have no means of paying for it.'

The restaurant's perky, Italian-American playlist filled the pause, taunting us.

'But,' said Ange, 'you really need this trip right now.'

I stared back at her, lost for words.

'If I were in your shoes,' she continued, 'if I'd already sunk a few grand into the deposit, I would find a way to get my hands on the rest of the cash, come hell or high water.'

Did she not understand? Hell and high water had both come and gone. We'd been fried, drowned. We had nothing.

'Ange…' said Beth softly, a warning.

'I'm sorry but I just think Liv should treat herself,' said Ange defensively.

Beth sat back in her seat, arms folded, her glass of wine perched in the crook of her elbow. It read as a gentle vote of no confidence. Binnie sat back too.

'For god's sake, girls!' said Ange. 'You're supposed to be Liv's friends!'

'We are!' Binnie retaliated. She turned to me and spoke more calmly: 'We are, Liv, you know we are.'

'Then we have to find a way to make Corfu happen,' said Ange, 'for all of us.'

We looked down at the table, children chastised. We were disappointing Ange with this show of pessimism.

'So, I'll pay,' she said.

I thought Ange meant the restaurant bill.

'I'll cover Liv's remaining balance for the holiday.'

Beth and Binnie looked up, stunned.

'What? No!' I protested.

Ange closed her eyes, one palm thrust towards me. 'Yes! I'm doing it. I've decided.'

'Oh, come on. I mean, it's sweet of you, sure, but' – this was not an outcome I had prepared for – 'you can't, because I haven't a clue when we could pay you back, or if we ever could.'

'I'm not listening,' Ange said, hands over her ears. 'You can pay me back in ten years, twenty years, whenever, never. It doesn't matter. It's happening.'

She meant it. And I knew she could probably afford it. The holiday was catastrophically expensive – thousands per family – but still it was a fraction of what Ange had spent on that kitchen of hers, with its copper sink and church windows. It was a trip barely equal in value to one of her beautifully tiled bathrooms. To Ange, it might even be considered small change.

'We'll call it The Liv and Pete Comeback Tour,' she said, warming to her campaign. 'It'll give the holiday a real purpose.'

Beth's and Binnie's expressions of shock had dissolved. Binnie was shaking her head in amused disbelief like she had when Ange first suggested the three-week trip. Beth shrugged at me, as if to say, *Why not?*

'Okay,' I said. 'Okay. I'll come.'

Ange drummed her hands on the table, cheering. Beth and Binnie joined in – a full rhythm section. The noise drew an anxious waiter to our table – was everything all right?

'We're just fine,' I said, a phrase I'd been using a lot and not meaning at all. But I meant it then. The misery of the last few months hadn't allowed me to imagine an outcome as wonderful as this – for my friends not only to dismiss the idea of replacing me on the trip, but to make me its new focus. I was overwhelmed by their kindness.

'We'll get t-shirts printed!' Ange said, bobbing in her seat. Her enthusiasm was infectious; we bobbed along with her. 'On the back they'll say, *The Liv and Pete Comeback Tour* and on the front...' She mapped out the slogan across her chest. '*The. Only. Way. Is. Up.*'

The restaurant was on the edge of a popular bay, the sand crowded with umbrellas, the shallows a soup of Lilos and rubber rings. We took an elevated position, superior, on the restaurant's covered veranda. An ancient olive tree craned towards the water, screening us from the eyes of any nearby sunbathers.

The other diners were predominantly yacht owners, all Hilfiger stripes, popped collars and chestnut tans. It was an international crowd – loud American superlatives dancing over a bassline of deep Russian vowels. Out at the mouth of the bay, there was a whole pageant of yachts, from the compact and quietly chic, to the huge, shiny and ridiculous, rocking with the waves, sails furled. The small boats that had brought ashore their owners, our fellow diners, jostled against the restaurant's pontoon below.

We ate grown-up food – deep-fried courgettes stuffed with cheese, seafood linguine that coiled unctuously around your fork. With no kids to please, we swerved the hummus, pitta and chips, and let soft, baked squid melt on our tongues, washing away the tensions of the preceding twenty-four hours with crisp white wine.

Ivy and I had reunited with the group after their breakfast, the pair of us jumping straight into the pool and instigating a game of volleyball – a demonstrative act. *Look at us, completely grudge-free, having so much fun!* The others joined in – adults and kids – and we commandeered the whole pool with our raucous, good-natured competitiveness. Throughout I was desperate to swim to Ange and put my arm across her shoulders, tell her that we were good now, that I'd drawn a distinct line under their Berlin trip. Instead, fate gifted us a moment: Ange and I teamed up to score a particularly pleasing point, and we hugged and high-fived in its wake. It was implicit; nothing needed saying. We were good, more than good.

When it came time to wave the children off on their kids' club trip to the beach, we slathered them white with sun cream, issuing stern caveats to behave. We headed back to our rooms, ostensibly to dress for lunch, but with a couple of hours to kill before our taxis arrived, I knew the others would be shagging. Open-plan family rooms were not conducive to holiday sex – you had to seize your opportunities. Pete and I were used to sharing a 'family room' at Nigel's house, and we had also become well-versed in leaving one another alone, for reasons beyond our sleeping arrangements.

Around that restaurant table though, my guard came down. I let Pete rest his hand on my knee, didn't brush it away. We were relaxed – sighing our appreciation for the setting, enjoying the pauses between courses, ordering the next round of drinks without thinking twice. The children would have merely tolerated such a leisurely lunch, their forbearance a ticking timebomb. Without them there, we let the meal stretch towards four p.m., polishing off plates of baklava with coffee, feeling no inclination to leave. So, Jason ordered champagne for the table, making a grand, noisy gesture of it, further marking our separateness from the yacht crowd, who drank their dusty vintages discreetly.

With the champagne served, Ange rang a spoon inside her empty water glass demanding the table's attention. The other diners on the veranda hushed as well, turning our way. Ange feigned embarrassment at this, but still she slipped off her strappy heels to climb onto the raffia seat of her chair, tall enough then for the whole restaurant to see. She wobbled in place a while, a giggly kind of merry. Binnie tugged at the leg of Ange's broderie anglaise playsuit, which had ridden up indecorously high.

'Firstly!' Ange announced. 'As everyone knows, it's my honey-bunny's birthday...'

We responded with a sweetly sarcastic, 'T'aww!'

Dev ruffled Jason's hair.

'My darling baby Jason, the most wonderful father to my three gorgeous boys, has hit the big four-five...' I topped up my champagne glass from the dregs in the bottle, settling in for one of Ange's Facebook commemorations – live and in the flesh! I gestured to the waiters clustered by the cash desk that we would be needing more champagne. Their focus was already on our table, a conference taking place about how long they would let the intoxicated Englishwoman balance precariously, making a spectacle of herself.

Kenny also had ideas about cutting Ange short. 'Happy forty-fifth birthday, Jay-Co!' he interjected in a roar, glass aloft. 'You're halfway to death and you don't look that bad for it.'

'Halfway to death!' echoed Dev.

'Halfway to death!' we all chimed, leaning over the table to strike one another's glasses.

But Ange wasn't stepping down. She wasn't giving in. She put a finger to her lips like a nursery teacher commanding an unruly class.

'No, but seriously,' she said, 'but seriously...'

Beth provided back-up. 'Come on, guys!' she scolded. 'Just listen!'

I did my part at our end of the table, quietening Kenny and Pete, sharing a matronly bit of tut-tutting with Binnie, as if we hadn't been as loud with the toast as everyone else.

Ange cleared her throat to continue: 'So, this holiday isn't just about Jason's birthday. We're all here for another really important reason...'

She looked at me. I froze. I'd been prepared for an Angela Addison Facebook tribute, but not to be the subject of it. Was every tragic detail of Liv and Pete's fall from grace about to be drunkenly delivered to the international yacht crowd? I returned her smile feebly.

'When I first suggested we do this three-week trip' – Ange pressed her hands girlishly to her breastbone – 'I confess, I had an ulterior motive.'

This embellishment was classic Ange. Pete hadn't lost his job when she first proposed the trip; the decision to dedicate it to our comeback came later. But, of course, Ange was going to tell it this way; it played better.

'I packed swimsuits and shorts in my suitcase, sure, but' – her voice grew mischievous – 'I also packed something else.'

Oh, god, I thought, the t-shirts. Ange was going to bring them out *now*. I drained my glass of champagne.

'I also packed a beautiful, *beautiful* dress,' Ange said, 'which my gorgeous friends helped me choose.'

This pulled me up. It made no sense. Ange had bought me a *dress*?

She inhaled deeply, increasing the pressure of her hands against her breastbone, her eyes damp, her lip trembling. This was not classic Ange.

'I also packed three stunning flower-girl outfits for Amelia, Paige and Ivy, who have been absolutely amazing at keeping quiet.'

A murmur travelled though the restaurant. Everybody else had grasped what was about to happen, while I, stuck on an old story, a phony one, remained lost.

'And don't ask me how I managed it, Jason, but I sneaked your best suit into my case as well.' Ange performed a curtsey up on her perch. 'Though I realise now that we're here, it's totally too hot for you to wear it.'

Beth gave a titter of laughter. I caught her eye and she beamed back, squeezing her shoulders close to her ears, as if I were sharing her excited feeling, as if I knew what on earth was going on.

'Jason...' Ange's voice went low; she fanned the beads of sweat collecting at her temples. She was nervous. Jason stared up at her, his expression equal parts admiration and bafflement. 'I love you to the moon and back,' she said, 'and I know you feel the same about me because you keep talking and talking and talking about making it official. So, I give in, babes. You know me too well. I'm a doer not a talker.'

The soft murmurs on the veranda gave way to an anticipatory silence. Ange savoured the moment, took her time.

'That's why we're all here, on this stunning island.' She threw one arm towards the view, as if everything we could see belonged to her. Though my head and my eyes followed this sweeping gesture, I had left my body. I was floating above the scene, unable to get a grip on reality.

'Beth and Binnie have organised the lot, a gorgeous ceremony at this romantic spot up in the hills. There are flowers, there's food and...'

A pyramid of champagne saucers, I thought.

Ange stopped to take a dramatic, shuddery breath. 'Oh, god, I bloody hope you're on board for this, babes!'

Jason reached up for her hand, giving her a sombre nod, a sign that she should continue. The Greek chorus on the veranda regained its voice, issuing squeaks and little *oh*s of delight. Inside of me rumbled an entirely different kind of *oh* – one like thunder.

'I love you so very much, Jason Connors,' Ange intoned. 'Will you do me the honour of becoming my husband?'

He rose from his seat, fierce, solemn. The diners held their breath, as if Jason's answer were ever in doubt.

'A thousand times yes!' He grabbed Ange about the waist with a force so intense I had to look away. I knew what that kind of passion felt like. I knew what it was to lose it. My head turned, I saw instead the confetti landing on our discarded napkins and empty plates: hundreds and hundreds of tiny pink and red cut-out paper hearts, thrown by Beth and Binnie, clutched in their fists beneath the table all along. Everyone whooped. Everyone cheered. The whole restaurant. Except for me.

Jason suggested it. He led the hysterical race down to the restaurant's pontoon, hollering the dare, 'Jump! Jump! Jump! Jump!' He didn't pause to shed his shoes but ran full pelt the whole swaying length of the platform, his grasp tight on Ange's wrist, so she couldn't chicken out at the last minute. They leapt high, briefly silhouetted against the blue before splashing into the water with yelps of delight. On the veranda, applause rang out. The diners were up on their feet, craning for a view of this crazy celebration. Beth and Binnie jumped next, shrieking as they took flight. Then went the boys – Kenny, Dev and Pete – the three of them clattering down the planks together, launching in unison, Dev attempting a somersault and not quite nailing it.

Me, I stood rooted to the land end of that floating pontoon, feeling the nauseous roll of their aftershocks. I could hear them laughing and splashing in the sea beyond the tethered boats and knew I should be in the water too, being gracious, rinsing away my expectations. What did it matter that this wasn't *The Liv and Pete Comeback Tour*? I'd never believed in that anyway. Wasn't I grateful just to be on the island, at that expensive restaurant, tanned and replete?

No, because now I understood exactly *why* I was there. I had to be. Ange would never have considered replacing us. She didn't want a wedding, she wanted *my* wedding, like she wanted *my* trip to Berlin, *my* friends. She didn't need those things like I did, but she was going to steal them anyway. The joy of it for her was having me watch. I could hear my mother's voice, shrill in my ear. *Eat the cake, Liv, just eat the fucking cake!* But I couldn't, wouldn't. If Ange had been standing beside me at that moment, I'd have taken hold of her arm and bitten down. I'd have drawn blood.

Pete, I assumed, would be furious.

I found him in his dad's oven of a conservatory, a room he had started referring to as his 'office'. I hung back in the doorway as I relayed my exchange with Ange – her offer, my acceptance – and was ready for his anger. When Kenny had suggested he cover just one of our restaurant bills, Pete had been humiliated. Yet he greeted the news of Ange's gift of a luxury holiday by leaping from his seat, grabbing me by the waist and swinging me around. We hadn't touched one another intentionally, with affection, for months. This show of passion threatened to overwhelm me. It made me breathless for what we'd lost.

'The Liv and Pete Comeback Tour!' he echoed, exultant with it. He stroked the hair from my face, demanding to know why I wasn't smiling.

'Because we'll never be able to pay it back,' I said.

'But you said Ange didn't want paying back.'

'Come on, Pete, it's *thousands*. We'll have to eventually.'

He shrugged. Not a problem. Some freelance consultancy work had come his way via an old uni contact; we'd be out of the woods in no time. I recognised that tone of voice, the bluster. I wasn't going to fall for it again. I extricated myself from his embrace, annoyed that I had let his touch convince me we were close again. All Pete did while he hunkered down in that conservatory 'office' was adjust the margins and the font size of his CV. Mostly, he stared through the smeary windows at the dandelions growing tall, at the flurries of goldfinches Nigel lured to his bird table with sunflower seeds. I was taking a forensic interest in our joint account now; nothing was going in from Pete. We'd cancelled my phone contract but maintained his for 'business reasons', and it never rang. One day as it charged in the kitchen, the lockscreen lit up with another message from Becky: *always here for you x*

I didn't confront him. It wasn't that I feared the truth; I just knew Pete wouldn't give me it. He was sticking solidly to the story that his job had been axed in company-wide cuts, that he was last in, first out. But a redundancy with no pay-off? A redundancy that had seemingly rendered him unemployable? None of it added up.

It was down to me to bring in the money. My public libraries experience, I discovered, was about as useful as a qualification in lion-taming. Our local library had closed. The one in the next town was staffed by self-serve machines. My translation work was too sporadic, and while I might have advertised myself as a languages tutor, there being an endless supply of pushy parents in the neighbourhood desperate for their kids to ace their GCSEs and A-levels, it would only have occupied me in the evenings and at weekends. More than money, I wanted to be out of the house, away from Pete. My fingers burnt with the desire to grasp and shake him, to slide my hands around his throat, to lift him high above my head and launch him through the smeary glass of that godforsaken conservatory.

I fell back on another proven skill – espresso-making. Gabi had given me that at least. Her tutorials at the Winter Gardens café, like the woman herself, had been intense. (Clean and dry the portafilter between each extraction. Measure out the grind size *exactly*. DO NOT FORGET to warm the cup.) I had been a barista before being a barista was even a thing.

The café was on a high street much like ours, two towns east. I couldn't work anywhere close to home. If Beth, Binnie or Ange had walked in wanting a flat white, it would have been excruciating. For them, more than me. Nigel let me borrow his X-reg Astra occasionally, a car he playfully described as vintage, but I couldn't use it all the time. Pete's 1990s road bike with its curling racer handlebars was living with the spiders in Nigel's shed so I liberated that to cycle the nine-mile journey into work.

It was cool, the café, at least it thought it was, with its raw wood panelling and uncomfortable chairs. Chirpy Motown rang from the speakers one moment, nihilistic triphop the next. Unexpectedly, this attracted baby boomers in the main, stopping off after a mid-morning dog walk, people old enough to call me 'girl', as in 'I gave my order to the girl at the coffee machine,' even though I was the oldest member of staff, including the manager. In another life, this might have been embarrassing, alienating, but I hadn't taken the job to be liked. I rolled up my jeans and the sleeves of my t-shirt as a gesture towards fitting in with my millennial co-workers, knotting a bandana in my hair. I ladled out gluten-free soup, toasted vegan paninis and brewed one hundred lattes a day, trying not to think of the French novels packed away in a cardboard box in Nigel's garage, focusing instead on the cash I was slowly accumulating. The mindless routine of it numbed me.

When the café installed a fridge of artisan beers and began opening later, I took on split shifts, cycling through the five a.m. streets, alone but for a foraging fox, to open for the breakfast shift, heading home for a nap in the middle of the day, then returning late afternoon to serve the evening crowd, mopping the floors after closing. As I cycled home, I'd see the same fox skittering into the hedgerow.

Once I got back to the dark, silent house, I'd pet Ivy's head as she lay sleeping on the camping mattress, then quietly undress, climbing into bed beside the deep-breathing mound of duvet that was Pete.

Days could go by without me speaking to Ivy. The school run, Ivy's playdates, her tea – Pete sorted all that. He was the one who got to call her Spud without her complaining. In the few hours I spent with my daughter each week, she'd tell me about the schoolfriend who had new trainers, the schoolfriend throwing a horse-riding party, the schoolfriend whose mum didn't have to work and was always there.

But it was for the best. I wasn't a nice person to be around. I was sullen and bitter, my rage at Pete eating me up inside. I couldn't share that with anyone, and especially not the girls.

To be included in the trip to Corfu, Pete and I had to be a couple, one working towards a miraculous comeback. Our marriage had always been a keystone of the group, the wedding written into the folklore of our friendship; it was untouchable. Allowing myself to admit aloud that Pete was lying to me would, at once, make it real. I'd be the duped wife, the terrible fool – and then what? I couldn't leave; I had nowhere to go. Yet.

When I really went for it, working seven days in a row, taking extra shifts and covering colleagues' duvet days, I could bring home nearly seven hundred and fifty pounds a week. There was no mortgage to pay, no utilities. Nigel refused my offers of rent.

'Save what you have,' he said, 'otherwise you'll never get back on your feet.'

And I'll never be rid of you, was what he meant. His girl-friend, Sheila, wasn't keen to stay over anymore, not with Pete, Ivy and me sleeping on the other side of Nigel's thin plasterboard bedroom wall.

So my bank balance gained zeroes. I shifted the bare minimum across to the joint account to cover essentials. What remained, I considered mine – all mine. I wasn't saving for the prophesied Liv and Pete Comeback. A small, insistent voice in my head told me what that money was really for: *You're saving up to run away.*

I divulged a little bit about my savings to the girls on our shopping trips – the ones I could manage around my shifts. I told them I was working hard, getting close to some kind of equilibrium, and was beginning to feel hopeful. Ange would persuade me to try on clothes that I liked, just to see, and if something looked good, she would encourage me to buy it.

'Treat yourself,' she'd say, resting her chin on my shoulder, grinning at me in the mirror. 'You deserve it.'

I liked her for saying that, because I *did* deserve it, but I always resisted.

When we ate out, I would lie and say I wasn't hungry, that I'd had something before I'd got there. *Nigel made this massive lasagne, and I couldn't say no.* Then I'd order a Coke, or a glass of wine if I was feeling extravagant. I knew it was rude, accepting the invitation, then sitting there, watching the others eat.

'We'll pay if you need us to,' Beth said, 'if that's what stopping you.'

It was and it wasn't. I didn't want to make even the smallest dint in my bank balance, but also, I liked denying myself – it was the only power I could wield with absolute confidence. I was living for that trip away in the summer. It would be a comeback, as Ange said, but not for my marriage, just for me. I'd have three whole weeks without working, time to think, time to remind myself who I was. I'd rooted around in the boxes in Nigel's garage and decided which French novels to take. My energy would go on those girls and our friendship, because with their support, I believed I could summon the strength to strike out on my own, without Pete.

At every opportunity, I thanked Ange for paying our balance, for giving us that wonderful boost, a chance to free ourselves from the rubble of the past year. I thought of it like a student loan, a debt accruing negligible interest, one that could be deferred and deferred until it was finally manageable. But also, I was a realist. A holiday was more than just the flights and accommodation paid for in advance. There would be bar bills, excursions, meals out. Pete's mythical freelance consultancy income wouldn't cover it, and there wasn't a bank in the whole wide world who would trust us with a credit card. It was up to me. I decided on a figure that felt safe, a good shock absorber, considering the extravagant tastes of the company in which we were travelling. Mentally, I prepared for that amount to be deducted from my escape savings.

Then, Binnie came knocking.

Pete was with Ivy at an after-school football match. I was on the way back from work. Nigel had invited Binnie inside to wait the twenty minutes until I returned – an awkward twenty minutes I surmised from the atmosphere in that living room when I walked in. Binnie was perched on the very edge of an armchair, as if it were contaminated. Nigel's house was homey and cluttered, sure, the décor tired and naff, but it wasn't that dirty.

'I'll leave you two to it,' Nigel said, heading off into the garden to tinker with something that likely needed no tinkering with at all.

Binnie gave my cycle helmet and rolled-up jeans a swift once over.

'Look, Liv,' she said, 'this is hard, so I'm just going to come right out and say it, okay?'

'You don't want a coffee?' I asked. 'A tea?'

Binnie shook her head. I watched her slip on that metaphorical jacket, her tough, legal-eagle persona.

'You need to pay Ange back what you owe her,' she said.

'Right.' I shrugged the rucksack off my back and freed myself from the cycle helmet. 'Of course. That's a given.'

'No, I mean, you need to pay her back, like, now.'

'But...' I rubbed at the skin of my forehead where the cycle helmet always left its mark. I felt as though I was returning to a soap opera after not watching for years, trying to piece together the plot. Or rather, I'd been cast in that soap opera and was performing without a script, without lines. 'But Ange told me ten years,' I said, 'twenty years, it's been, what...'

'Six months.'

'Right, six months.'

Binnie held her silence. I'd never been in a confrontation with her, in all the years we'd known each other, not a serious one. Was this a confrontation? I wasn't sure. Out of nervousness, I laughed.

'I'm not joking, Liv.' She mumbled it.

'I know,' I said, 'I can tell. It's just...' I sank into the armchair opposite. 'I just don't know what to say.'

Binnie offered me her palms. 'Ange is really upset.'

'So why hasn't she come to me and—'

'She couldn't bring herself to. She didn't want me to say anything today either.' Binnie rolled her eyes. 'You can imagine.'

I could imagine: Ange sitting sad-faced at her varnished-wood kitchen island. *I'm sorry but I was only trying to be nice*, she would say to Beth and Binnie. *A loan is a loan, though, and at some point, it has to be paid back.*

'Look,' said Binnie, 'Ange is aware that you're having a few financial difficulties at the moment...'

'A few, yeah.'

'… and she wants to be sympathetic, but you've been earning money for months now, you keep telling us how you have this ton of savings and—'

'I mean "a ton" isn't quite—'

'—and you know Ange didn't really mean it, that thing about paying her back in ten years or twenty. It was just a silly turn of phrase, a thing people say.'

Did we all know that? Was it a thing people said? I was certain Ange had told me whenever, or never. She'd said that the money didn't matter.

Binnie sighed. 'I'm totally guilty of it too – seeing Ange as some kind of fairy godmother who will swoop in and make everything all right, but she can't keep you afloat right now.'

Keep me afloat? I was mortified.

'Don't say anything to her,' Binnie went on, 'but I think Ange might have a few money worries of her own.'

'Of course,' I replied, urgently rummaging in the rucksack for my phone, praying that I had some data credit, desperate for Binnie to stop talking.

'She just couldn't bring herself to ask,' Binnie went on.

'Of course,' I said. 'Of course. I must have misunderstood. I must have just…'

'God, this is *so* embarrassing!' Binnie said, letting go of a great gasp of pent-up air.

'So embarrassing,' I said, nodding in agreement, my voice a whisper. I held her eye for a moment so she would know that I was sorry, and that I was grateful for the intervention. Binnie would smooth things over with Ange, I was sure of it. She'd vouch for me, explain the misunderstanding, make everything okay.

I held my phone out, my thumb obscuring the available balance. I didn't want Binnie to see how much was in my escape fund, how little would be left afterwards – hardly anything, two hundred pounds, if that. I entered the amount owed to Ange for the holiday – eight thousand, one hundred and fifty pounds – and, as if understanding the enormity of the figure, my banking app asked one final question. *Are you sure this looks right?*

Binnie placed a reassuring hand on my arm, and I hit *Confirm*.

I said, 'Congratulations!'

And, 'I'm so excited for you guys!'

And, 'Yes, I know I should have jumped off the jetty too, but it's just that I have this phobia about swimming in the sea.'

Then I shrank, I hid away. That next day by the pool, I kept my head down, sunglasses on, the peak of my tired baseball cap tweaked low. I disappeared into one of my French novels, immersing myself in the machinations of another world, where order had been imposed by the author, consequences meted out as they should be.

While I read, Beth, Binnie and Ange replayed the proposal over and over, turning it into a fiction of their own, something puffed up and schlocky.

'I'm sorry but wasn't it the most romantic thing you've ever experienced?' said Beth, poking me to reply.

'Yes,' I said, because it had been romantic, in the sense that it was fanciful, unrealistic, absurd.

Inside, I seethed, desperate to scream, *Can't you see what she's doing?* Desperate to slap both Beth and Binnie across the face, before dragging them into a taxi headed straight for the airport. But they had to want to be freed from the cult of Ange, and they didn't. They were smitten, too far gone. So, I retreated into almost silence.

That evening we caught a boat to Corfu Town, the island's capital – sixteen cheap tickets on a clunky, chugging party bus across the waves. The sun was still hot in the sky as we left the north-eastern headland, the coastline of Albania playing out to our left across the sea – a distant horseshoe of golden, Lego-block buildings.

I made the effort that the trip demanded, putting on an outfit not yet worn on the holiday – a black cotton, button-down dress with a nipped-in waist, part of my fast-fashion bulk buy, the swing tags tucked into the back of the bodice, a dress that put me in mind of Audrey Hepburn in *Roman Holiday* when I'd picked it out. I too could be a girl escaped, royalty disguised as one of the masses. I'd dedicated the requisite half an hour to blow-drying my fringe in place. I took several attempts to get my eyeliner just right, before pausing to wonder what the girls would say if I turned up for our night out wearing no make-up at all. Because did I truly enjoy it, the primping and peacocking, the hours spent in front of the mirror working against the certainty that our natural, unadorned selves were not good enough?

This question continued to nag me out at sea. I stared down at my red sandals against the vinyl floor of the boat. I'd bought those sandals two summers ago because they were similar to a pair owned by Beth (who had bought hers because they were similar to a pair worn by Ange). Did I like them? If I'd had absolute freedom to choose, what would I have put on my feet that evening – on my body, on my face? The terrifying conclusion: I didn't know.

At the prow of the boat, Ange and Jason posed in *Titanic*-style clinches against the railings, Beth and Binnie laughing along, capturing the moment, their embellished iPhone cases glinting in the sun. My own phone was still at the bottom of my rucksack in our apartment, turned off. I had no photos of the holiday so far, no memories recorded – which was probably for the best. Why would I want to remember this, a trip organised by a woman I could barely bring myself to look at, a woman who had lured me close only to eat me up?

Ivy and I sat on moulded seats on the covered lower deck where the chain-smoking chief mate had put on a playlist of bouncy Euro-pop and opened a makeshift bar. He lined up his limited offerings on the countertop as a visual menu – a carton of apple juice, a can of Coke, a bottle of Smirnoff Ice, a stubby of Alfa beer. Pete gestured to each drink in turn as he waited to be served with Kenny and Dev; Ivy and I shook our heads at every option.

Ivy was feeling seasick. We should be out on the upper deck, I told her, where we could see the water and get our bearings, but Ivy insisted we remain below. In the cigarette fug of that under-belly disco, I was beginning to feel queasy too.

'So, are you looking forward to being a bridesmaid?' I asked my daughter.

'Flower girl,' she corrected.

'Right.'

I left it a moment, not wanting to seem too invested in her answer.

'So, are you,' I asked again, 'looking forward to it?'

She shrugged, noncommittal. 'I suppose.'

Ange would have pounced when I was working, when Ivy was on a playdate with Amelia and Paige. She must have considered leaving Ivy out, treating her as an extension of me, before realising that assimilating my daughter into her wedding plans without my knowledge would make her victory all the crueller.

'Did you know about this?' I had demanded of Pete when he emerged from the water after that jump from the restaurant pontoon. 'Did you know Ange was going to propose?'

'No!' he said, shaking water from his hair, grinning, ecstatic, as gullible as a Labrador. 'Wasn't it amazing!'

I left another judicious pause before asking Ivy, in as light a voice as I could muster, 'So how come you didn't tell me?'

'Because it was a secret,' she replied.

I nudged her playfully in the ribs. 'And can't I be trusted with your secrets?'

She turned to consider me for a moment. I couldn't tell if her serious expression was in response to my question or the motion of the sea.

'Ange said I mustn't say anything to you.'

I hung on for dear life to my smile. 'Why ever not?'

'Because if someone tells you a secret then you have to keep it – Ange said, "That's girl code."'

'Girl code,' I repeated.

Ivy nodded, dropping her chin. She was ashen, green almost.

'Do you think that you might actually be sick?' I asked.

'Maybe,' she replied.

At Corfu Town harbour, we walked the sloping gangplank down to dry land, the skipper bellowing instructions for the return journey. We were to be back by nine-thirty.

'You not here, I leave without you!' he barked, as if we'd already gone and done it, turned up late, messed him around.

Like so many English sheep, we followed the movement of the other passengers along the smooth, brick pavements towards a cluster of cafés. Our small flock halted on the graduated steps of a clay-coloured church to make plans for the evening. Rather, we listened while Ange told us the plan she had already decided upon. I zoned out, peering up at the church, at the white, zigzag rays radiating from its round, central window like a child's drawing of the sun. At primary school, a boy had upset our Religious Studies teacher by pointing out that god couldn't be both almighty and good, because bad things happened all the time. I agreed with him, but stayed quiet for fear of getting into trouble – for fear of being struck by lightning. Ange's plan went unchallenged. The boys were to find a café where they'd be happy drinking beer, somewhere that also served hummus, pitta and chips for the kids. Us girls would, of course, go shopping.

If I'd had freedom to choose, I'd have started my evening with a look inside that church, before wandering to the rocky promontory we'd seen on our approach by boat, where there was a sixteenth-century fortress, a museum and the promise of beautiful views. But I didn't have the freedom to choose because I'd signed up for this. I'd handed over the reins to Ange long ago, I could that see now. It had been a slow, stealthy and comprehensive take-over. I was lucky to have retained the smallest sense of who I used to be and what I cared about. But had Beth? Had Binnie?

We took to the narrow lanes running between the town's high Venetian buildings, made narrower by racks of natural sponges and woven friendship bracelets, olive oil hand creams and traditional wool slippers with bright pompoms sewn onto the toes. By necessity, we walked in single file through this Greek souk, Ange at the head of the snake. Our prey was Gucci fakes, specifically the most convincing knock-off t-shirt we could find for fifteen euros.

The displays of coloured scarves and strange musical instruments we ignored, the carved wooden toys and the embellished religious icons too, all the things worth browsing out of sheer fascination. That the girls could afford genuine Gucci goods back home was not the point. Our quest was about getting more for less. It was about making those fake t-shirts the official souvenir of our trip to Corfu – not the *Liv and Pete Comeback Tour* t-shirts that Ange had promised but never delivered.

They spied their quarry in a shop selling tie-dye dresses and hooky football kits. We headed inside and the girls set about pulling apart the neat piles of shirts on the shelves, searching for their sizes.

'Why can't I find one that will fit me?' complained Beth.

Ange was fast with her response: 'Well, what do you expect after two vaginal births!'

There was an odd pause.

This wasn't Ange's joke. She had never tried to use it before. The events of the past twenty-four hours had clearly emboldened her. But she wasn't doing it right, her timing was off. Beth and Binnie eyed Ange cautiously beneath the shop's unforgiving strip lighting. They would see her for what she truly was now, I was sure of it. She was a land-grabber – Berlin had been annexed, my bank account emptied, demands for a bigger and better wedding had been dumped on Beth's and Binnie's shoulders. Now Ange was trying to muscle in on our shared jokes too.

But they didn't see it like that. Binnie scrambled for the dropped ball, barking out a laugh. Beth chuckled, smoothing away the awkwardness of that initial pause. The browsing resumed. T-shirts were pulled on over cami tops and strappy dresses, then the three of them lined up, identical, in front of the shopfloor mirror, Ange in the middle, arms slung possessively across Beth's and Binnie's shoulders, one knee cocked. They pouted at their reflections, Binnie capturing this image on her phone.

'You buy now!' The harried shop owner arrived at their side, Ange the main cause of concern – she had chosen a size Small and the trademark red and green Gucci stripes were distorting across her generous bust.

'I was going to anyway,' Ange replied primly, lifting the top up and over her head, rolling her eyes at the three of us as soon as the shop owner turned her back to tidy the ransacked piles of shirts.

'And you must get one too, Liv,' said Beth, stepping away from the confrontation, 'these things are, like, three hundred and fifty pounds back home.'

I shook my head.

'Come on!' she urged. 'Then we'll match. It'll be hilarious.'

'It's just not something I would wear,' I said.

'Oh.' Beth appeared stung. She looked about her for Binnie and Ange – a child searching for its parents in a crowd.

'They're at the cash desk,' I said.

'Right.' Beth didn't follow them. 'Are you okay?' she asked.

'Why would I not be?' I replied.

This wasn't the reassurance Beth was after; it was tough love. I wanted her to join the dots for herself, to wake the fuck up, and that wouldn't happen if I only played nice.

We left the shop, the girls clutching a plastic bag each. My empty-handedness, for once, felt like success. As we continued through the narrow streets, Ange initiated a takedown of the shop owner. 'I'm sorry but is it an actual crime to try on a top before you buy it?'

Binnie delivered the requisite, 'No, it absolutely is not.'

'Who did she think she was,' said Beth, 'actual Gucci?'

This was where I was supposed to chip in, call the woman a 'greaseball' or select some other element of her character to inflate and abuse. Pete was right – I didn't like who I was when I was with these women. But who would I be without them? I'd be alone – that was the only certainty.

Our focus shifted. Ange needed 'something new' for her wedding outfit, and the girls decreed that this should be jewellery. We entered a bright, clean, open-fronted store with displays behind locked glass, no prices on show. The others headed straight for an upright cabinet of dainty chains and charms. I was drawn to the low counter where there were rings set with large nuggets of rose quartz, jade and tiger's eye. A single tray lay on top, unsecured, and I plucked at it, magpie-like, choosing a chunk of milky turquoise stone on a thick band of antique silver. This was it, I thought, threading it onto a middle finger, this was the sort of thing I would wear if I had the choice, if I had the money. I held up my hand, fingers splayed, an action that caused an assistant to slide into view, her smile wide and white, her English almost accentless.

'This looks beautiful on you.'

'It is gorgeous,' I said with a sigh.

'And that band is very slim-fitting. Not many people can get it over their knuckle.'

I was being sold to, flattered – *The glass slipper, Cinderella, it fits! It fits!* – but I didn't care; I was in the market for this kind of attention. I felt a hand at my back and assumed one of the girls had come over to admire this perfect union of turquoise, silver and my slender middle finger – until I felt a tug, and a snap. I spun around. Ange was holding up the swing tickets to my dress, smirking.

'Look what you did!' she cried, loud enough for the whole shop to hear.

She offered me the tags, the price printed in bold type: £24.99. Nothing at all, but also, far too much. I snatched at those little pieces of card, shoving them into the pocket of the dress.

'Just like you, Liv,' Ange said with an affectionate shake of the head, using the same tone she used to accuse me of making grand entrances. She didn't qualify her statement this time and tell me which of my intrinsic traits I was laying bare. Was I forgetful, careless, a cheapskate, all of the above?

Beth and Binnie called to Ange – a fresh tray of necklaces had been released from its cabinet – and she went skipping back across the tiles with a fluttery little clap of her hands. I slipped the ring off my finger and dropped it into the assistant's waiting palm, before making for the exit. I didn't know if I was going to cry or rush across the shopfloor to grab Ange by the back of her neck, to thrust her face-first into one of those glass displays. I rested my back against a sliver of wall in the packed alley outside, to collect myself. The lamps were lit now, everything dowsed in a warm, artificial glow.

And then there she was – in the shop across the alley, the actress, dressed in red linen. I watched her lift portioned paper sacks of herbs to her nose, inhaling their scent, deliberating – dry grassy dill, or fennel with its aniseed bite? She rejected both in the end; she wasn't buying. Her indecision was only a performance.

She left the shop, passing close to me, and I experienced a shudder, a prickling of the skin. I might have reached out and tapped her on the arm, but then what? I'd have said something banal, killed the moment. Still, I couldn't help myself – as she moved into the crowd, I peeled my back from the wall and followed, convinced that her appearance there, then, was destiny, that she had come to save me.

The actress moved confidently, swinging her arms, a ballerina's turnout to her gait, a way of walking that suggested the streets were familiar to her – this lane would lead to the next, no surprises around the corner. We passed the sweet, nutty temptations of a crêperie, and a tobacconist's no bigger than a cupboard. A tall display of counterfeit rucksacks dominated one alley, tourists pointing up at their choices, the shop owner using a long pole to hook them down like they were prizes at a fairground. The lane opened out onto a wider, expensive-looking avenue, no wares spilling onto the pavements here. The actress made for a clothing shop whose window featured thin, white mannequins in floral prints, their rigid hands clutching bags either ludicrously large or improbably small. I loitered at the mouth of the narrow lane to watch her through the glass.

Inside, she worked her way along a rack of colourful shirts, stroking the fabrics. She took a plaited belt and ran the length of it across her palm, before selecting a wide-brimmed floppy hat, taking it to the mirror and putting it on, teasing the brim into a shape that pleased her, an assistant dancing at her shoulder, scattering compliments I could not hear. The actress removed the hat to examine the detail of the lining before positioning it on her head once more at a different angle. As with the herbs, she was making a show of being interested, savouring the emotions of it. This was the enjoyable part after all – the possibility. How buoyant Beth, Binnie and Ange had been sorting through those piles of shirts. Once they were paid for and in their hands, the fun was over.

Leaving the shop, the actress wandered some distance along the avenue, the red of her dress allowing me to track her journey through the crowd. She stopped in front of a café that seemed beige and unappealing, but she claimed a table with no hint of indecision. A waiter was immediately at her side, greeting her joyfully, reaching down to kiss her on both cheeks.

I walked her route and entered the cool, perfumed interior of the clothes shop. I caressed the silky shirts and ran that plaited belt through my own hand, releasing its musky scent of leather. I took the same floppy hat to the mirror, pressing the soft felt over my blow-dry, which had long ago collapsed in the evening heat. Could I be the sort of person who wore an extravagant hat?

'This is very popular tonight!' said the assistant at my shoulder. Like the woman in the jewellery store, she spoke with barely an accent.

'How much is it?' I asked.

'Four hundred and twenty euros,' she replied.

I didn't baulk. Taking my lead from the actress, I tipped my head from side to side, as if considering a purchase.

'Hmm, I'm not sure,' I said eventually, handing the hat back.

I stepped out of the shop – and the actress was gone.

Despondency struck. There was no hope that I would reconnect with the girls that evening, and my game of chase had finished far too soon. I trailed over to the actress's table and sat down, the woven plastic of the seat still warm. When the waiter came, I pointed to the ice melting in the heavy tumbler on the table.

'What was in that?' I asked.

'Bourbon,' he said – something that I would never drink, but I ordered it, nonetheless. Maybe I was the sort of person who liked dark, oaky spirits, neat on the rocks. I wouldn't know until I tried.

I kicked off my red sandals and stretched out my feet, exactly the way the actress had the day she arrived at the pool bar. I smoothed down the skirt of the dress that I now permanently owned whether I wanted to or not. Did I like it? I thought perhaps I should. It had given me the *Roman Holiday* experience I'd craved when I'd put it in my online basket – I'd escaped for a short while, been given the chance to be someone different.

The bourbon tasted like cough syrup, but I enjoyed the way it soothed my mind. I studied the people passing by: were they being their authentic selves, hanging in the right tribes, laughing at jokes they genuinely thought were funny? Which of these people were holding hands with someone they truly loved, and which were gripping tightly to the closest, easiest person, someone who had been right for them once, but wasn't anymore and had become difficult to shed? Noticing the pretence in others, their efforts to make do, I felt better about my own situation. I ordered another bourbon and considered a third until I checked my watch. Nine-twenty. I shrieked, leaping from my seat, drawing stares. The boat left in ten minutes and I had no idea where I was, no clue how to get back, no map to guide me. I lodged a ten-euro note beneath my glass, thrust my feet back into the red sandals and ran, the smooth stone of the pavement slippery beneath my soles.

At every loitering group, I demanded directions to the harbour, wasting no time on anyone who hummed and hawed, or began searching for an answer on their phone. I followed fingers that were pointed decisively, even though it felt like I was running in circles through that maze of streets, the trinkets on display in every shop so similar, repeating, echoing, until I came upon the steps beneath the clay-coloured church. I sprinted down them, then along the familiar pale pavement that led to the waterfront, jigging between parked cars on the square. I could hear a twang of music from tinny speakers and spied a strip of lights on a raised upper deck – our boat, still there.

That was my moment to make a dash for it, face up to the wrath of the skipper for making him late, have the other passengers applaud me ironically – *Just like you, Liv, always making a grand entrance!* But instead, I stopped dead beneath the trees of the square, hidden in the shadows.

Pete was on the gangplank, hand in hand with Ivy, the chief mate trying to usher him aboard, and not politely. Pete was refusing to move, doing the equivalent of holding the doors on a train, ensuring the gangplank stayed in place until I arrived. My watch said nine-forty. They should have set off ten minutes ago. The skipper came to the stern, gesticulating wildly, shouting what appeared to be an ultimatum. I held my breath as Pete made his decision. Still hand in hand with Ivy, he walked towards dry land. He wasn't going to leave without me.

Then a woman's voice cut through, a higher register. Ange had come to the stern to appeal to Pete. And though I couldn't quite catch her words, I could imagine what they were. *Think of Ivy*, she'd say. *You need to get her back to the hotel. You can't wander the streets all night with a little girl.* She would make it sound so reasonable, as if she cared. *Liv's a grown woman. She knows how to tell the time. I'm sorry but why should you and Ivy have to suffer the consequences of her actions?*

Ivy cast a searching gaze back towards the Old Town. Pete's shoulders drooped. Ange had convinced him – of course she had.

'Yeah, fuck you, Ange,' I muttered as Pete, resigned to the fate that she had decided for him, walked Ivy back onto the boat. The chief mate quickly lifted the gangplank so Pete couldn't change his mind. The boat's engine grew louder. It pulled away.

'And fuck you too, Pete,' I added.

I was alone and stranded, the exact same way I would have felt if I'd stayed with those girls all evening and boarded the boat. The fairy lights of the upper deck disappeared across the water. The jangly music faded to nothing. Above me, a roosting bird fluttered in the branches as a thread of smoke curled through the air. There was the smell of weed. Someone was sitting on a bench beneath the trees.

I turned – and there she was, the actress.

As we locked eyes, she slowly raised both her hands in the air, the roll-up gripped between her teeth.

'You caught me!' she said, with a grin.

3.

I walked into the breakfast room barefoot, my red sandals hooked on one finger. Beside me, also barefoot, walked the actress. We made straight for the buffet.

As she plucked a peach from the still-life display, lifting it to my face and brushing the fur of its skin against my cheek, I held her eye. Then I selected a red apple for myself, taking a big greedy bite, wiping the juice from my chin with an action that was almost obscene.

We turned to our audience. They were seated at the long table in the middle of the room, quietly staring. The urge to bow, to make them applaud, was strong.

'Catch you later, darling!' the actress said, planting a lingering kiss close to my ear before exiting via the patio doors.

I took a fortifying breath; there was nothing left for me to do but join the others. From a nearby unoccupied table, I dragged a chair, inserting myself next to Ivy, who glowered at me over her chocolate cereal. She was the furious mother; I was the daughter who had not come home when she was supposed to. I played along, acting childish, crossing my eyes and sticking out my tongue until Ivy sniggered.

The rest of the group would not be so easy to win over. They were silent, waiting for me to speak. Beth tilted her head enquiringly. Binnie's eyebrows rode high. Ange made the slow, cow-like chewing of her toast an accusation. I willed her to say her usual line, which would, for once, have been accurate – *Just like you, Liv, always making a grand entrance.*

Pete broke the stand-off. 'So?' he asked.

The skin beneath his eyes was as dark as a bruise; he hadn't slept. I shrugged in response, taking another large, messy bite of the apple, swallowing my guilt with the acidic pulp.

'Are we going to get an explanation?' he continued coolly. 'Or an apology, perhaps?'

'You go first,' I replied. I was still a little drunk; I was feeling plucky. 'You were the one who left me there alone, to spend all night in a strange town.'

Ivy stopped spooning cereal, tuning into the awful hum of tension. I stroked her arm to absolve her from any blame.

'It didn't look like you were alone,' said Pete. His face twitched, infuriated. That lingering kiss had been an improvised addition, a step too far, perhaps.

'Yes, do tell us, Liv!' Ange could resist no longer. She called out her contribution from the opposite end of the table. 'Who is your new friend?'

'Huh?' I leant forward, sinking my teeth into the apple again. I'd heard Ange well enough; I just wanted to make sure she had heard herself, how pompous she sounded.

'I *said*' – she was haughtier still, shameless – 'who is your new friend?'

Ange delivered the word 'friend' like it meant something despicable. I sat back in my chair, flicking creases from the lap of my dress.

'Her name,' I replied plainly, 'is Clara.'

Her name was Clara and I had caught her. If she knew that I had been chasing her across Corfu Town all evening, she didn't say so, and I didn't ask, but there was an unspoken understanding that a game had been played, and that our meeting by the harbour was its finale.

'It's medicinal,' Clara said, explaining the roll-up between her teeth, extracting it to examine the smoking tip. 'It cures my disappointment.'

She patted the bench beside her and I sat down, sharing the joint, letting the dust settle on what I'd just done – deliberately missing the boat. It was an easy silence. I might have been back on the flat roof of my uni house, marvelling at the stars with Gabi.

'So,' Clara said, and she mimicked my voice – sweetly, not mean-sounding: '"Fuck you, Ange" and "Fuck you, Pete".'

'You heard that?'

She nodded. Close up, her eyes were a glassy blue, her freckles so distinct they looked painted on. I thumbed anxiously at my lower lids where I was sure there would be smudges of mascara.

'Pete's my husband,' I said.

'Got it. And Ange?'

'Ange is...' I took a long drag, searching for the right description. 'Ange is a grade-A fucking narcissist.'

Clara erupted with laughter, dousing my simmering anger, forcing me to snort with laughter too.

'Oh, we are so going to need a drink,' she said, taking a swipe at my thigh, as if we were age-old *amigos* with years of catching-up to do.

'But what about *your* boat?' I asked. Surely that was why she was at the harbour: she was waiting to leave.

'I skipped mine as well,' she said, springing to her feet, crushing the stub of the roll-up beneath her plimsoll. 'Great minds think alike!' She grinned impishly. This was not the finale of the game after all; it was only the beginning.

Breakfast done, Ivy went to the pool with Beth and her girls, so Pete and I could return to our room and argue privately – loudly, gloriously – something we'd been deprived of for months living with Nigel, his ear always there on the other side of our bedroom wall.

'It's you who should be apologising, Pete!' We launched straight into it the moment the door closed behind us.

'You ran off, Liv! You gave the girls the slip, they were out of their minds with worry.'

'Oh, bullshit!'

I stripped off last night's dress, throwing it to the floor, pacing in my underwear, no idea what to do with myself. I needed a shower. I needed to sleep. I wanted to be with Ivy. I wanted to see Clara. My desire to fight Pete won out though; it was like electricity in my veins.

He stood in the doorway to the lounge and kitchenette, containing me within the bedroom, keeping his distance.

'They had no clue where you were,' he said, 'or why you'd gone.'

'Really?' I came close to his face. 'Those girls had no clue why I might have had enough of them?'

'So, you did run off?' He raised his finger; a point scored.

I slapped that finger away. 'You're on their side now, are you? I see. Quite the turnaround. I thought you said those girls were a bad influence.'

'That's not what I said.'

'They tricked us, Pete! Why are you not fucking angry about that?'

He let his arm fall limply by his side, lost at this turn in the argument.

'We were fooled!' I laughed at him, at us. 'Fooled into spending thousands of pounds – thousands! – that we just don't have, because that selfish, manipulative woman needed us to be two more little cogs in the wheel of her stupid fucking wedding!'

Pete was confused. 'You're upset because Jason and Ange are getting married?'

'I'm upset that they lied about it.'

'It wasn't a lie; it was a surprise.'

'Too fucking right! A total surprise – for Jason, and for us, but no one else. For god's sake, even Ivy knew what this whole trip was about before we did.'

Pete shook his head. 'I don't get you, Liv. Your expectations of people are like...' He drew a mountain in the air. 'Something's got mixed up in that head of yours. It's like you insist on the same kind of commitment from friends that you'd get from, I dunno, a parent or a...' He had wandered onto quicksand. Sinking down on the bed with a sigh, he tried again. 'Ange wanted you here for her wedding because you are one of her best friends. Why would she have gone to so much trouble to get us to come if that wasn't the case?'

It was an amateur argument. I sneered. 'That's precisely how she wants you to look at it. But I'm telling you, Ange would never in a million years have proposed to Jason if we hadn't been here, forced to cheer and applaud while she did it.'

Clara led me back through that maze of narrow alleys. I marvelled aloud at her sense of direction, and she brushed the compliment aside.

'Our lot spend every summer here,' she said. 'Have done since I was a little girl. Daddy insists.'

'Daddy' was the mahogany-skinned patriarch and her 'lot', as she called them, included her elder siblings Andrew (fine-featured 'Hugo' who we had seen calling the shots at the restaurant) and Alice (the harassed-looking woman from the sun deck, Clara's early prototype). In recent years, their annual trip had incorporated her siblings' respective partners and their growing broods, though fearsome Aunt Mari was a constant from childhood – the elderly matriarch Binnie had accurately pegged as a sister to 'Daddy' and not his wife.

'The Empress,' Clara titled her, ominously.

'And where's your mum?' I asked, as we walked along the wide avenue with its expensive boutiques and pavement cafés.

'Mother is dead,' Clara intoned, a teenager using tragedy to impress.

I reached for a 'sorry', but the moment had passed. We were outside the beige café once more and the waiter was calling to Clara: 'Back so soon?'

She took my hand, pulling me towards an empty table.

'Christos!' she cried. 'This is my new friend, Liv!' I was pushed forward for his approval – Clara's brilliant find. He made no mention of my earlier visit to the café as he delivered a kiss to both my cheeks, but also he didn't need to ask what I wanted to drink.

'Two bourbons on the rocks,' he said, wiping our table clean.

'Wait,' said Clara, turning to me, 'do you like bourbon too?'

'Absolutely,' I said.

She narrowed her eyes – suspiciously perhaps, or conspiratorially. 'The coincidences just keep on coming, don't they?'

The first coincidence was the decision to strand ourselves in Corfu Town overnight. Clara's 'lot' had chartered a private speedboat to take them to the capital for the evening – no chugging party bus for them.

'Won't your family be cross?' I asked. My mind was occupied with thoughts of what Pete would say, what the girls would do, once I eventually made it back.

Clara shook her head. Her absence at their scheduled departure time was less a gesture of rebellion, more an annual event.

'Seriously, they'd have been disappointed if I *had* shown up,' she said. 'They rely on me to inject some drama into this godforsaken holiday.'

She slipped into some stuttering yet spirited Greek when Christos returned with our drinks. He steered her towards better pronunciation, Clara accepting his corrections with good grace until finally she threw up her hands.

'Off you go!' she cried. 'We're speaking English from now on!'

Christos retreated, smiling, and I was left with the feeling that Clara and handsome Christos knew each other more intimately than just the exchange of kisses on the cheek, though it was an unlikely pairing, a waiter and Lady Clara.

'Sorry,' she said. 'I'm hopeless at it, even after all these years of coming here, but I just love languages.'

'Are you ready for another coincidence?' I said, and told her about my MRes, speaking of it in the present tense – still studying, still translating – because it felt absolutely right and true, in keeping with the spirit of the evening. She shrieked at the mention of one of the novels I was working on.

'I love that book! I mean, obviously I haven't read it in the original French like you, but the main character' – she gasped, a hand at her chest signifying the emotional impact – 'I sometimes I think I *am* her.'

'What, Cécile?'

'Yes! I know we're not supposed to like her, not really, or at least not identify with her so absolutely, but I rather think that's the reason why I do, because others won't.'

'Same!' I replied, meaning it. I too had wondered if my affection for the protagonist was strange when there were so many reasons to find her objectionable.

'It's because we're contrary,' said Clara, leaning close, then tipping back her head for a burst of delicious laughter. 'How amusing that we should be agreeing on that! On our contrariness!'

The bourbons continued to arrive without our asking as midnight came and went. Christos slipped a curl of till roll beneath the glass ashtray with the drinks orders he delivered to neighbouring tables, but he didn't do that with us. The suggestion being there would be no bill to pay at the end – thank goodness. I had just thirty euros in my wallet; it wouldn't have covered my share. We watched the tourist crowds ebb then disappear, replaced by young locals who yelled to one another along the length of the avenue. Mopeds sped past, their exhausts trumpeting, boys driving, clinging girls riding pillion. We were the last drinkers left when Christos said he really must close up. It was nearing three in the morning.

'Oh, but we have nowhere to go,' Clara said, a trembling hand at her brow.

I joined her in these drunken amateur dramatics.

'We're marooned!' I cried. 'Forsaken!'

Christos would not be swayed and there was no invitation back to his place either. He suggested instead that we try a small boutique hotel nearby. His friend worked as the night manager and would likely take us in until the water taxis started running again. Clara and I linked arms, weaving slowly down the now quiet alleys, giddy at the prospect of finishing our stopover in style. We repeated our damsels in distress performance for the dishevelled night manager, whom we had clearly woken from a nap. He was no match for Clara's doleful eyes and persuasive English vowels. There was no bedroom available for us, but the residents' lounge had a couple of comfy sofas, if we agreed to be quiet.

We'd be like mice, we promised, as he led us up the stairs, tiny mice who didn't even know how to squeak. We sniggered as we made these vows. We shushed one another loudly.

'And could we possibly get some coffee and bourbon?' asked Clara, as we were led into a cool, panelled room with great swags of curtains. Her request was delivered so politely, so reasonably, that the night manager was once again powerless to refuse.

We sprawled on our backs on the two parallel sofas, a tray of drinks on the low table between us. 'Tell me more about Ange,' said Clara, and I slugged at the laced coffee, describing warm, invested Ange, and organised, aspirational Ange, and also the Ange who was skilled at administering everyday abuses, stuff hardly worth mentioning, a constant series of little nothings that had inoculated us against the larger abuses to come.

'Like when she snapped the tags out of your dress in front of everyone in that jewellery store,' said Clara.

I rolled onto my side to face her. 'You saw that?'

It gave me a thrill to think Clara had been watching me first, that she had pretended not to see me in the alleyway between the shops, allowing me to grab the baton and take my turn watching and following her.

'We outliers have to stick together,' Clara said, rolling onto her side too so she could look me in the eye. She was fond of a wise pronouncement, something pithy delivered with a twinkle to the eye, but this time she was deadly serious. 'People don't under-stand us, Liv. They treat us like we're difficult or weird. But we are ourselves, truly ourselves, and to others that's scary, in case we reveal the truth in them too. Why should we apologise for being honest? Why should we justify ourselves to them?'

Her words connected to something deep inside of me. This was the teenage sleepover I'd never had. This was it. I'd found it.

'But a wedding!' Clara squawked. 'What a masterstroke!' she said. 'Isn't it just the perfect way for Ange to deal with her terrible envy of your relationship with Pete?'

'Oh, I don't know about that,' I said, reaching for more of the bourbon-charged coffee.

My argument with Pete, up in our room, was ultimately unsatisfy-ing. It had crossed my mind as I paced in my underwear, swollen with rage, that we might have fucked, if only in frustration. Had Pete chosen to see me in that moment – really see me – my anger spilling free, all the hurt I had pushed down inside of myself finally released, we might have grasped one another physically, discov-ered some common ground in the flesh at least, before finding a way to talk about how our relationship had slowly disintegrated. Because we had always had that. Sex. When the girls complained about the tumbleweeds rolling through their bedrooms, the way petty arguments and the piles of laundry smothered every spark of passion, I always kept quiet. If pressed, I'd be as humble as possible: 'I'm sorry but me and Pete never really struggle with that.'

'That woman does nothing but bicker with her partner,' Clara said. She had been watching Ange too, watching all of us. 'She orders him around like he's staff. I can only imagine what strange kink she must be servicing.' Clara was enjoying herself now. 'Yes, that'll be it – some truly, out-there, super-kooky kink that only Ange is willing to accommodate. Why else would someone like him be with someone like her?'

I pulled a face. I didn't want to be thinking about Jason's kinks. I didn't want to be thinking about any kind of lust between him and Ange. The way he had grabbed her around the waist after she proposed, the fierceness of it, still haunted me. It felt like yet another thing that Ange had stolen – my passion for Pete, my love.

'I actually find him quite attractive,' Clara said, employing a stage whisper for effect.

'What, Jason? No!'

'Yeah – in a rough kind of way.'

Objectively, I could see that he was the most attractive male in our group, if you liked brick-built men, Statue of David kind of stuff. That Clara considered him rough, though, was hilarious; he was more privileged than the rest of us.

'You should go for it,' I said. Any man offered the choice would surely opt for the beautiful, refined woman lying on the sofa in front of me over Ange. Clara was Rokeby Venus kind of stuff. 'Nothing would please me more than seeing someone steal Jason from that woman. Give her a taste of her own medicine.'

'Yes!' said Clara, grasping hold of the idea, eyes widening at the possibilities. 'Every girl needs a bit of holiday romance, doesn't she?'

I shrugged. Clara caught the whiff of sorrow.

'What is it?' she asked.

135

'You have it wrong about Pete and me,' I said.

I had told her everything else and she had not pitied me, nor thought me a fool; there seemed no reason to hold back on this, and I was so desperate for the relief of disclosure.

'Pete lost his job,' I said.

Clara nodded; she was listening, this new friend of mine, this brilliant find.

'And he's pretending to everyone, including me – even to himself, I think – that he was made redundant. But I know he wasn't.' I took a breath, ready to say it aloud and make it real, ready to begin whatever lay on the other side of my admission. 'He was fired,' I told her, 'for having an inappropriate relationship with an intern.'

When I think of the knots I tied myself up in, I cringe.

I'll send flowers to make amends, I thought, and agonised over the bouquet. What would convey 'sorry' the best – tulips or stocks, freesias or snapdragons? And could I really justify spending thirty-three pounds of much-needed cash on a fistful of blooms and some seasonal foliage? Yes, I decided, filling in my details on the website, then Ange's, faltering only when it was time to click *Buy* – was this too grand a gesture? Would I be heaping embarrassment on embarrassment? I clicked away from the site and went and wrote a letter instead – handwrote it.

Dear Ange,
You have always been so generous to us girls, and lately to
me in particular, both with your time and with your money.
I would never want you to feel unappreciated. I'm just as
embarrassed as you are about the misunderstanding over
the loan for the holiday. I had no idea I had overstepped the
mark. I wish you had said something so that we could have

I screwed up the letter and threw it away. I'd wanted it to sound like one of Ange's Facebook missives, but my tone was all wrong. You could hear me clinging to the belief that I had done nothing wrong. Ange would see right through this half-hearted effort straightaway. Her open letters gushed. They put the recipient on a pedestal, then showered them in glitter. Before Pete was won over by her, he'd said that Ange's letters read like a psychopath mimicking normal human behaviour. So, what did that make me – a psychopath mimicking a psychopath?

137

I would wait, I decided, and say something to Ange face to face, find a quiet moment at our next dinner, top up our wine glasses and pull her aside. After all those afternoons we'd spent at her kitchen island, just the two of us, planning my house extension and sharing our private thoughts on Beth and Binnie, I was certain we could find intimacy again. I'd explain the mix-up, Ange would express the awkwardness she had felt, and then we might both cry, but eventually we would hug it out, emerging from our conversation closer than ever.

The only hitch was that there were no get-togethers marked in the diary – nothing for weeks. Which was strange, knowing Ange. I considered messaging Beth, something short and casual. *Hey, stranger, what's up?* But even in that, Beth would recognise the anxious subtext. *Am I being left out again? Have you started a new messaging group without me?* I would not go back to playing the victim and sobbing in coffee shops. So, I didn't text. Though I wish now that I had. That fallow period in our social diaries fell around May – the month the girls went to Berlin. The trip would have involved a fortnight of preparatory meetings and a fortnight of debriefs to which I was not invited. Had I fired the arrow of a plaintive message to Beth then, it might have found the target of her conscience.

At the beginning of June, a message arrived from Binnie. Our local cinema was doing a singalong screening of *The Wizard of Oz* (Binnie: *My fave!!!!*), should she get tickets for all us girls plus kids? I pounced right in with my *Yes!* thinking only of the opportunity it would give me to see Ange and clear the air. I watched the bubbles pulse in the chat, nervous that maybe she might count herself out. Ange's three boys weren't likely to be interested in yellow brick roads and cowardly lions. Eldest Duff, who had left prep school and started at a private secondary, was eleven going on seventeen. During a playdate trade-off, organised while I was working at the café, he had taken it upon himself to tell the younger kids about how babies are made – a horror version.

'And when you do it, the lady's blood spurts everywhere!'

Ivy was savvy enough to be suspicious, relaying Duff's explanation over dinner like a physicist forced to narrate the theory of a flat-earther. Pete and his dad coughed and spluttered over their beans and waffles. It landed to me to set Ivy straight, or rather confirm that, academically, her understanding of the subject was far more robust than Duff's.

Ange did sign up for the cinema trip. But as predicted, her boys were not interested in the film. Emboldened by the sing-along nature of the screening and the permission that gave them not to be quiet, Brady and Beacon, led by Duff, bellowed rude lyrics to 'Over the Rainbow' and heckled constantly. Long before the Wicked Witch of the East had been squashed flat by Dorothy's house, the nice, polite families around us were making their complaints known via passive-aggressive staring and loud exhales. Ange's response was to leave her seat and buy her sons yet more mollifying snacks.

I saw my opportunity and offered to help.

We descended the stairs together in the darkness, making for the double doors, and I spoke as soon as we hit daylight in the lobby, lest my nerve should desert me.

'Ange, this issue with the money for the holiday – can we talk about it?'

I was prepared for bluster, a sweeping aside of the subject, or even for Ange to snap at me. But instead she shrank away, she squirmed, her chin sinking low. Her reply wasn't the anticipated whip-crack; it arrived limp and reedy.

'What, here?' she said.

We crossed the popcorn-littered carpet to the refreshments counter.

'You're right,' I said, doubting myself immediately, thrown by her uncharacteristic meekness. I was clearly being too much. 'Now's not the best time. It's just, I haven't really seen you since Binnie came to my house and told me how upset you were.'

She cut me dead, her voice still small but clipped, even a little venomous. 'I'm not upset.'

To the girl at the refreshments counter, Ange spoke brightly, as if she had flicked a switch, ordering three sharing bags of Minstrels and three large cups of Pepsi – no 'please', no 'thank you'. She thumbed through her wallet for a card, studiously avoiding my eye.

'No,' I said. 'Okay.' I took a pause. 'Because I would totally understand if you were. Upset, I mean.'

I got another clipped retaliation, the consonants sharper. 'I'm not upset.'

'But when you talked to Binnie about—'

Ange came at me full force then. 'For god's sake, Liv! You know Binnie and how she loves to create drama!'

That shut me up.

I helped Ange carry her drinks and sweets back into the auditorium, more fuel for her boys and their interjections. From then on, the film was just colour and sound to me; I couldn't concentrate. For someone who wasn't upset, Ange seemed pretty distressed about something. Had she not wanted the money back? Had Binnie got that wrong? Could we have waited to repay her? The idea that I had transferred all that indispensable cash made me feel sick. Though I was sicker still at how I had dropped Binnie in it. She was only trying to help, but I'd made it sound like she came to my house to gossip. I'd amplified her reputation for creating drama – a reputation to which, until Ange's outburst, I'd been completely oblivious.

We went our separate ways at the end of the screening. No one wanted to spend a moment longer in the company of Brady, Beacon and Duff. I didn't get a second chance with Ange.

I texted Beth later: *I think I might have upset Ange today by talking about money.*

Beth replied: *She seemed fine to me.* Then: *Did Ivy like the film?*

There would be no satisfactory resolution.

I told Beth that Ivy had loved *The Wizard of Oz*, but she hadn't. On our walk back to Nigel's house, Ivy picked holes in the plot, rabbiting about all the things she would have done differently from Dorothy. Her biggest grievance was with the Wicked Witch of the West's foot soldiers and flying monkeys. If they had always hated their mistress and what she stood for, then why did they run her errands and do her dirty work?

I struggled for an answer. 'Because of... I dunno, fear?'

Ivy laughed. No, that wasn't it, because the flying monkeys outnumbered the Wicked Witch; they could have defeated her whenever they wanted.

'Well, maybe they didn't understand how evil their mistress was until Dorothy came along.'

Ivy shrugged her grudging agreement.

I see the comparison now, of course I do. It's stupidly, blindingly obvious.

'Maybe they needed Dorothy to show them what they were capable of,' I added. 'She was the one who proved how easy it is to make a witch melt.'

Once again, our days were lazy, pool-bound, but now, I spent them with Clara.

I took my towel, my sun cream and my book to the bleached wood sun deck where Clara was always able to secure a pair of loungers in prime position. This is the speciality of the truly privileged – getting what you want, when you want it, every time. I benefited by association.

The others maintained their usual, inferior sunbathing spot beneath the pineapple palm. I caught them peering over at us every now and again. They were confused by my desertion – and I was glad about that. Let them have a taste of rejection, I thought, of exclusion and punishment, and let it force them to their senses.

We enjoyed our uninterrupted view of the sea in satisfied silence. Clara pitter-pattered at her laptop, a seam of concentration creasing her forehead as she leant into a screen barely visible in the sun. ('What are you writing?' I asked. 'Thinly veiled fiction,' came her Dorothy Parker reply.) I made translation notes in the margins of my books without fear of being called a show-off. Clara even asked me to read aloud from the novel we both loved, so that she could hear it in the original French.

'Are you understanding any of this?' I asked, after a couple of paragraphs.

'Not a word,' she replied. 'But please don't stop because I'm about to come.'

We cackled loudly and I hoped the others would hear.

They kept their distance, all of them, except for Ivy. She was unfazed by my setting up camp with Clara and frequently crossed the picket line to visit us, clambering onto my lounger, breaking the calm with her melodic chatter, bringing along things to show and tell. On one occasion, she produced a sundried snakeskin.

'George and Henry's dad found it on the rocks in the bay,' she told us breathlessly, displaying the skin reverentially on her two spread palms. 'Touch it,' she instructed, 'it's horrible.'

Clara and I did as we were told, stroking that dark, crispy, shucked-off thing.

'So, the snakes *do* exist,' I said.

Ivy nodded with a grin.

On another visit, as she sat on my lap, soggy from a recent swim, narrating the arrival of the small boats around the green headland, rating each day-tripper sailor on their ability to dock at the jetty in the bay, Ivy pulled up short to demand of Clara 'the names of the children'.

'Which children?' asked Clara.

Ivy pointed to the gaggle of grandkids on the pebbles below. Euripides – Rippy – was acting as site-manager while his brother, sister and cousins built a castle from the stones. The littlest ones in the troop ran around completely naked, peeing at will. A relaxed attitude to nudity was clearly a family trait.

Clara provided Ivy with a swift inventory of her young relatives (I remember there being a Homer, and that the blonde girl was called Cordelia, Dee-Dee for short) and Ivy silently echoed each name, as if it were important that she committed them to memory. As I watched my daughter's lips form these unfamiliar shapes, I realised that she *did* need to memorise them, because she was going to be tested later. The voice she'd used to ask Clara her initial question was a borrowed one – and it had been familiar. Ange's jokes about calling your kid Euripides must have run dry. She needed some new material.

'Clara,' Ivy said, setting up another question; this one without doubt had been planted on her, a bomb designed to detonate across enemy lines. 'Why', she wanted to know, 'does your bikini only have a bottom half and not a top?'

The heat climbed during that second week of the holiday. Something had to give.

Binnie was the emissary sent to attempt a reconciliation. I was at the pool bar, ordering Dirty Martinis, the hour having ticked past five, when she approached with stealth, claiming the stool beside me. She wore a sarong wrapped around her swimsuit, knotted at her shoulder then again at the waist – a rectangle of fabric somehow transformed into a dress. Binnie had always been good with things like that.

'Hey,' she said.

'Hey,' I replied.

We watched the bartender work, holding the olives back in their jar with a spoon as he poured a dose of brine into his silver shaker.

'It's really hot, huh?' said Binnie.

I nodded, feeling a pang of sadness. Was this how we spoke to each other now, me and one of my best friends in the whole world, like awkward strangers at a party?

'So…' said Binnie expectantly, as if my next line were obvious, as if it were I who had summoned her there, to pass on some urgent news.

I shrugged, wordless, uncertain which version of Binnie was sitting beside me. Was it smart, droll Binnie, generous with her Clarins masks, always ready with a killer Pointless answer, the woman I had fallen in love with right at the start? Or was this legal-eagle Binnie, who knew precisely which emotional buttons to press when it came to recouping a loan, a woman on a mission to challenge my friendship with Clara, to stop it overshadowing Ange's precious nuptials?

Binnie glanced back towards the pineapple palm. Pete was watching us, arms folded, brow furrowed with concern.

Up in our room, he and I spoke to one other in razor-sharp sentences. The last two evenings, he'd gone to dinner with the group without me. I'd eaten a club sandwich at the pool bar washed down with more Dirty Martinis, listening to Clara's stories about her very own Wicked Witch of the West – Aunt Mari, the 'Empress'. As a teenager, Mari had dropped out of the family to tie herself to railings in the name of feminism, peace, the environment, whatever cause was considered cool at the time, before entering a long-haired groupie phase, shagging rock stars and band managers, and taking her top off for notorious photographers. Once she hit thirty, though, she U-turned, breaking out the twinset and pearls, and fully embracing conservative Knightsbridge life. She now took residence on the moral high ground, running the family like a dictatorship, adopting Clara as her personal project.

'Apparently, I need saving,' said Clara with a dark look, followed by a burst of laughter. 'You see, the Empress gave up on her true self decades ago and now lives a life of utter regret. What she wants is for me to descend to her level, because the lonely old spinster needs the company.' Clara shook her head. 'No, thank you!'

I ate up these scything takedowns as hungrily as that club sandwich with its side of fries.

Meanwhile, Pete seethed. 'What are me and Ivy supposed to do while you're off with your *friend*? You're making things impossible!'

'Go eat with your *friends*,' I told him plainly. 'I don't see what's so impossible about that. Ivy can join me if she wants, but she'd much prefer to be with Amelia and Paige.'

Pete was used to being the reasonable one; this turnaround had unmoored him.

'You do know that I love you, don't you?' he pleaded.

I nodded, thinking, *Do I? Do I know that?*

The bartender affixed the lid to his cocktail shaker and began rattling its contents.

Binnie took another run-up. 'So...'

I did want us to talk, to find some common ground, because being punished or doing the punishing – neither was pain-free. *Pete says you're upset about the wedding plans*, Binnie might have offered as her opening gambit. Or, *Why did you run away from us that night in Corfu Town?* If she had been genuinely interested in what was going on with me, if she'd said anything that pushed us towards a meaningful reconciliation, perhaps we would have worked things out that afternoon under the canopy of the bar. Perhaps the holiday would have taken a different turn.

Binnie lowered her voice and pinned me down with one eye.

'So,' she said, 'what did you two get up to all night in Corfu Town?'

The question dripped, oily, lascivious even. Ivy could be excused for asking a planted question, she was nine years old; Binnie knew better. She hadn't come seeking common ground. As Ange's proxy, Binnie only wanted drama. So, I gave it to her.

'Well, we found a hotel,' I began, measuring out my words. Binnie's eyebrows commenced their ascent towards her hairline. 'And then... We spent the whole night licking out each other's fannies. Is that what Ange wanted to hear?'

Binnie reared back as if slapped. The bartender looked up from straining the Martini, spilling some across the countertop.

'Okay, Liv. Okay.' Binnie slid from her stool, her face pinched. 'It's not my fault that you can't get along with Ange. That's your shit. Please don't take it out on me.'

She remained there, a hand resting on the seat of the stool, as if waiting for me to spar some more, or to apologise. I didn't want to do either. I wanted us to speak to one another like we used to, have the ease of our old friendship return, but I didn't know what I could say to make that happen.

'Right. Fine,' Binnie said, finishing a conversation that was already over. 'I'd actually come to invite you to our recce of the old town tomorrow, up in the hills. Ange has hired a car. We were going to make a girls' day trip of it, have lunch, plan the ceremony, but I can tell you're really not interested at all.'

It was a lure, a good one. I felt the threat of missing out like a knife to the throat.

'Thanks for thinking of me,' I said, signing for the drinks, charging them to Clara's room as she'd instructed. 'But I already have plans for tomorrow.'

This wasn't a lie; I did.

The following morning, I went to Clara's room on a lower terrace, an apartment identical to ours, except Clara had it all to herself. On the tiled floor lay her suitcase, open and half-unpacked, unfeasibly small for a long summer trip. On her bedside table there was a stack of books (Salinger, Dostoyevsky,

147

Camus – proper showing off) alongside a bottle of perfume, the name of which I had never come across before. She connected her phone to the small speaker in the room and began playing the sounds of the rainforest as I relaxed back on the bed, freshly made by housekeeping. I closed my eyes.

The previous day, on the sun deck, Clara had told me she could do Reiki. While on a holistic retreat in California, she had bonded with a girl called Priya – 'who, you would not believe, lived just a few streets away from my family in London'. Priya was a Reiki master and believed Clara had a natural gift for energy healing, so she trained her in the art.

'And this is what you do?' I said, registering how strange it was, how indicative of time spent with Clara, that I was only now getting around to asking such a first-base question.

Clara looked lost.

'I mean,' I clarified, 'is Reiki your job?'

'Oh, no!' She chuckled at the idea. 'Reiki is just something I can do.'

I waited for her to fill in the obvious blank – tell me her actual profession – but she turned away, back to staring at the sea.

'You know, I thought you were an actress when I first saw you,' I confessed.

'Did you?' She smiled at that, but still she didn't volunteer anything more.

I went for it. 'So, what do you do then?'

'Darling!' Clara dragged out the word, playing a heightened version of herself. 'One does not ask a person of my ilk what they do, they just are!'

It was a pretentious thing to say, and she knew it, but it was also true. I hadn't told Clara that I worked in a café, in part because it was a detail wrapped up with our dire financial situation, which I had no wish to share, but also because I didn't want to be defined by what I did either. I also wanted to just be.

As the Amazon rain fell and the animals chirruped to one another in the trees, Clara hovered her palms above my forehead, my cheeks, my neck, my chest. I could sense her journey down my body, the heat of it, though she didn't touch me at all.

'Some people see pictures,' she said. 'Some hear words. Whatever you get is a message. Pay close attention.'

I was sure I wouldn't hear or see a thing. Reiki was a load of old nonsense; so much woo-woo talk and a lot of waving of hands. I was only humouring Clara by letting her treat me, and I was enjoying her attention, the communion of it. But then came the large shard of glass lodged in the heel of my foot – a striking vision that was oddly soothing to begin with; the blood that flowed needed to be let. But then I wanted the glass to be gone. Clara made sweeping gestures down my legs and I found myself sitting at the sea's edge, hoping the waves would loosen the shard from my foot. At no point, in this dream state, did it occur to me to reach down and remove the glass myself.

On the balcony afterwards, feeling fluffy-limbed and tearful almost, I recounted to Clara what I'd experienced. She had made us tea from a Ziploc bag filled with what looked like bark and leaves, pulled from a hidden pocket in the lining of her suitcase. The drink was dark and oily, on the verge of being unpleasant.

'My recurring vision when I'm on the table,' Clara told me, 'is that I am a tall proud cactus in the Mojave Desert. And I know there is a way to be content as a cactus, but I just can't make it work.'

'It's because we're prickly people,' I said, going along with her vision, speaking in solidarity.

'Yes!' she chimed, ready to dig deeper, when a voice broke through our conversation – a woman, high-pitched and vexed. We could make out the silhouette of her on the neighbouring balcony through the woven screen.

'Well, I have been diligent about it,' she said, 'not putting paper down the toilet, as they asked.' She spoke like it was a huge imposition, like she was doing the hotel, not to mention the entire Greek plumbing system, an enormous personal favour.

Our sniggers halted her monologue.

'And I expect some returns soon!' hooted Clara, imitating the woman's voice, making her bustle back through her patio doors.

We both roared with laughter.

149

'This place!' said Clara. 'The people! It's all so...' She searched for the word, nose wrinkled. 'It's all so *base!*'

I was on board for this – a trashing of the hotel Ange had taken such pride in finding, a place she spoke of with a peculiar kind of ownership, like all its luxurious touches were down to her, an extension of her somehow. But then it struck me: Clara wasn't joking, not in the slightest. The lush lawns, the striped parasols, the fawning staff... they were nothing to her. In Clara's eyes, this decadent hotel complex was a two-bit, rinky-dink holiday park. She was absolutely slumming it.

'Then why do you come here every year?' I asked.

'Oh, we don't usually come *here*!' She looked appalled at the suggestion. 'We tried a place in the hills last year, which was perfectly lovely, but just so remote and too far from the sea. Daddy thought this place would be on a par but...' Clara pulled a face. 'He's trying to match perfection, you see, and it's a losing battle.'

She became thoughtful. A green aura developed around her head, pulsing gently.

'We've always stayed with Daddy's cousin, since we were babies. But we can't do that anymore. And it was just so wonderful there, I can't even begin to describe it.'

The aura expanded. It began to flame, turn yellow.

'Jesus,' I said, looking down at the dregs in my cup, 'what the hell was in that tea?'

'Oh!' She grinned mischievously. 'Just something to soften our spikes.'

She reached out her hand, as if trying to touch something floating in front of my face.

'You have stars on you,' she said distractedly, before returning to the subject of the cousin's house. 'I can't even begin to describe it,' she repeated, though she forged ahead with an attempt, the detail of it lost on me, petals on the wind. I was too mesmerised by the swells and surges in Clara's glowing aura. She leapt from her seat, suddenly gripped by a brilliant idea.

'Oh my god, I know!' she said. 'I could show you!'

What followed wasn't a hallucination. I know this because the consequences were very real.

We drove fast along the coast road in a pretty, vintage two-seater – cream with a red interior, the roof down. Clara was the very vision of a femme fatale, dilated pupils hidden behind white-rimmed sunglasses, her hair held back by a printed silk scarf. (I caught the words *Hermès Paris* as she twisted it into a length and tied it in place.) The car belonged to Daddy. He kept it garaged on the island but had recently had it delivered to the hotel for his use. Clara was persuasive as ever, despite the influence of that trippy tea, when she told the hotel receptionist that she was permitted to take the keys.

Should I have got into that passenger seat – as a grown woman with a husband and daughter, with responsibilities, with good sense? Probably not. Clara's driving seemed confident, but I was no reliable judge, having drunk the tea as well. I felt no fear, though, only exhilaration. And victory – a fulfilment of my life's search. Beside me was my soulmate, the one I had longed for, another version of me, a friend who understood the need to escape yourself every now and again. I raised my hands high, as if I was reaching for the twitching lasers in that Berlin club again, riding the crescendo of the music, making contact instead with the force of the wind, letting it slip through my fingers like liquid. No resistance. I was totally free.

We swung inland, taking a narrow lane, Clara doing battle with the gears on the ascent. The road hairpinned back and forth, past private plots and gated villas, each one more impressive than the last. Eventually we were met by a pair of tall gates, the initials *P.R.* incorporated into the wrought iron. Clara pulled up too far from the intercom and had to kneel on her seat and lean over the door edge to speak into it, giving me a close-up view of her soft, tanned buttocks below the frayed hem of her denim shorts.

'Joe?' she enquired.

The intercom crackled. A tentative, Greek-accented voice replied, 'Yes?'

She whipped her head back around to me, hissing a celebratory 'Yes!' of her own.

'Joe! It's Clara,' she said.

There was no response.

Clara persisted. 'Open up, would you, darling?'

Still no reply.

'I promise you, Joe,' she said, 'it's very, very important.'

For the longest time there was only static. I could feel Clara deflating. Her aura turned milky, dispersing in the afternoon heat. Then there was a *clink* and the gates began their mechanical yawn. Clara whooped as she dropped back into the driver's seat. She jammed her foot against the accelerator, making the engine growl with anticipation until the gates opened wide enough to let us pass.

The driveway went on forever – the smoothest stretch of tarmac I had seen on the whole island, flanked by dense, dry pine forest. We arrived at a vast courtyard where verdant palms bowed in welcome. Beyond them lay a mansion – a castle! – with white-rendered walls and a burnished red-tile roof. The veranda was supported by impressive timber columns, and in the tranquil shade beneath sat plump sofas and low dark-wood tables, a wind chime above, singing the tune of the breeze. It was a page ripped from the property section of a society magazine, price on application.

'*Et voilà!*' said Clara, parking at a jaunty angle and cutting the engine.

There was silence – pure, expensive silence. We stepped out of the car.

'My god,' I said.

Clara had been right. The hotel complex *was* just a two-bit holiday park compared to this.

'Please tell me we live here now,' I said, and as Clara threw back her head, laughing, the arc of her neck and shoulders left a kaleidoscopic image in the air. I revelled in this optical wonder, open-mouthed, snapping back to attention only when she gave a yelp.

The car! It was rolling away from us. Its immaculate cream paintwork was bowling backwards towards a bank of mature prickly pear. Or was it? Was this part of a joint delirium? I couldn't chance it. I sprang into action, running, then putting myself bodily behind the bumper, with no thought for the vehicle's weight or how it might knock me down. Grunting with effort, giggling too,

I heaved the car back to its parking spot. Had the tea made me into Superman? I wondered aloud. Could I have stopped it with just one finger? Clara leant down and fixed the handbrake; it was by the driver-side door, where you least expected it. Then she seized my hand, holding it aloft – I was a champion!

With that same grip she led me across the courtyard and we tap-danced down a set of stone steps at the side of the house, discovering at their foot a grand, kidney-shaped swimming pool and a mind-blowing vista of the flat, blue Ionian Sea.

'Oh, my fucking god!' I said, prompting another gale of laughter from Clara. To her, my awe was hilarious.

She didn't waste a second. She kicked off her shoes and pulled her t-shirt up and over her head, showing no inclination to wait for our hosts. I followed her lead. We dropped our shorts, our underwear, the lot, and sprinted for the pool, naked and shrieking, as if the palace did indeed belong only to us. We surfaced from our jump exhilarated, just laughing, laughing, laughing. A pair of vivid, iridescent dragonflies skimmed the water around Clara's head, and I was about to ask her if she saw them too, so I would know if they were real, when a figure appeared at the pool edge – a short, brown-skinned man in his fifties, dressed in crisp slacks and a buttoned-up polo shirt, a uniform not that dissimilar to the one worn by the staff at our hotel.

'Joe!' Clara cried, delighted.

I sank down, my mouth at the waterline, wrapping my arms around myself, covering what might be visible of my body through the blur of the water. Clara did the opposite; she threw herself onto her back and floated, her headscarf drifting away from her like a slow-moving, colourful fish.

Joe fixed his gaze on the horizon.

'Alex, he gone,' he said. His accent was thick, his tone blunt.

I tried to think of a Greek name that could be shortened to 'Joe'. Was there one? Or had this man's employers renamed him, with something easier to remember and to say?

'I know, Joe!' said Clara, relishing the rhyme. 'I know that's so, Joe! Alex, he go. Oh no, oh no, oh no!' She dipped beneath the surface – a comedy flourish – spouting water as she remerged.

'And Mr Philip,' said Joe, 'he very sad.'

'We're all very sad, Joe,' said Clara, with a sudden bite of anger. She bookended her words with a threatening smile.

The dragonflies, real or not, were spooked; they made their exit.

Joe shuffled restlessly at the pool edge. 'And he be back soon,' he said.

'I'm sure, I'm sure,' said Clara, throwing herself into another backward float. 'How convenient that Uncle Philip should be in Nice for the whole time we're on the island.'

'No. He at Kouloura,' said Joe.

'What?' Clara righted herself, suddenly sober.

Joe was wringing his hands now, his anxiety peaking. 'He have lunch at Kouloura and he be back soon, Miss Clara.'

I laughed, maybe at the mounting tension, maybe at that obsequious title – *Miss* Clara.

'Mr Philip,' Joe persisted, 'be back at two. Not very long now. He be very unhappy to see you like this. It not right, Miss Clara.'

Clara's chin began to quiver, though she couldn't possibly be cold. I thought she might sink like a rock to the bottom of the pool.

'But why...' she stuttered, 'but why would you... why would you let me in, Joe?'

'You say very important,' said Joe, waving forward a female member of staff who had, until then, been cowering by one of the timber columns of the veranda, a bundle of towels in her arms. 'I thought you come to say sorry, to make things good, but this bad. You are very bad, Miss Clara.' Urgently, he beckoned for her to swim to the pool edge and she did, front-crawling swiftly, hauling herself from the water in one strong, definite movement. The female member of staff tried to place a towel across Clara's shoulders, but she shrugged the woman away.

'He told us he was in Nice,' Clara said, slapping wet footprints across clay tiles, repeating the words over and over – a spell to make it so. 'He said he was in Nice!' She thrust her sopping skin into underwear and shorts. 'Liv,' she barked without looking back at me, 'we need to go.'

I had become suspended in time, body-less, as though I was only watching the strange drama unfolding in front of me, not participating in it.

'Now!' yelled Clara.

She gathered up my clothes and made for the stone steps. I dragged myself inelegantly out of the water and ran after her, Joe trailing us – my bare backside – his manner still obsequious, even though we were trespassing, even though, as he put it, Clara was being 'very bad'.

'What I tell him?' Joe called after her. 'What I tell Mr Philip?'

She paused on the steps, allowing me to snatch back my things, to throw on a t-shirt at least. The rest I would do in the car.

'You won't tell him anything,' Clara instructed.

Joe looked down at his feet – that wasn't going to be possible. His loyalties obviously belonged to Mr Philip.

'It'll be your fault for letting me in!' Clara spat. 'He'll punish you for that!' Then she pivoted, mercurial, dashing up the steps towards the car.

We hurtled back along the coast in silence, my eyesight still glitching from the effects of the tea. Rainbows zigzagged in my peripheral vision. Water droplets fell from my hair in slow motion, exploding dramatically on the dimpled skin of my thighs.

It didn't seem right to ask until we were almost back at the hotel: 'Are you okay?'

'He said he was in Nice,' she said, a sphinx behind sunglasses. 'I thought Joe could be trusted.'

'What happened?' I ventured. 'Why can't you go there anymore?'

She gave a tight shrug. 'Because of Alex. He and I... We... We liked to have...' She glanced across at me, the tips of her hair whipping against her freckled cheeks. I saw her change her mind, decide not to tell the truth. 'We had fun! Adventures!'

I smiled like I understood.

Clara turned back to the road, as if to say I hadn't understood at all.

We were on a blade edge, I could feel it. One wrong question and Clara would become furious, maybe even swerve the car off the road. There was a darkness to her on that journey back, a nihilism.

'Alex is gone,' I said, tentatively repeating Joe's words.

'Yes, but Daddy isn't one to admit defeat.' She gave a snort of deathly derision. 'So here we still are! Trying to summer on the island like we always did!' Her mood took another dive. 'And failing miserably.'

We pulled into the driveway of the hotel, to the sight of Aunt Mari, seated upright and magisterial, by the steps of reception, on a dining-room chair that had certainly been fetched at her command.

'Oh, shit,' Clara muttered, sounding genuinely afraid.

As we parked, Aunt Mari rose, revealing the full Frida Kahlo glory of her embellished smock. She stalked across the gravel in platform sandals and, when she reached the car, snatched at her niece's white sunglasses, Clara flinching as if she had expected a blow to the head. With bird-talon fingers, Aunt Mari prised Clara's eyes wide – a doctor checking for signs of life.

'What did you give her?' she demanded.

Once again, I'd slipped into the role of observer, suspended in time. With a jolt, I realised the Empress was talking to me.

'What? Nothing! I... Nothing. I only—'

Aunt Mari cut me off. 'Okay, get out.'

It didn't seem right to scurry away and leave Clara with this old woman who was surely going to eat her alive. But Clara shoved at my thigh; I was to do as I was told. I opened the car door and stepped out, considering for a moment the damp print of my backside on the red fabric of the seat.

I raised my gaze to receive the Empress's judgement.

'You stay away, you understand?' she said, steely-voiced, terrifying. 'The last thing Clara needs right now is someone like you.' Incrementally, she lowered her voice – 'Some freeloader, some hanger-on' – so that I had to lean forward to receive her final whispered insult. 'I see you,' she said. 'And I know what you are. You're a parasite.'

I recoiled, stung, waiting for Clara to leap to my defence, but she remained quiet, head down, hands lying limp in her lap. I took this for agreement. Aunt Mari was right. Who the hell did I think I was, rejecting the only solid group of friends that had ever accepted me, drunk on the belief that I could stroll unchecked into the realms of the one per cent and claim my place amongst their clique? How hilarious. How pathetic.

There were no rainbows in my vision as I walked away from Clara and Aunt Mari, back towards the holiday I was supposed to be taking with my husband, my daughter and my friends. I was seeing clearly for the first time; all illusions gone.

I was a parasite.

After all that time spent watching others, someone had seen me, *really* seen me for what I was – a parasite with a reptilian brain, a snake compelled to keep shedding its horrible skin, a chameleon with no fucking clue what colour it was supposed to be. I was a creature that subsisted on the attributes of others, learning them then reflecting them back – the only method I knew for winning acceptance and love. I went through the world exactly as my mother had instructed: by eating the fucking cake, by shoving huge slices of it into my mouth and swallowing them whole, like a crazed Alice in Wonderland devouring anything that might gain her access through that door.

On the flat roof of my uni house, I smoked roll-ups, not because I liked the taste of them, nor the woozy high; I did it because Gabi did it. Gabi had confidence and chutzpah, qualities that I wanted for myself and thought I could gain by association. We'd lie on our backs and she'd monologue about the stars and I wouldn't correct her once. *Actually, I think you'll find that's Jupiter and that's Saturn. They're not stars, you know, they're planets.* Instead I bit my tongue and played stupid, pretending to be more stoned than I was.

'Wow,' I'd say, all dozy, 'it, like, really makes you feel small, huh?'

When she asked me, stretched out on that same roof, how many girls I'd kissed, I didn't give her the truth then either. (*None at all. I'm pretty much into boys.*) I gave Gabi what she wanted to hear.

'Shit! I dunno,' I said, 'I've completely lost count!'

Because I needed that invitation to Berlin. I knew what Gabi expected of me, how she saw us – not as friends, as *more* than friends – but I had to go. Clara seemed to doubt that I understood the meaning of adventure, its value, but I wondered the same about her. Could someone who has been gifted everything – beauty, intelligence, courage, privilege, money – have a desire as strong as mine to escape who they've become?

I transformed into what Gabi wanted me to be, I changed the colour of my lizard skin – finding rapture in that warehouse club, losing myself to a different culture, to the music, the atmosphere, and to whatever it was Gabi put in her roll-ups. The game got harder, more complex, but I carried on playing, extending my tenuous leave to remain. Everyone kissed everyone that night. So, when the shaven-headed girl put her mouth on mine, I went all out, because I knew Gabi was watching, intently. I wrote cheques I couldn't bring myself to cash later in the dark intimacy of Gabi's room.

She told me to leave – of course she did – but I found a way to make it Gabi's fault. I blamed it on her presumptuousness: confident people can be so self-absorbed, don't you find? So rude, so careless of others. She was the villain; I was the good guy. I shed that skin and slithered away.

With Beth and Binnie, I didn't get a chance to put on a disguise. They saw me first and chose me anyway. They proved that the real, unguarded Liv might be acceptable after all.

It was Ange who spoilt everything. Funny, ballsy Ange who, it turned out, was neither of those things, only vain and mean, a psychopath mimicking normal human behaviour. No wonder Pete's description stuck with me. I recognised Ange as one of my own – both of us were imitators. Maybe I should have shared this knowledge with Beth and Binnie, made it a moment of revelation. I could have shown them the ways I altered my character and denied my feelings to make people like me, ending with a final unveiling of my true self – my *true* true self. If acceptance followed, I'd have warned them about Ange: she was an iceberg heading straight for us and there was still time to steer our boat from her course. But animal instincts are so hard to override when survival is the predominant goal.

I fell back on dependable bad habits. I ate the fucking cake. My friends heaped their praise on Ange, and I watched and I copied, so consumed by the task that I came to believe the things we were saying: she was a born organiser who only ever wanted the best for everyone, a fairy godmother who swooped in and made everything all right. I joined their arms race for better schools and bigger houses, flashing blue, then yellow, then pink with purple spots, anything to stop my friends seeing that beneath it all I was probably a dull, repulsive green. Pete didn't like who I was when I was with those girls and neither did I, but I tell you who I liked even less: the person I was without them.

A parasite needs a host.

So, thank goodness for Clara and her bourbon, and her Dirty Martinis and her foul, hallucinogenic tea. She gave me the chance to escape who I had become yet again, unwittingly leading me back to who I was at the start – a nine-year-old girl holding her own at an awful birthday party, refusing to take any kind of shit from a goofy-toothed kid in a frilly fucking blouse. When I sank my teeth into that girl's flesh, drawing blood, I liked the taste. That was what frightened me – the idea that I had power, that I was bad, that if provoked I would attack, and when I did, it would be poisonous, deadly. Aunt Mari saw it – the beast within, the one I kept caged and pacified with cake.

It was time to embrace my animal instincts. I would always be a parasite, a snake adept at caudal luring, able to conceal the full extent of myself while waving a piece of enticing tail, drawing close unsuspecting prey. It was time to reframe this as my most impressive skill.

With this understanding inside of me, with a willingness to use it to my advantage now, I knew I had to make some kind of peace with Ange.

That night I rode dreams like they were lurching fairground rides, thanks to the residual effects of Clara's tea. In one, I conducted a long, impassioned phone conversation with my mother about everything that had happened so far while we'd been in Corfu. She did not speak, only laughed maniacally – because is there any other way people laugh in dreams like that?

On waking, I was struck by the sickening idea that the phone call had really happened, so when Pete and Ivy left for breakfast, I went scrabbling for my phone in the bottom of my ruck-sack. It was still powered off. Relief washed over me. I plugged in the phone and waited for the battery to gain enough juice to come to life, then watched the notifications scroll – *Mum Voicemail, Mum Voicemail, Mum Voicemail, Mum Voicemail* – daily updates on what my no-good, waste-of-space dad had done now. I dismissed the alerts, connected to the hotel Wi-Fi and used every available minute of my allotted lie-in to search for an olive branch for Ange.

They weren't there, beneath the pineapple palm, when I went to find them. But their detritus was: damp towels, sun cream, rainbow Lilos and blow-up donuts lodged beneath sunbeds. The ice in their drained and cloudy milkshake glasses was still solid though, so I knew they couldn't be far. Delighted cries from Ivy pierced the air and I used these as a homing signal, following the sound of her voice down the wooden steps to the cove.

The girls were sitting in a row on the pebbles, their swimsuited bottoms sharing a single towel. On their heads, they wore similar wide-brimmed hats. *The three amigos*, I thought, as a deliberate act of self-harm. The hats were new, likely bought during one of their evenings browsing the shops in the bay after dinner, or on that girls' trip to the old town in the hills – a trip I could have gone along on too, I reminded myself, because there would be no more playing the victim from now on.

'Hey,' I said, sitting down next to Beth, making her squeal in surprise.

'Omigod!' Her hands flew to her chest. 'You nearly gave me a heart attack!'

'Sorry,' I said. I touched her arm, leaving my hand there longer than was necessary, so she understood that this *sorry* wasn't only for the moment just gone, but all the many moments before. Beth put her hand on mine in acknowledgement, letting her earlier fright, the overreaction of it, dissolve into a cackle of embarrassment. I smiled. This was the Beth I knew and loved. Her laughter felt as good as the hot Greek sun on your skin.

Binnie and Ange did not acknowledge my presence. They continued to stare out to sea, to Dev troubleshooting George and Henry's leaky snorkelling masks, Jason refereeing a swimming race between his three boys, to Pete and Kenny launching Ivy, Amelia and Paige high out of the water in turn, the girls making star shapes at their point of suspension, beads of water shooting from their fingers and toes, turned to diamonds by the sun.

I had something sparkly too, designed to turn a magpie's head.

'So,' I said, lowering my voice, drawing them in, 'who wants to hear the *real* reason why the poshos are staying in this hotel?'

There was a twitch from Ange, a brief glance. I continued, relaying a version of our trip to the cousin's house – describing the splendour of the place, Clara's outrageous skinny-dipping, and that dramatic expulsion by Joe. I omitted much of my own participation, painting myself as a bewildered onlooker, which wasn't exactly a lie, shaping the whole escapade to sound like a scandal-seeking mission from the start, all of it building up to this moment of disclosure to the girls on the beach.

'It turns out there's a deep family rift,' I explained, as if I had the full picture. 'They're not invited to stay there anymore. The cousin even pretends to be in Nice when they're on the island so he can avoid seeing them.'

The girls raised their eyebrows and puckered their mouths. Beth and Binnie waited for Ange to lead the vocal response to this brilliant piece of gossip – but she stayed tight-lipped. I was not yet deserving of a cluck or a squawk. Not yet. I looked down at our variously painted toenails against the grey shingle; mine pink and chipped, the girls' decorated in shades of purple, the finish still shiny and intact. All of us had a pleasing colour to our skin though, the tanned ridges of our toes contrasting with the paler skin in between.

'Isn't that her now?' said Ange, breaking the silence.

She nodded towards the jetty. Clara was walking down it, wearing a short white voluminous dress, the ties of a pair of leather sandals criss-crossing her shins – items of clothing I hadn't spotted in that open suitcase on her apartment floor. Her face was made-up – we could tell that from a distance, her lips a bold red – and she was walking arm in arm with Aunt Mari, also well turned out, though the Empress had yet to demonstrate a casual setting. The entire family followed in their wake: Daddy, Andrew, Alice, their respective partners, the gaggle of grandchildren, with Cordelia – 'Dee-Dee' – trailing at the end, skipping to catch up.

'There they go,' muttered Binnie, 'the von Trapps of Corfu.'

'Where are they off to?' Beth asked, turning to me for the answer.

At the end of the jetty bobbed a sleek, private speedboat. The driver offered his hand to Aunt Mari and Clara in turn as they stepped aboard and found their balance. Clara wasn't smiling; she had the look of a hostage. Did she need rescuing? I found myself wondering, despite the way we had parted the day before. She had saved me that night in Corfu Town; was it my turn to save her back?

'No clue.' I shrugged in answer to Beth's question, feeling a thin seam of guilt develop for trading Clara's secrets for a ticket back into my old group. Someone of Clara's ilk was never going to be truly friends with someone like me, Aunt Mari had made that patently clear, but seeing Clara again invoked the feeling I'd had when I first laid eyes on her – that she was another version of me, destined to be my soulmate.

Beth sensed my despondency.

165

'T'aww, Liv,' she cooed. She slid an arm across my shoulder and pulled me close. 'It's good to have you back,' she said. The swell of our breasts in their swimsuit cups pressed together. *Bosom buddies*, I thought to myself. Then I reached for my second sparkly thing.

'I was thinking, Ange,' I called down the line, unlocking my phone, 'will you be having readings at your wedding? Because, if so, I would love to contribute something... if you have room, if it's not too late.' I dared a quick look in her direction. Her face gave nothing away. I scrolled. 'I could read some French poetry maybe? Baudelaire could work well, though he can be quite raunchy. And a bit dark. Or maybe Victor Hugo? He's the *Les Mis* guy. His stuff is a bit saucy too, but he's very romantic...'

Ange did not respond. I ploughed on. This was all I had, my last offering, a means to demonstrate that I would, as she wanted, be one little cog in the wheel of her wedding. I pulled up the words for 'Since I Have Placed My Lips' and began to read. The girls were listening, I could feel it; their attention was almost tangible. Except for that first, drunken night on the patio when I had sung '*C'est si bon*', they'd never heard me speak French before. Why would they? I would never show off like that. Speaking it in the service of Ange and her wedding, though, was defensible, necessary even.

'Obviously, I can translate,' I said, 'if you'd prefer that? If you want me to do it in English on the day.'

I was quiet then; my audition done.

Fish schooled in the stretch of shallow, translucent water before us. George and Henry floated above, arms splayed, faces down, like small, snorkelling corpses.

'That car Clara was driving yesterday,' Ange said, 'it was a Sunbeam Alpine.'

'Was it?' I replied. 'If you say so.'

Cars were Ange's thing.

'I saw it outside reception,' she went on. 'A Mark Five, I think, late nineteen-sixties.'

'Right,' I said, unsure where this was going. Had I included some detail about the car in my story about the cousin's house and inadvertently exposed my lies of omission? Was Ange about to use that detail to call me out?

'I love it,' she said, her voice as appreciative as that hand stroking the dashboard of our brand-new BMW. 'I'm looking for a bridal car to take me up the mountain,' she added.

There it was: Ange's price for settling my debt.

'Sure,' I replied. Buying my way back into the group was my only goal; the logistics of the deal, I'd figure out later. 'I'll ask Clara,' I bluffed, as if that was possible after yesterday's drama. 'I'm sure she'll say *yes*.'

That evening, the boys were sent to forage at the supermarket in the bay. Dining out every night, Ange said, had become too much. Not the expense of it – Ange and Jason could throw their restaurant bills onto any number of platinum credit cards – it was calories that she was worried about.

'I've put on so much weight this holiday,' Ange whimpered, driving the heels of her hands into her belly, 'I swear I won't be able to get into my wedding dress.'

Beth got there first. 'Oh, please!' she said. 'Your dress is going to look amazing.'

Binnie went next. 'I'm sorry but that's bullshit, Ange. If you want to see some proper weight gain, behold my thighs! I'm calling that layer of fat my wine-shorts!'

It was my turn. 'Yes,' I trilled, 'tell me about your dress, Ange! Or even better, show me!'

We stepped from the shared patio into Ange and Jason's apartment, Ange drawing the long, pastel curtains behind us, bringing an early dusk to the room, making sure Jason couldn't catch a glimpse of her bridal outfit. A trio of expensive scented candles burned on the dresser, doing little to counteract the musky air. The top note was cheap, teenage body spray, the base note: armpits – the smell of too many boys living in a confined space.

Ange opened her wardrobe and lifted out a dress carrier, laying it on the bed with gentle ceremony. I expected something white. Wouldn't that be just like her, to denounce the pomp and frippery of weddings for all those years only to succumb to a full, ivory meringue? But, of course, it wasn't white. She unzipped the carrier and revealed something red, long and sleeveless. Wearing it, Ange would resemble a very curvy bottle of wine.

'Wow, it's...'

Ange grinned, tonguing the corner of her mouth provocatively. We both knew the right adjective – *familiar*. The dress was remarkably familiar.

'It's stunning,' I said, meeting her eye. 'It's just what I would have chosen.'

Then, I laughed. Who knew it would be so funny, coming face to face with the truth and recognising it for what it was? Ange laughed too, an acknowledgement of the new terms of our relationship. A pressure released. We were polite enemies – that's how it was going to be. If I had been drinking, I might even have raised a glass to that.

Binnie was the one who wanted to abstain. Ange needed a breather from indulgent dinners; Binnie needed an evening off the booze.

'My liver is screaming,' she said.

I offered to keep her company. Clara's tea had left me out of kilter, and I wanted a clear head for my first night back in the fold.

Beth was disappointed. 'What, not even a glass of wine with the food?'

She looked imploringly at Ange – were alcohol calories being rationed too? If Ange was staying sober, then Beth was duty-bound to join her. This would be a three-line whip.

'Well, my boys have been a complete nightmare today,' Ange said, proud of her endurance, 'so there is absolutely no way I'm not having a drink.'

Our dinner was cheap and improvised, making it easy for Ange to fool herself that it wasn't as greedy as a meal at a restaurant. We crowded around the pushed-together tables on the patio to tear great hunks of bread from several end-of-day loaves, softening their crusts in pots of rich, creamy deli-counter dips. We demolished numerous packets of feta cheese and cured meats. We shovelled up handfuls of crisps.

The mood was loud and silly from the get-go, but after the kids went to bed, the night took a particularly raucous turn. Everyone was very drunk, except for me and Binnie, and everything was hilarious; nothing out of bounds. Jason mimicked my retort to Binnie at the pool bar when she had asked what Clara and I got up to all night in Corfu Town. *We spent the whole night licking out each other's fannies.* We screamed with laughter at this vulgar line removed from its context – 'I mean, who says *fannies* anymore!?'

Binnie scolded Jason for his indiscretion – an indiscretion that had exposed hers – but I smoothed over the issue, kept things light.

'Of course you told them what I said. Why would you not?'

Binnie let it go. Jason did not.

'So, tell us, Liv,' he said, 'what does aristocratic pussy taste like?'

The girls gasped with fake horror. The boys applauded, hooting, even Pete.

Earlier in the evening, Pete had drawn his chair close to mine. His hand had wandered onto my knee and, without thinking, I had rested my chin on his shoulder. This could be solvable too, I thought, somehow.

At the mention of Clara's name, I checked over my shoulder, looking across to the pool bar to make sure she wasn't there, that she couldn't hear this. I was grateful for my clear head.

'Surely you know what aristocratic pussy tastes like, Jason,' I replied, pretending confusion. 'Or are you not doing your bit for Lady Ange?'

There were more squeals of laughter, Ange joining in.

She was less enthusiastic when Beth (very, *very* drunk) demanded that I (entirely sober) perform some French poetry for the group.

'It's so sexy,' she slurred, directing this observation to the boys. 'Honestly, Pete! You lucky man!' We smiled at one another, sharing the awkwardness. 'It must be like living with...' Beth halted, her wine-soaked mind unable to deliver the name.

'Catherine Deneuve?' suggested Binnie.

Beth shook her head, eyes pinched shut, both forefingers raised like antennae, hopeful of incoming signals.

'Gérard Depardieu?' said Jason, for the laughs, the biggest coming from Ange.

'Léa Seydoux!' This was Dev's offering.

'Who?' Binnie replied furiously, as if he'd just namechecked an attractive girl from the office.

Pete looked at me askance during this game of French woman bingo. Had he forgotten what I was good at? Couldn't he bring immediately to mind, like I could, that weekend we'd spent in Paris before Ivy came along, hardly leaving our hotel bed, me translating the soap operas and the news on the TV, debating items on the menu with waiters when we eventually did head out?

'Vanessa Paradis!' Beth yelled. That was the name she'd been groping for. A nostalgic, tuneless group rendition of '*Joe Le Taxi*' followed and, once done, Beth's proposition could no longer be avoided. She shoved me to standing and shushed any persistent singers. I won't pretend I wasn't touched by her support for this skill and passion of mine, something that was at my core, an honest piece of me. I delivered the same two stanzas of the Victor Hugo poem that I'd read from my phone on the beach and then curtseyed to a wild, sarcastic chorus of 'Phwoar!' and '*Sacrebleu*!'

Ange and I shared a moment of silent agreement as she slow-clapped my performance. *Enough now, Liv*, we concurred.

Our usual boy/girl division drifted in as the night went on. Beth got yet drunker, while Ange, keeping stride, seemed less affected. Binnie and I stuck to lime and sodas and Diet Coke despite plenty of coercion from Kenny.

Then it got weird.

I am sitting on Jason's lap, I remember, though I cannot recall the reason why. What follows is a great, yawning blank, until I feel the sharp sensation of the hotel lawn against my cheek. I am lying on my stomach in the dark and someone is calling my name – 'Liv? Liv?' They're at a distance, getting closer.

I try to get up, but one arm is extended above my head at a peculiar angle and it shrieks with pain. The voice comes to crouch down beside me, placing a hand on my back. I lift my head.

'Squeak, piggy, squeak!' I say, before vomiting all over their sandalled feet.

'Shit!' groans the crouching person, before returning to their earlier sense of urgency. 'I'm going to call an ambulance,' they say.

Then there is nothing, just black.

4.

I woke to no sign of Pete, no sound of Ivy. On the bedside table was a stack of books that were familiar but out of context, the titles on their spines blurry.

'She lives!' said a voice like a ringing bell.

I sat up abruptly, immediately poleaxed by nausea, stunned by the incredible weight of my head. On the floor was an open, cabin-sized suitcase, half-unpacked. At the foot of the bed: Clara, in her blue embroidered nightdress. The sun coming in from the patio doors outlined her slim body beneath.

'Where am I?' I said, each word a bowling ball rolling about my skull.

'You're in my room,' said Clara, coming to lie down beside me.

This I had grasped. What I meant was, where was I in time, in the story? The events of the previous few days rushed forwards, each recollection elbowing the last one out of the way.

I was a parasite.

I was not to be seen with Clara anymore.

I was back in the fold, part of the wedding.

I was Ange's polite enemy. And there's an honesty to that. An honesty worth drinking to.

If I had been drinking…

The thoughts stalled. I brought a hand to my neck, as if checking for damage.

'I'm naked,' I said, frightened of what that meant, tightening the shroud of Clara's bed sheet around me.

'You were sick all over your clothes,' Clara said. 'We had to take them off.'

'We?'

Jason's voice echoed in my mind – *So, tell us, Liv, what does aristocratic pussy taste like?* – and with it came the physical memory of sitting on his lap, Jason's thigh between my legs, the alien male scent of him in my nostrils. *Squeak, piggy, squeak!* I was saying, laughter rising high, Jason's face too close.

'You're lucky it was a female night porter on duty last night,' said Clara. 'I could never have got you up here and undressed all by myself; you were a dead weight.'

I exhaled a small zephyr of relief and stared down at the black, grubby half-moons of my fingernails against the white sheet, waiting for more sense to flower from the dark, swollen bud of the night just gone.

'You're lucky that you were sick and brought it all up,' Clara went on, 'or else you could have been less dead-weight, more actually dead.'

I showered in her room, scrubbing grass stains from my knees, dissolving the crust of vomit from my hair. Clara let me borrow a dress – a pretty yellow floral number that Aunt Mari was sure to recognise if we crossed paths.

'Leave the Empress to me,' said Clara as I headed off in search of my friends and my husband, the people who had left me unconscious and alone on that hotel lawn.

They were by the pool, drinking coffee in awkward factions. The boys – Jason, Dev and Kenny – were at our usual loungers beneath the pineapple palm, arranged like the subjects of a Homeric painting, pale and aggrieved, gazing off in different directions. By contrast, our children leapt joyfully about their flotilla of inflatables in the pool.

Beth and Binnie were at a table under the canopy of the bar, Binnie hunched over, Beth running a soothing hand up and down Binnie's arm. A few tables away, Ange was also hunched, and tearful it seemed. The person least likely to be comforting her was sitting at her side – Pete.

I made for Beth and Binnie's table, the nearest grouping, the safest to approach. Still, I'd rather have lain down in the grass again and done my dying properly this time. Ange never cried, which meant something truly terrible must have occurred. And if

Pete was providing consolation, it was no great leap to assume I had had some hand in that terrible thing. The idea became strong, thick fingers tightening around my windpipe.

'Hey!' I said, nearing Beth and Binnie's table, adopting breeziness as my armour. 'What's going on?'

'Oooh, you look nice!' Beth matched my tone, twisting in her seat to greet me. I was a diversion to be grasped at, I could feel it. Though the dress might have looked nice, I certainly didn't. Beneath my tan I was a queasy green.

Binnie lifted her gaze from her coffee – a proud and measured action.

'Jesus!' I gasped. One of Binnie's eyes was black, her nose swollen. A huge rectangle of white gauze obscured her forehead and butterfly strips sealed a tear in the skin across her left cheekbone. Beth twitched a glance in Ange and Pete's direction at my exclamation, nervous that I had disturbed them. The grip on my windpipe grew tighter. Had I done this to Binnie? Was that why they'd left me all alone on the lawn in the dark?

I slid into a chair.

My question was meek, whispered. 'Binnie, what happened to you?'

'I fell,' she said, taking a delicate sip of coffee.

Thank fuck! I thought. *She fell.* And waited for Binnie to elaborate. But that was it. End of story.

'But when?' I demanded, my voice rising. 'How?'

I was shushed by a glare from Beth.

'After midnight sometime, I don't know. I was drunk. I tripped and went head-first.' Binnie made a blade with the edge of her hand, bringing it to her face in line with her injuries. 'I hit the patio wall like this, full force.'

'Shit!' I said, wincing.

Binnie dipped her chin, ashamed.

Beth took over, masterfully shifting the conversation away from Binnie's disgrace with a show of indignation. 'Omigod, how tired are we? We had to wait *all night* in the hospital – just for stitches! It was supposed to be a private hospital but, honestly, it was wall-to-wall pissed-up English chavs from

177

Kavos, all blood and swearing and tattoos. I'm telling you – it was a nightmare.'

Binnie gave a glum nod of agreement. I looked down at her foot, curled around the chair leg, at the colourful hummingbird inked above her ankle. A middle-class tattoo, a middle-aged tattoo – it didn't count.

The waiter arrived and I ordered coffee and a Danish. He left, taking the momentum of the conversation with him. We were quiet. Samba music undulated from the pool-bar speakers. Residents loped past, their flipflops *thok thok thok*-ing against the paving. It seemed obscene that the rest of the hotel was going about its bright, banal business as we picked over the detritus of the night before. I looked across to see what Ange was doing. She was blotting her eyes and asking Pete to check for mascara smudges. I turned back to Beth and Binnie, expecting an explanation of this weird scene playing out between my husband and our friend. They remained silent.

'So,' I ventured, 'was it just you two at the hospital then, or ... ?'

'Dev had to stay behind and look after the kids,' said Binnie. 'He wanted to come but—'

'Oh, no, I wasn't suggesting that he... I wasn't suggesting anything.'

I peered at Dev. The mood amongst the boys had lifted marginally; eye contact was happening now. Returning my attention to Beth and Binnie, I caught the tail end of a mouthed exchange that was quickly halted.

'So,' said Beth, compelled to say something, 'are you and Pete all right?'

'Why do you ask?' I replied, those fingers tightening around my throat again.

The waiter interrupted with my coffee and pastry, which I snatched at, taking a big slurp and a large bite, desperate for the caffeine and sugar.

'Look, full disclosure,' I said, brushing flakes from the skirt of Clara's lovely dress. 'I can't remember anything after, I dunno, "*Joe Le Taxi*".'

Beth and Binnie nodded as if this spontaneous amnesia made total sense.

'So?' I prompted, exasperated.

'You got shouty,' said Beth, yielding but still reluctant. 'You wanted us to play a game where we sat on each other's laps and squeaked or something. But no one else wanted to join in and—'

'Except Jason,' Binnie interjected.

'Yeah, except Jason,' Beth confirmed.

'Who was being a total dick,' Binnie added.

'Yes,' said Beth, resigned now to recounting the whole affair, 'you and Jason were being total dicks, and you were really upsetting Ange, so Pete told you to pack it in, and that's when you started laying into him, saying horrible things, accusing him of all sorts.'

'Like... ?' I desperately wanted to know, and also I wanted to press my hands to my ears and run away.

Beth stalled.

'Like, sleeping with an intern,' Binnie piped up. 'I remember that bit.'

I groaned.

'So, Pete said he'd had enough, that he was going to bed and he didn't care what you did,' Beth continued. 'And because Ivy was asleep in Amelia's bed, and you were in no state to look after her, she stayed with us. Well, with Kenny, because I went in the taxi to the hospital with Binnie.'

'Thanks,' I said weakly.

We were quiet for a moment.

'Is that true, Liv?' said Beth gently. 'About Pete? Because we spoke about this ages ago, and you said it was a misunderstanding and that—'

'Of course it's not true!' My denial was too swift, too hot.

Pete and Ange were staring out to sea now – my polite enemies, both.

'So, why was Ange crying?' I asked.

Beth and Binnie became suddenly interested in the escalation of the children's riotous pool game.

'George!' Binnie called out. 'Less of that, please!'

179

'Is it because of me?' I pressed. 'Because of Jason and me? Do I need to go over there and apologise to Ange?'

That got their attention.

'No!' they hissed in unison.

'Don't go over there,' Beth said. 'She's really upset.'

'And you were so drunk,' Binnie added.

'But' – and this was the elephant in the room – 'I wasn't drinking. And neither were you, Binnie.'

They avoided my eye, Beth eventually giving in with a sigh. 'Your drinks were spiked,' she said.

'What!'

Beth's hands spasmed into the air. Once again, I was being too loud. She checked to see if Ange had heard us – seemingly not. Ange's gaze had narrowed onto middle son Beacon who was yelping at the poolside. Likely, it was a false alarm; the kid had a laugh that sounded eerily like crying. So many times that holiday it had tricked our sensitive motherboards into thinking a child was in pain.

'A few shots of vodka wouldn't have caused that, though,' I said, gesturing to the ground zero of Binnie's face.

'It wasn't vodka,' said Binnie.

I cocked my head.

'It was this stuff Jason got from the top shelf in the supermarket in the bay,' Beth explained. 'He'd stuffed it in the freezer compartment of their mini fridge and Ange didn't realise what it was—'

'Ange was doing the spiking!'

Frantically, I was shushed again.

'She just wanted you and Binnie to chill out,' pleaded Beth in whispers.

From Ange's direction came a quietly furious, 'Oh, for fuck's sake!' and the three of us jolted to attention, thinking that we were the cause. Ange levered herself out of her seat and headed for Beacon, who truly was in distress, squealing for mercy on behalf of his little brother Brady. Eldest brother Duff had Brady in a headlock and was dragging him towards the graded steps of the pool. Jason was nowhere to be seen.

'And what was it?' I demanded, making the most of Ange's distance from our conversation. 'What was this top-shelf drink?'

'A weird grain-alcohol-thing,' Beth said. 'I tried a sip. It didn't taste of much, but it was, like, eighty per cent proof, it turns out.'

'We drank the whole bottle between us,' Binnie muttered.

My jaw fell open.

'But it was only a small bottle!' Beth spoke quickly, tamping me down. 'Half a litre, not even that. And look at you. I mean, you're totally fine, so it couldn't have been that strong.'

Binnie joined in with this damage limitation. 'And Ange didn't know what it was, really she didn't, or what effect it would have. She's distraught about the whole thing. Honestly, she's been in tears all morning.'

'It's completely broken her,' said Beth, her face contorted with concern. 'I thought we were going to have to go back to that hospital for Ange and get her, I don't know, sedated or something.'

'But Pete seems to have worked his magic,' said Binnie, as if this were the happy ending to the story. 'He's made her calm again.'

Pete was also focused on the events unfolding at the poolside. Ange had grabbed hold of Duff in an attempt to free Brady, but she was being dragged towards the pool steps too. She lost her footing, performing the most inglorious stumble, almost toppling into the water, and at this, she snapped. Roaring with fury, she drove her long nails into Duff's bare upper arm, making the boy scream and release his little brother immediately, so that he might clutch at his wounds. My mouth fell open again.

Beth laughed uneasily, proving that we all do what Beacon does sometimes, confuse the sounds of humour and horror.

'What the fuck?' I said. Surely this was it – the end of Ange's rule. She had demonstrated very clearly who she was and there had to be consequences – for her cruelty to Duff, for Binnie's terrible injuries, for leaving me for dead on the hotel lawn. 'I mean, what the actual fuck!'

'Oh, come on, Liv,' said Beth, with a tense shake of the head, like I was the one being too much.

'It'll all settle down, I'm sure,' said Binnie, chin to her chest.

Ange had turned her attention to middle son Beacon now and was tickling him, ostensibly to cheer him up after his earlier distress, but the boy was curled tight like a bug on the pool's edge, gasping for breath.

'Mum, stop!' he wailed. 'Please, stop!'

'Let's just not talk about it anymore,' said Binnie. 'I can't bear it.'

Beth nodded in agreement. 'Let's not make Ange feel any worse than she already does.'

When I met Clara in the bay afterwards, I was breathing fire.

'What has to happen for them to see?' I raged. 'How far does she have to go?'

Ange's small, everyday abuses had done the trick. Beth and Binnie were now immune, so immune that they were willing to brush aside significant acts of violence, even recast Ange as the victim. I feared what that woman would do next, what else the girls would tolerate. 'I don't understand the hold she has over them!' I howled.

Clara took my hand and walked me away from the hotel to the far curve of the bay. I was a tearful toddler in need of pacifying. At a restaurant there, she leant into the outdoor chest freezer and bought two ice creams, letting me choose the one I preferred, guiding us to a place on the beach where we could sit down and eat them.

Once soothed, I relayed everything to her.

'Poisoned!' Clara declared, Shakespearean in her delivery.

'I mean, what if I'd stumbled into the pool and drowned?' I said.

'You were more likely to have choked on your own vomit,' said Clara matter-of-factly, pulling splinters of chocolate from the casing of her Magnum. 'Or imagine if a Nose-horned viper had come and found you, given you a friendly nip.'

'Ivy would have been thrilled,' I deadpanned. But I wasn't ready to let it go. 'What if something *had* happened to me, it would have looked like an accident, like it was my own stupid fault.' I bit a chunk from the Cornetto. *You have steel teeth*, Pete liked to say. *You have steel teeth and asbestos fingers.* 'This morning, Ange would have been crying about my death instead of Binnie's face, still making the whole thing all about her. Pete would have set aside his own feelings to work his magic and make her calm. Beth would be telling Ivy that, "Everything will settle down soon, you just see!" My name could never have been mentioned again. Because: "Come on, guys, let's not make Ange feel any worse than she already does!"'

I tossed the rest of my ice cream onto the pebbles, furious most of all with myself. How could I have so monumentally under-estimated Ange? She'd ostracised me, tricked us into a holiday that would likely bankrupt us, co-opted my daughter into a wedding designed to obliterate the memory of mine – and after all of those considered steps towards my annihilation, I'd still thought that we were merely polite enemies. There was nothing polite about any of that.

'What I don't get though,' I said, watching my ice cream melt into the gaps between the stones, 'is why she did it to Binnie too. She likes Binnie, I think.'

'Collateral damage,' said Clara, less Shakespearean, more Schwarzeneggean. 'It's about control, isn't it? Everyone must behave as she wants, drink when she says drink. Besides, I don't think that woman likes anyone. Not even herself.'

'Well, she likes your car,' I said. 'She wants to use it for her wedding. She asked me to ask you.'

Clara turned to me, aghast. 'You are joking, aren't you?'

I shook my head.

'The gall!' she said, with a shot of bitter laughter.

Beside us on the beach, a trio of mature Greek women lifted themselves from their sun loungers, grunting with the effort, their knees and lower backs disobliging them. Carefully, they picked their way across the pebbles to the water, wading in up to their thighs. They stood, hands on hips, generating a pitter-patter of conversation, the content unfathomable; the mood of it, the tutting especially, was understood. I had thought that Beth, Binnie and I would be like that, still inseparable in old age.

'So, I'm a parasite,' I said.

Clara's expression flatlined. 'Oh, Liv, look... The Empress, she... She can be over-protective, even downright clannish. That's the best way to put it. I think she does mean well, though it kills me to say so.' Clara chewed thoughtfully at her licked-clean ice cream stick. 'You see, I've had some... some issues, and Aunt Mari is holding me accountable for my recovery.'

'Oh, god,' I said, suddenly mortified by the thought of all the bourbon we'd sunk in Corfu Town, of our tea-time ritual of ordering Dirty Martinis. 'Are you an alcoholic?'

Clara laughed wryly. 'Probably! But it's the drugs that put a bee in the Empress's bonnet.'

'I'm so sorry,' I said.

Aunt Mari's disgust after our jaunt to the cousin's house was coming into clearer focus: Clara pulling up to the hotel, soaked through, eyes glazed, in a car that she had no right to take; sitting beside her, a stranger, an enabler, a pleb.

'If anything, I'm the parasite,' said Clara. 'I feel like I'm under constant surveillance, like I need to get away. This island for me has always been about blowing off a bit of steam, you know?' She shrugged. 'So, I latched onto you. That's how it is.'

I nodded. It was possible to be both, I was beginning to real-ise – parasite and host, perpetrator and victim, predator and prey.

'Anyway, you are now my "lame duck",' announced Clara, anointing me by placing her hand on my bare thigh.

'Excuse me?'

Clara grinned. 'Aunt Mari believes that everyone should have a "lame duck" to look after.' She pulled herself up tall and rounded out her vowels. 'It gives one focus and responsibility, gets one out of one's own head.'

I still didn't get it.

'I told her about everything that's been going on with you,' Clara explained, 'and then I nominated myself as your sponsor. In helping you, I'm helping me. So... now we can hang out.'

'For real?'

She nodded and I hugged her like a much-loved soft toy, lost then found. My soulmate had been returned to me. It was only when I let her go that I wondered what the 'everything' was she had explained to Aunt Mari. Everything about my friendships? My marriage? The prospect of being on the receiving end of the Empress's pity was somehow worse than being the object of her ire.

'Oh, you mustn't look so wounded, Liv,' Clara said, butting me amiably with her shoulder. 'I'm a lame duck too – I'm Aunt Mari's lame duck. Just let the Empress think what she thinks. What concern is it of ours?'

The women in the sea continued to babble and cuss. Tourists on paddleboards were coming too close, disturbing their wading. The women shooed them away, ferociously unapologetic. How would it feel not to care what others thought of me? I wondered.

'So, what form is this help of yours going to take?' I asked Clara.

'I will do whatever you desire, O mistress,' she replied, playing genie to my Aladdin.

'Well, you could start, O subservient one, by killing Ange Addison before she kills me first.'

'Why, certainly!' Clara bowed her head obsequiously, gave a flourish of her wrists. 'It shall appear as if it were nothing but a silly accident!'

This was fun. We riffed.

'Oh, dear, did the clumsy little poppet fall off a boat on a day trip, her body never to be recovered?' said Clara. She mimed a shove then pulled down the corners of her mouth into a frown.

'Oh, no,' I said, grabbing the baton, 'did she feel so ashamed of the bad things she'd done that she took far too many sleeping pills that were in no way crumbled into her dessert by us earlier?'

'I believe she was speeding, your honour, when she borrowed my daddy's lovely little car,' said Clara, her bottom lip fat, her face pantomime-sad, 'and that was why the poor darling simply couldn't brake in time.' She performed the car's tragic trajectory from a cliff edge with a slow-motion arc of her hand. 'Crash!' she said, such a sibilant word, so satisfying. It stopped us in our tracks. We looked at one another, then out to sea.

'That's the one,' I said, as we watched the sun begin its descent, 'that's how we'll do it.'

Let's not make Ange feel any worse than she already does.

I shouldn't have been shocked by Beth's words. Because hadn't this always been our unspoken mantra, the programme running silently in the background?

When Pete still had his fancy job, when there was a private-school prospectus lying on our coffee table and a shiny BMW parked outside our house, Pete's company threw a ball at a hotel in Mayfair – black tie, partners invited. This was around the time that Ange and I were especially tight and, on her advice, we planned an afternoon at Westfield shopping centre to find me the perfect outfit.

Slipping through north-west London on the train, rain blurring the windows, I described to her the dark column dress I imagined for myself.

'A kind of *Breakfast at Tiffany's* vibe,' I explained, 'minus the long gloves and the tiara.'

'You would look stunning in something like that,' Ange said, employing her invested voice, the one that could make you lop your hair off at a moment's notice.

I was itching to start the search but, when we stepped off the train, Ange wanted us to get something to eat. A snack, I assumed, it being neither lunchtime nor dinner, so I agreed, only to be steered through the doors of a pizza restaurant.

'My treat,' she said, disarming me with generosity, ordering a bottle of prosecco as soon as we took our seats, directing me to go for the largest pizza on the menu as she did. When the food arrived, handmade crusts spilling over the edges of wooden serving boards, I asked the waiter if we could take home what we couldn't finish.

'Such negativity!' cried Ange, tearing into her Fiorentina with her hands, egg yolk dripping, nodding at me to do likewise. When did we ever get to eat a whole pizza like this, she said, without kids or husbands demanding their share? Finishing every scrap was an obligatory demonstration of our worth. I unfastened the top button of my jeans as I put away the last slice.

In Burberry, the perfect column dress materialised – navy, slinky, with a chic halter neck. Of course, I couldn't fit into it, my belly so distended by dough and cheap fizz. Taking a size up didn't help; the dress fell loose around my rib cage while still pulling tight across the middle.

Ange commiserated with the assistant as I eyed myself in the tall mirror. 'I think you reach an age,' she said wistfully, loud enough that everyone in that shop would hear, 'when you just have to accept that you no longer have the body you had in your twenties.'

I think I laughed, a humiliated bark, before scuttling back into the changing rooms, to my everyday clothes and my self-loathing. It seems obvious now that I should have challenged Ange. *You can fucking talk!* I might have spat back because surely I could have been forgiven for being catty in return. Or could I?

Ange was the one who battled the most with her weight. She was the shortest too – no length in her limbs. Beth, Binnie and I were reprimanded if we made any kind of effort to get slim; it was a crime against the sisterhood, Ange said, a weakness in the face of society's unrealistic expectations of women. Yet Ange dieted, feigning food intolerances as cover. She'd even had plastic surgery. Her ears were pinned back in an operation that was reframed as a victory over the bullies who had teased her as a child, while the procedure to correct her Caesarean scar, we all knew, had effectively been a tummy tuck. She talked about the upkeep of her appearance like it was an all-consuming, essential chore, one that Beth, Binnie and I simply couldn't understand, because we were not operating at Ange's level where perfection was expected. She was a goddess. We were mere mortals. Yet we were simultaneously expected to feel a little bit sorry for her, just enough to make her bulletproof. Just enough that I would think twice before bringing her down a peg or two in that shop. Because how would it have looked if I had hissed, *You can fucking talk!* to my small, dumpy girlfriend who was only trying to help? It would have looked like I was the one being the bitch.

I went home empty-handed from Westfield and made a hasty online purchase – a cocktail dress with fussy straps that I spent far too much time adjusting in the pink curlicued toilets of that Mayfair hotel.

Summoned to Ange's kitchen for a debrief in the days after the ball, I provided a description of the chandeliered dining room and the beautiful food. I made it sound glamorous, because it was, visually, in all its composite pieces, and also because that was what Ange needed to hear. I was her debutante reporting back. If my night had been a marvellous success, it was down to her, my mentor.

In reality, those events are always ninety per cent anticipation, ten per cent strained talk with people you will never meet again. I struggled to provide distinguishing characteristics when describing Pete's colleagues; all of them were white men in their forties in identical suits – Paul, Martin, Rob, Steve. But there was also a girl, Becky, in her early twenties – an intern, I assumed. She sat across the round table from me at dinner, dewy-skinned and for the most part mute. Asked a question, she was slow to answer and a little dull when she eventually did, though no doubt she found us dull in return, pedalling through our usual middle-aged, middle-class conversations about where our kids went to school, and what the house prices were doing in our area. Becky came alive after dinner as she chatted at the bar with people from other tables and when she danced unselfconsciously to the covers band. I saw her talking to Pete at several points in the evening. They were jokey with one another, playful. There was, I remember, some touching of arms.

With Ange's encouragement, I was critical in my rundown of the outfits worn by the other wives.

'Her legs weren't good enough for a dress that short.'

'The outfit was way too casual for black-tie.'

'I liked the shape but the colour – ugh!'

When I got to Becky, though, I was complimentary about her lacy maroon gown, the kind of thing you buy for your graduation ball then recycle in the years after. Her sandy-blonde hair was woven into several plaits then wrapped across the top of her head, Swedish milkmaid-style. Online tutorials would have been involved, whole cards full of hairgrips. I went overboard relaying to Ange how lovely Becky had looked, how put together she was.

What I was trying to convey, in my indirect manner, was how scrappy I was by comparison, and how I too could have been as polished as Becky, if Ange hadn't scuppered my shopping trip. This raising up of Pete's colleague to subtly bring down Ange was my much-delayed retaliation for making me eat all that pizza and then humiliating me in Burberry. It was, I believed, the only method of retaliation I had. But it's amazing how many avenues for payback open up once you let go of the idea that someone is untouchable, a goddess, that you aren't allowed to make them feel any worse than they already do. It's liberating to realise that, in some circumstances, being the bitch is perfectly acceptable, enjoyable even, a means to a necessary end.

That third and final week of the holiday was a missile hurtling towards its target. Everything we did was in service of Ange's big day.

We took up our usual spot beneath the pineapple palm and made tanning our sole objective. Ange told us about a friend of hers whose bridesmaid had spoilt their wedding photos by being too pale – 'like blue, you could see her veins' – pulling focus in every shot. The moral of this tale was implicit: we were to remain supine, avoid movement, rotate at intervals. Lying there obediently, I wondered about these nameless friends who populated Ange's stories. When justifying her micro-planning of our holiday, she had said previous experience taught her that a schedule was key to success. But where were they now, these friends from group holidays past? I'd met several of Beth's and Binnie's schoolfriends, uni friends, the odd ex-colleague too, but Ange hadn't introduced us to anyone from her previous life. Had she discarded them, been discarded, or had they never existed in the first place? And what about her family – why weren't they joining us for the wedding? Ange took such relish in the gossip about my dad's gambling, but was that only to throw us off the scent of her own family shame?

I stuck to the trusted maxim: keep your friends close and your enemies closer. To all outward appearances, I was a dutiful solider in Ange's pre-wedding, poolside dictatorship, but whenever possible, I tossed a grenade of rebellion, disguising it as a benevolent gesture. In this, Ange had taught me well. If all went to plan, my small, everyday attacks would leave her sick with unease as the ceremony drew nearer. She would be weakened and vulnerable, ready for our final, vengeful blow.

Early that week, Binnie decided to remove the large square of gauze from her forehead. It was too conspicuous, she said, and it was irritating her skin; she would take her chances with infection. No one had the heart to tell her that the gnarly gash beneath, the many black and wiry stitches of it, was yet more conspicuous. Binnie was hard to look at, but I did look, using that shocking wound as a totem, a reminder of why I was lying there, being ostensibly polite to a woman who had tried to finish me off. It kept me focused on my goal – the downfall of Ange.

'We should all move into the shade,' I proposed when Binnie's gauze came off. 'Sun is really bad for scars.'

I didn't wait for the others' agreement; I just did it, shunted my sun lounger back a few metres onto a shady patch of grass. Until then we had been resolutely *not* talking about Binnie's injuries, in case we brought up the events that had caused them – or *who* had caused them. My talk of scars was a toe edged over the line. Maybe that was why Beth leapt up straightaway to move her lounger too – to stop me from saying anything more – though I think we were all craving a break from our tanning regime. The sun was so hot that week it had its own heartbeat.

Binnie got up as well, a tentative hand held to her stitches, and scooted her lounger alongside us. I collected the little side tables that held our bottles of water, sun lotion and magazines.

'Are you coming as well, Ange?' I asked brightly.

Of course she was; Ange wouldn't risk missing out on any of our chatter. But she endured barely half an hour in the shade before behaving like a self-serving president tired of the sober advice of their health minister.

'I always tell my boys to get as much sun as they can on their cuts and grazes,' she announced into one of our silences. 'Sun's a brilliant healer. It dries out the skin and makes the scabs form quicker.'

'And it causes hyperpigmentation,' I said, keeping my nose in the overpriced edition of British *Vogue* bought by Beth from the supermarket in the bay.

'But does it though?' Ange said.

Beth lifted her head from the pillow of her arms, anxious at this hint of tension.

192

I closed the magazine, put it down.

'Tell you what,' I said. I made my voice light, can-do, address-ing everything to Beth, as if we were a nursery teacher and her assistant deciding how to deal with a particularly demanding child. 'I'll move back into the sun with Ange, so she has someone with her while she works on her tan, and you can keep Binnie company in the shade.'

My suggestion had the surface appeal of resolution. Beth nodded eagerly.

'Oh, I didn't mean it like that!' cried Ange, in the high, naïve tone she adopted in these kinds of situations. 'I just don't want you to feel like you're missing out on the sun for no reason, Bin.' She leant forward to speak past me, giving Binnie her most down-cast, puppy dog expression. 'All I want is for you to get back to your usual self as soon as you possible can.'

It was an own goal. Ange had mentioned something none of us had dared acknowledge since Binnie removed her gauze – that she was never going to get back to her usual self, sun or no sun. Binnie's face would always bear a branching pattern of silvery striations, like the rocks in the clear water of the bay, etched by fossils of what had gone before.

Sticking close to Ange and the others beneath the pineapple palm allowed me, once again, to observe Clara from a distance. All four of us watched…

Clara reclining on the sun deck, opening the lid of her laptop with the gravity of an Egyptologist rolling away a stone at the mouth of a tomb.

Clara stretching languorously before posting her arms into the blue embroidered nightie and following her family across the lawn towards the bay for lunch.

Clara lying back topless and staring out to sea, somehow managing to seem monastic in this pose.

'But, honestly, does she really have the kind of boobs that are worth showing off?' Ange posed her question as if she were addressing the Oxford Union.

'Ange!' I chided. 'She's arranged for you to borrow her father's lovely car!'

'So!' she shot back in a plea of unassailable innocence. 'Does that mean I can't have an opinion on her wandering around in front of our children half-naked?'

I responded with a shrug. *On your head be it*, I thought.

That same day, late afternoon, I told the girls I was going to my room to practise my reading for the wedding. Instead, I went to Clara's balcony for a smoke. If caught by Aunt Mari we would be fine; she tolerated Clara's roll-ups as the lesser of many druggy evils – as a cure for disappointment. We sat at opposite ends of the balcony's rattan sofa, our legs up on the cream cushions, feet mingling, and we burnt citronella candles to mask the mossy scent of the weed.

We worked through logistics. Getting Jason drunk would be no problem – he managed that every night all by himself; getting him close to Clara once he was in that state was the challenge. Our group did most of its drinking on the shared patio, away from other residents.

'What if he doesn't take the bait even when you do get us two together?' asked Clara.

'Oh, please!' I said. 'Look at you!' There wasn't a dimple to the olive skin of her thighs, no whisper of a spider vein. The curled-up ends of her bobbed hair directed you to the smoothness of her freckled cheeks and the noble curve of her lips. 'You are all of Jason's birthdays and Christmases come at once.'

'But he's devoted to Ange, you say.'

I did say, and so did Jason, often and loudly, as did Ange, but like everything about that woman, I was now considering a different view, a more sober assessment. Take the night when my drink was spiked. Jason's question about the taste of aristocratic pussy had come with a heavy-lidded gaze, with genuine, prurient interest. Regardless of the amount of alcohol slipped into my Diet Coke, would I have willingly sat on his knee after that? Yet I had found myself there, lassoed by a strong arm, his thigh pushing up between my legs. Any demands for a game of Squeak, Piggy, Squeak were likely only a tactic to change the tone, to escape his grip.

It wasn't the first time Jason had misbehaved. Back home, when we went out as a group, he was famous for being a dick after a few pints. Ange would turn her back on his heavyweight flirting with other women at the bar, pretending she didn't care.

'That man is absolutely devoted to me,' she'd say with a confident swagger. 'I've got nothing to worry about.'

But now I wondered what kind of screaming and vase-throwing went on when they got home.

On a boys' night out, Pete said, Jason had taken things further: enjoyed a cheeky sort-of snog with another woman. 'Yeah, but he would never actually cheat,' I'd said, back then, when I was indoctrinated into Ange's version of reality

'You just need to wind Jason up and let him go,' I told Clara, and we debated how far that should be. Clara dismissed my concerns for her safety. She was happy to go all the way.

'A good fuck is what this holiday is surely missing,' she said, trying to impress me by blowing smoke rings.

'Yeah, but not with a total dick,' I said, 'and a married one, to boot.'

Clara corrected me with a wag of her finger. 'Not married,' she said. 'Not yet. Not if we have anything to do with it.'

The second joint had us sinking lower into the cushions of the balcony sofa, our talk shifting from good fucks to real love. Had Clara ever experienced it? I wanted to know.

She nodded serenely. 'With Alex,' she replied, taking a long, hungry drag on the roll-up before passing it to me. She exhaled with a sense of yearning. 'He was so free and wild,' she said. 'I've never felt so alive as when I was with him.'

'And he...' – after our tetchy exchange in the car driving back along the coast, I understood that I needed to venture carefully else I would scare this subject away – '...lived at the house we went to?'

She nodded again. 'Uncle Philip's son.'

'What, he was your cousin?' I spoke too quickly, without thinking.

Clara was prickly in return. 'Philip is *Daddy's* cousin. Uncle is a term of endearment. So, Alex was only my second cousin, actually.'

'Sorry,' I said, though it still seemed too familiar to me, a second cousin as the love of your life. 'I didn't mean to upset you.'

'I'm not upset,' she said, though she clearly was. She gave a quick shudder of her shoulders like a horse righting its mane. 'Anyway,' she said, 'it's your turn. Tell me about Pete.'

Maybe it was the tender way in which Clara had spoken of Alex, or the softening influence of the weed, but I found myself describing the moment I first laid eyes on my husband, on the platform of the Gatwick Express. Clara looked confused by this sentimentality; I trailed off.

'I meant,' she said, 'tell me about Pete and the intern.'

'Oh,' I replied. Then I burst into tears, violent sobs that I was sure would destroy me.

We had circled each other like battle-scarred strays in the days after I outed his affair to the others, that night on the shared patio. We communicated, in the most part, via Ivy, parenting in a showy, declamatory way, using our daughter as a channel for our anger, something we'd observed other parents do and promised we never would.

'Tell your mum that she's going to make us late for dinner. Again.'

'Tell your dad that it is possible for a child to drown in a pool if someone doesn't keep a proper eye on her like he said he would.'

After just a day of this passive-aggressive sparring, Ivy perched on the edge of my sun lounger and asked in a tone that was heart-breakingly practical, 'If you and Daddy split up, who will I live with? Him or you?'

Clara embraced me as I cried, stroking my hair and shushing me gently. I saw her wipe away tears of own, though I knew they couldn't be for me and Pete. They had to be for Alex, who had gone, though where and why I still did not know because I had screwed up my chance to ask.

On the Tuesday, beneath the pineapple palm with the girls, I laid some groundwork for what Clara and I had planned; I feigned concern for Jason's nerves. Was he having a wobble about the wedding? I wondered distractedly.

'What do you mean?' said Ange. Her voice was fierce, but I heard it crack; fear had got in.

'Oh, god,' I said, swamping her with apologies. 'That came out completely wrong! Jason is absolutely devoted to you – of course he is! I just wondered if he was nervous about the ceremony itself. Maybe Pete could give him a pep talk. He was as cool as anything on our wedding day, wasn't he, Beth? Wasn't he, Bin?'

On the Wednesday, I enthused about a vintage Yves Saint Laurent suit Clara was borrowing from Aunt Mari – the cut of the starched, white fabric, how Clara alone had the figure to carry off the flare of the trousers. It was, I gushed, just the perfect outfit for a wedding chauffeur. I watched Ange's face blanch, certain that the phrase 'aristocratic pussy' was echoing through her mind, spoken in the lustful tones of her future husband.

'What, Clara is driving the car?' said Ange. Panic coloured her words, more than just a tinge.

'Well, yes,' I replied. 'Who else?' Clara was looking forward to it, I went on, she was honoured to be taking part.

'But she can't wear white,' countered Ange.

'Whyever not?'

Beth came to Ange's rescue. 'Because it's bad manners, isn't it? Only the bride can wear white at a wedding.'

'Oh.' I left a beat. 'Remind me again what colour your wedding dress is, Ange?' I asked as if I really had forgotten, as if the memory of that red dress laid out on her bed for my inspection had been wiped away by what was slipped into my drink in the moments afterwards.

That same afternoon, I told the girls I was going for a walk in the bay to stretch my tight hips, promising to bring back chocolate for everyone. I stopped by the supermarket to buy various slabs of Ritter Sport before joining Clara at a sticky table in a shadowy corner of the sports bar – somewhere I knew the others would never venture. This was why people had affairs I was beginning to realise. It wasn't the newness of the other person nor the glimpse of another possible life; it was the sneaking around that provided the hit of dopamine. I could have shared this revelation with Pete, we could have bonded over it.

The large screens in the bar were showing Spanish football, the ecstatic commentary galvanising no one – the bar was all but empty at this prime sunbathing hour. We ordered a jug of one of the lurid cocktails and drank the lot as we picked over our strategy for an incriminating meet-cute between Jason and Clara. It would take place the evening before the wedding, we'd decided, leaving Ange and Jason as little time as possible for reconciliation before the ceremony. Clara reasoned that it would be easier to lead Jason into a compromising situation if they had already met and spoken before that night, if only briefly.

'And an audience is important,' she said, doubling down on the details, sucking up her glass of lime green cocktail with a straw. 'It's crucial that Ange sees us but that others do as well, preferably you guys, so that *you* control the narrative, not Ange.'

'She'll probably still go ahead with the wedding anyway,' I said. I could feel gloom descending. 'That ceremony is all about her. Jason's presence is pretty much beside the point.'

'It will still be a victory though,' Clara argued, 'if Ange is filled with doubt when she recites her vows. Especially with all of you standing there, pitying her, because you've witnessed cast-iron evidence that Jason is absolutely *not* devoted, like she says he is.'

'I suppose,' I said. 'But is it enough?'

'Enough for what?'

'To make us even. For everything Ange has done to me.'

Clara topped up our glasses from the jug of Melon Sunrise or Grasshopper Piss, or whatever it was called. 'Well, then you just continue when you get home. You move on and attack another section of her delicate fortress.'

I ditched my straw to drink straight from the glass.

'But I'll have to do that alone. Without you.'

This was the root cause of my melancholy: the creeping realisation that the holiday was ending, that soon Clara would not be there. Every girl needs a bit of holiday romance, she had said, and wasn't that effectively what we'd enjoyed? Someone of Clara's ilk didn't hang out with someone of mine back home, in the real world.

'What on earth are you talking about!' she exclaimed. 'You're not getting rid of me! You're not allowed! I saved you from the brink of death on that hotel lawn. That makes us friends for life. Inseparable!'

She ditched her straw too, chinking her glass against mine, and we took hearty gulps, wiping our mouths clean with the backs of our hands, simpering like idiots. She was right. How could we go through what we'd been through, what we were about to do, and then never speak again?

'Or I tell you what,' said Clara, holding my eye, 'we could just make sure that wedding car never makes it up the mountain.' She repeated her mime from the beach – a slow-motion hand travelling through the air, demonstrating Ange's tragic trajectory. 'Crash!' she said, and at that precise moment the football crowd on the TV screen erupted into cheers. The coincidence widened our smiles; it spurred us on. How would we do it – make that car leave the road in a way that seemed purely accidental? Clara could set the vehicle on its lethal course, but then she'd have to dive free at the final, crucial moment. The idea of stunt-rolling across a dusty mountain path in Aunt Mari's *haute couture* suit thrilled Clara. She leapt to her feet to pull some martial arts moves, a straw clamped cutlass-like between her teeth.

'That would be far too risky,' I said, with action-thriller seriousness. 'Ange needs to be behind the wheel' – I held up my fingers like scissors – 'and then all we need do is snip the brake cables.'

Clara sat back with a stubborn shake of her head. 'No way. Daddy would *never* agree to that woman taking his beloved car without me.'

We held one another's gaze, grinning, silently challenging each other to arrive at the perfect solution.

'Argh!' cried Clara, collapsing dramatically onto the sticky tabletop in defeat. 'It's like that riddle,' she said, sitting up again, making a play of it on the table with a balled-up napkin, a branded book of matches and a two-euro coin. 'You have to get the fox, the chicken and the sack of grain across the river without the fox eating the chicken, or the chicken eating the grain.'

'And are you the chicken?' I asked.

'I suppose. And that makes the car the bag of grain.'

'We can't save the car?'

'No.'

'But it's beautiful,' I said. 'Your dad will be so upset.'

Clara belted out a laugh.

'What?' I asked.

'Listen to us – commiserating about a car, but not about Ange.'

I laughed too, if only to let myself off the hook. Because beneath the surface of this fantasy scheme, I had caught a glimpse of the knife. Violent acts of revenge, I assumed, sprang from blind rage, from red mist. But deciding to kill someone could be as simple as sliding a two-euro coin from one side of a bar table to another, and then saying it should be so. No thunder was required, no fury, only a calm kind of certainty. Every one of us is eminently capable of that. We all stand at the end of the jetty, considering the jump, the coldness of the water below. It just takes one big breath, a second of courage. A courage, I told myself, I was fortunate not to have.

We emerged from that grimy bar into the vivid intensity of the day, to waves lapping and to children playing, their happy cries curling through the air like kites – and to the sight of Pete and Jason negotiating with the father and son who ran the water-sports hire.

Jason spotted us immediately. 'Hello, hello, hello,' he cried.

We froze on the decking of the bar, caught out.

Clara was the first to snap to attention, to realise that this was less a disaster, more an opportunity.

'Why, hello, sailor!' she said, drawing out her vowels in much the same way Jason littered his speech with glottal stops whenever there was some attention to be had. 'Getting paddleboards, are we?' she said. 'I *am* impressed.'

We stepped off the decking towards them. Jason was beaming; my husband's face was made of flint.

'What's going on?' Pete demanded, no pleasantries to spare. It was the most direct thing he'd said to me in days.

I swerved his question, adopting the charm of a game-show host introducing their contestants. 'Guys,' I said, 'this is Clara. Clara, this is my husband Pete...'

He ignored the hand she offered for him to shake.

'And this...' I paused; gave it weight '... is Jason.'

Naturally, Jason grasped Clara's hand, holding onto it for just a little too long.

'Liv and I were getting together for a spot of wedding planning,' said Clara.

I saw how both men held their breath as she spoke, delighted by her, and also, at the same time, afraid of what she might demand of them.

'Oh, yes, that,' said Jason, tossing the subject aside. He was behaving just as I'd said he would. Clara flickered a glance my way in acknowledgement.

'But it's a secret!' I said, wide-eyed, clamping my fingers around her arm. The car *was* a secret; Ange didn't want Jason to know. She wanted to make an entrance. 'We can't say another word.' I zipped my mouth shut with finger and thumb.

'Intriguing,' said Jason, his attention only on Clara.

'And now I must go,' she said.

I shot her a look – *go? Already?*

She leant close to whisper in my ear, made it sexy.

'Leave them wanting more,' she said, only for me, and then she was off. We watched her head back towards the hotel, swinging her hips as she walked; she knew our eyes would be following her.

'Missing the taste of aristocratic pussy, were you, Liv?' Jason said, guffawing at his own tired joke, delivering a slap to Pete's back.

Pete remained rigid. 'We're not good enough for Liv anymore,' he said.

I stared him down.

'Oh, no, I stand no chance with Clara,' I said. 'It's *you* she finds attractive. In a rough kind of way.'

'Me?' said Pete, his voice constricting.

'No, not you, lover boy,' I said wearily, watching his ego collapse and enjoying the view. I turned to Jason. 'You. Clara seriously has the hots for you.'

Jason's smirk slid from his face, to be replaced by a kind of terror. It was frightening, it seemed, to be pursued by a woman like Clara, someone so completely out of his league.

'Clara was very surprised to learn that you were the groom-to-be.' I laid it on thick. 'She's had her eye on you for a while because she assumed you were a single dad and that you might be up for, well, some aristocratic pussy.'

201

'You bitch!' Pete spat.

'Whoa!' said Jason, holding up his hands. 'Where did that come from, mate?'

'Who the fuck are you?' said Pete, ignoring Jason, drilling down on me. 'I really don't know who you are anymore.'

'Ditto,' I fired back.

Jason edged away. 'Okay, guys, I'm going to... I don't know what this is, so... I'm just going to...' He was off.

Pete looked me up and down, standing there holding my thin carrier bag filled with melting chocolate. He sneered. 'What the actual fuck are you doing, Liv?'

'What do you mean?' I said,

'That woman does not fancy Jason.'

'Why not?'

'Oh, come on!'

'It happens, Pete. Younger women do fall for old fuckers sometimes. You should know.'

Pete gave a baleful laugh. 'Oh, yeah, of course, this intern I've supposedly been shagging. Thanks for that, Liv. I truly love being humiliated in front of our friends every time you get drunk.'

A hand appeared on Pete's shoulder; it was the father from the water-sports hire.

'You take this somewhere else,' he said, friendly but firm, 'yes, please.'

All around us, people were gaping. The mum of a family returning their canoes shook her head at our language, ushering her young children out of earshot.

Pete snatched my arm and dragged me along the alley that ran between the hire shop and the neighbouring café, the customers at the front tables turning to watch our exit. We emerged in a clay-dust car park, walled in by chicken wire and cacti. I wrenched my arm free from his grip, seeing my shadow self on the dry ground perform the same action.

'I was not *drunk*, Pete!' I said, pushing my face close to his. 'I was *poisoned*, by Ange.'

'Did someone else make you drunk now?' he said with a leer. 'Because I can smell it on you. You're hammered.'

'I was drinking *Coke* and lime and soda – all night!'

'Ah, okay, so what other excuse do you have for climbing onto Jason's lap?'

'You know that Clara found me unconscious on the lawn, don't you?'

'Yes, the amazing, topless Clara!'

'I could have died, Pete. Where the hell were you?'

'I dunno. Was I off fucking an imaginary intern?'

'Imaginary!' I all but screamed it. 'Imaginary! Becky is not imaginary!'

Pete paused, genuinely confused. 'Becky?' he asked hesitantly.

'Becky,' I repeated, a name too prosaic to be a curse, though that was how it felt. 'Becky the intern.'

'Becky was on the graduate scheme.'

'Oh, was she?' I snorted at the ridiculousness of his correction. 'Oh, well, that makes it okay then.'

'Makes what okay?'

'That you lost your job, that we lost everything, because you were fucking Becky from the fucking graduate scheme.'

Pete's jaw worked soundlessly.

'All that pretence about being made redundant! But *she* was the reason – the reason you can't get a reference for another job, and why you refuse to talk to me about what really happened.'

Pete reached forward. I dodged him, scuffing up a plume of red dust.

'Don't you touch me,' I said. 'Don't you dare.'

'But that's not it,' he said. 'I lost my job because I sucked at it.'

'No.'

'Yes. I just wasn't good enough. I was completely out of my depth. And I couldn't talk to you about that because I felt like a total…' He choked, swallowed. 'Like a total fucking loser.'

The impulse to comfort him was strong; I shook it off.

'I saw the texts,' I said. 'I saw you two at the ball together, it was obvious.'

'Obvious that she was my only real friend at the company, the only person I was on a par with, skills-wise? Yeah, that's about right.'

'No, that's bullshit.'

'I tell you what's bullshit, Liv,' he lunged, his anger not spent, 'you putting all the responsibility on me, to earn everything, enough to pay for a car and an extension and school fees.'

'You told me I should go to college! You were the one who convinced me to do it. And you wanted all those things as well.'

'Did I?'

'I dunno. Maybe not, because clearly you didn't want me, otherwise you wouldn't have cheated.'

'I did not cheat!' He took a breath to make his voice firm, level: 'I did not sleep with Becky, Liv. I took lunch breaks with her and I was nice to her – yes. She was nice to me too, even when it was really clear that I was getting canned and that I'd be absolutely no use when it came to helping her with a job at the end of her scheme. She was the only one who messaged me to see if I was all right afterwards. The only one.' He let that sink in, for himself more than me. 'Oh, god, Liv, seriously, I don't understand what's happened to us. I thought that we were...'

'Forever?' I offered, taunting him.

He took it at face value. 'Yeah. That's exactly what I thought. How could you believe that I would do something like that?'

'Because I was told,' I said.

'Told? But... By who?'

'By Beth.'

'How would Beth know anything about me and my work, and... How is that possible?'

'Beth knew because...' I paused to untangle it, the thread of information and how it had reached me. And once I had, I stopped dead. 'Oh,' I said. Then, profounder still, 'Oh.'

I wasn't standing at the end of the jetty anymore, on the brink, considering the jump. The cold water was rushing up around me. It was filling my nose and my ears.

This was the end of Ange. It was already done.

News of my husband's infidelity came to me via a bag of second-hand clothes.

There had been a month of preparatory meetings at Ange's house in the run-up to the holiday, and I was diligent about attending every single one, even if it clashed with a shift at the café. I'd haggle with one of the millennials for a swap. It was important that I was there, that the loan disagreement wasn't raised from the dead in my absence, fed and watered anew with sentences beginning, *I'm sorry but...* The debt was settled, Ange had been paid off; I needed that to be the end of it. I also needed to stay in the loop. No way was I willing to arrive in Corfu unprepared, everything decided without me. I refused to be a stowaway on my own comeback tour.

Though we were all going to feel like stowaways to some degree. The trip had been Ange's idea in the first place; she had just very kindly invited us all along. She controlled everything from a file – one of those old-school, cardboard concertina affairs, with various neon Post-it notes rabbit-earing out of the top – and that meant we only knew what Ange chose to share. None of us had the name of the hotel, nor a link to its website. We were sent odd pictures and slices of marketing copy pasted into the body of emails. Ange played it like she was building up our excitement for what lay ahead. I did reverse-image searches and Googled the phrases she sent, desperate to land on some clues. Binnie outright asked for a URL at one of our meetings around Ange's kitchen island.

'Oh, Binnie,' Ange cried, 'it's actually quite adorable how much you hate surprises!'

'I just want to know if there's going to be a hairdryer in the room,' Binnie countered.

Ange pulled her close for a lip-gloss kiss to the cheek. 'Relax, Bin. You're allowed to, I swear. Let me take the load.' As she released her hold, Ange added, 'But, yes, you will need to pack your BaByliss Big Hair.'

I didn't push for any more information than Ange was willing to give. Like an addict chasing the euphoria of their very first high, I was doing everything I could to get back into her good books, to feel the warm glow of her attention once again. I accepted Ange's D-notice on the sharing of holiday details absolutely, in part because Beth and Binnie, on the whole, were doing the same. Though I realise now that was because they knew about the wedding. To them, right from the start, it *really was* Ange's trip to which we had all been very kindly invited.

At one meeting, Ange drew up a list of the items each person would be responsible for packing. There was no sense in wasting valuable suitcase space bringing duplicates of the things we could share. Beach tennis sets were thrown into the ring, a travel edition of Battleship. Beth offered up a paperback guide to the Ionian Islands, an unexpected contribution from someone who believed her phone held the answer to everything, but a strange, auction-like atmosphere had developed while we slugged rosé, Ange keeping score in her wild, looping cursive. Everyone was eager to put forward something more useful, more impressive than the last. *I take your set of French boules and I raise you a full-size, inflatable crocodile.*

Ivy, I said, would bring along a comprehensive art kit; the other kids were welcome to make use of her felt-tip pens and coloured pencils during the flight. Ange quietly tut-tutted and shook her head as she wrote that down. Only a Smug Mother Of Girls would suggest such a thing, she said. Her three boys would be doing parkour across the aeroplane seats while my angel Ivy did her colouring in. It was a shove-back, a slap across the face, I see that now. But did I feel it then? I think I had taught myself not to feel, or rather I'd learnt that what I felt wasn't important – a crucial distinction.

We moved on to discussing the outfits we should pack. Ange wanted us to wear long, flowing kaftan dresses for the journey, so that we could arrive in style, start as we meant to go on. I knew there was nothing suitable amongst the tangle of t-shirts, leggings and bras I kept in a cardboard box in Nigel's back bedroom, so I kept quiet, and my lack of participation in this conversation did not go unnoticed. I returned home from work a few days later to find a large, stiff, putty-coloured carrier bag waiting for me in the hallway. Nigel had taken receipt of it.

'She said that she was getting rid of some old things and wondered if any of them could be of use to you for your holiday wardrobe.'

Holiday wardrobe was not a Nigel phrase. I didn't need to ask who 'she' was. The carrier bag was an expensive one. It was branded – Burberry.

'How nice,' I said, because that's what you're supposed to say when someone gives you a gift. But was this a gift? Or was it another loan with an unspoken clause? I could imagine the scene if I wore any item of clothing from that bag on our trip. Ange would point it out, regale everyone with the reasons why it hadn't been good enough for her and why she'd had to throw it away. Yet I couldn't refuse these offerings either. That would be rude, a snub.

I stepped around the bag and picked up another hot potato instead. Pete was fetching Ivy from school. I had Nigel alone.

'Does Pete talk to you?' I asked.

'Talk to me about what, love?'

'About how he lost his job.'

'Well, they had to make cuts, didn't they? It was last in, first out.'

The answer to my question then was 'no'. Pete was palming off his dad with the same lie he'd told everybody else.

Earlier that week, I'd tried to hack into Pete's laptop, using every combination of dates, names and football teams to crack his password, hopeful of finding some revealing documentation from his former employer, some answers. Had Pete stolen from them, committed fraud, got into a physical fight in the office? I'd even started to wonder about sexual harassment. Was he capable of that? Did I really know who my husband was when I wasn't around? But I got locked out, all my password attempts were used up.

It was Beth who came to collect the bag of clothes. Ange was too busy.

'Things are insane for her right now,' said Beth. 'She's got three end-of-year school awards shows to attend. Three!' Beth ran through the accolades being bestowed upon each of the Connors boys – medals for fortitude, kindness, patience – qualities I'd seen no evidence of in the kids themselves. But I inferred what I was supposed to; those medals might as well be given directly to Ange, for she was the sun and her children merely moons reflecting her light.

'So, was anything useful?' Beth asked of the bag of clothes, as we made our way through to the kitchen.

My focus was on negotiating a successful rejection of Ange's 'gift'. I knew that my every word, its tone and accompanying action, would be handed back to her along with that rope-handled Burberry carrier. Beth would effectively be my ventriloquist dummy and I needed to perform well.

'I couldn't fit into anything,' I said, feigning embarrassment. 'It was all far too tiny for me.'

Beth looked unconvinced. I reminded her how tall I was compared to Ange, how proportionally I was always going to need a bigger size. Ange, I knew, would be delighted with this outcome. *I just can't stop thinking about how Liv couldn't fit into any of my clothes!* she would marvel at every available opportunity. But I could live with that.

'Oh, no, what a disappointment!' said Beth.

'Isn't it?' I replied, setting down a cup of tea in front of her.

'Where's Pete?' she asked.

'In our room, on his laptop. Shall I tell him you're here? Do you wanna say hi?'

'No!' Beth yelped it. 'No, no. It's okay.' She heaped two sugars into a drink she usually took without.

'What's up?' I asked, joining her at the kitchen table.

Beth inhaled deeply. I thought she was about to share a problem of her own, something she didn't want Pete around to hear.

'God, Liv,' she said, 'I've been going over and over in my mind whether I should tell you this.'

'You can tell me anything,' I assured her.

'I just came to the conclusion that if you knew something about Kenny, something like this, then I would absolutely want you to tell me.'

'Oh,' I said at this ominous shift in the conversation.

Beth, I realised, was about to reveal what I'd gone looking for in Pete's laptop. Therefore, I had to be ready for it – the truth. I put my hands beneath the table so she couldn't see that they were shaking.

'Right, well,' she began, 'you know the boys went out for beers the other week?'

'Yes,' I said.

'And, well, I never get anything out of Kenny about what they talk about when they're all together.'

'Boy code.' I smiled weakly.

'Boy code, right.' Beth's smile in return wouldn't stick. 'But Jason, he's a bit more open with Ange.'

'Right.'

'And Pete was being pretty open with Jason that night – about losing his job.'

I couldn't breathe. I had been so hungry for answers for so long, but right then I just wanted to run from that kitchen, from Beth, so I might keep my illusions intact.

'And?' I prompted.

'I mean, I'm sure it's totally nothing,' she said, 'but...' Beth closed her eyes and delivered it fast: 'Pete mentioned an inappropriate relationship with an intern.' She opened her eyes again. Her expression was that of a dog who has chewed up your favourite shoes.

My mind immediately lurched to the black-tie ball in Mayfair, to the joking, the arm-touching. *They seem to get along so well,* I had told Ange.

Still, I prepared my denials – *Oh, what, her? No, no, that's nothing!* I was determined to salvage some semblance of dignity amidst our humiliating existence, living out of cardboard boxes in Nigel's back bedroom.

I would have said anything to make Beth stop talking, to have us change the subject, to have her get up and leave. My focus was now entirely on saving face, so I didn't spot it, truly I didn't, how Beth was already doing her ventriloquist act. When she delivered the final damning detail, by giving me the intern's name – 'Becky' – I never once saw Ange's lips move.

We took the pale, slim road that winds its way up the foothills of the mountain.

But this was only a rehearsal, the ceremony before the ceremony, a practice of the service and a test of the food before doing it all over again in two days' time, for real.

Ange insisted at the last minute that she travel in a taxi with Pete, Ivy and me, leaving Beth and Binnie, dressed in their finest, forsaken on the hotel steps. There would be no 'girls' taxi' after all; Beth and Binnie would have to suffer the company of their own husbands and children on that journey up the mountain. Ange had caught the scent of something on Pete and me – the heady perfume of reconciliation, of happiness, of renewed lust – and there was no way she was going to tolerate that.

Ivy slept over with Amelia and Paige the evening after Pete and I argued in the red clay car park, allowing us some time alone to level the land.

Pete's superiors *had* described his friendship with Becky as 'inappropriate' – that was the small nugget of truth he had unwisely confided to Jason, which had been passed on to Ange, hammered into the ugliest shape, then delivered back to me. At his exit meeting, Pete's bosses ran through all the performance-review targets he'd failed to meet, then offered a little extra friendly advice: taking lunch with the graduate showed a lack of ambition. By some, it might even be viewed as 'inappropriate'. Pete should have been looking upwards for a mentor, playing golf with his peers. Except Pete had clocked early on that he had no comparable peers. His colleagues were in a different league. He couldn't do what they did. He just couldn't do the job.

So, there he was, aged forty, with no decent reference or recommendation, no coherent story to tell on his CV, no sense of what he was capable of anymore, his confidence spent. He was a boy of the eighties who believed he should be providing for his wife and daughter, and was in denial about his inability to do so, slowly drowning beneath extension plans and private-school prospectuses, hire-purchase car agreements and big bills from fancy restaurants, all the emblems of success we thought we must acquire. He was drowning and not waving.

'But who the hell are we if we decide that none of that matters?' Pete asked as we lay in bed together. (Clara was right, a good fuck was what that holiday was surely missing.) It was a genuine question.

I reminded him of how the group used to be – the easy, natural way of things before we started striving for stuff we didn't need. Specifically, how joyous it had been before Ange. It could be like that again, I was convinced of it, if only we removed her. She was the shard of glass lodged in the sole of our collective foot.

'Yeah, right,' said Pete, 'over Ange's dead body!'

'I'm okay with that!' I replied, laughing.

As we waited at the front of the hotel for the taxis, Pete's hand wandered from my waist down to the curve of my backside. I rested my hand at the back of his head, toying with the hair at his nape. This got Ange's attention – not her warm, glowing consideration; something hotter, more magnified. The cars pulled up and Ange slotted her arm through mine, scooting me towards the rear doors of one of the dusty saloons. I responded to Pete's look of trepidation with one of reassurance. Ange was as irresistible as always – no one made you feel like she did when she fixed the full wattage of her spotlight upon you – but I was in on the trick now. No woman gets sawn in half if there are two women in the box from the start.

Pete took the front seat. I was in the back, in the middle, Ange on one side of me, Ivy on the other. As we exited the hotel gates, I saw Clara make for the Sunbeam Alpine. She would follow our cavalcade up the mountain under the pretence of timing the journey for her chauffeur role on the big day. While she was there at the old ruins, should she bump into Jason, she would place a hand on his arm, maybe share a joke, and I would be sure to see it and point it out to Ange, this small scene in the narrative we were building, all of it leading to a grand finale of unfaithfulness from Jason the night before his wedding.

We left the coast road and began the climb; that was when Ange initiated the attack I knew was coming.

'So, we're all made up now, are we?' she said, her tone teacherly, her words seasoned with just the right amount of doubt, enough to say, *I really don't believe you and Pete will ever be happy*, but not enough that her question couldn't pass for well-meaning.

Pete leant an ear towards our conversation. I glanced down at Ivy beside me whose faraway gaze was on the brown hills rising around us and the clear blue sky above. She would be absorbing everything.

'Yes,' I said. 'All made up.' I sent Pete a dreamy smile, one that he wouldn't have been able to see, but Ange saw it. She was quiet for a moment. She wasn't done.

'But, what about... ?' Her voice fell to a whisper. 'What about... *the intern?*'

I was supposed to snap at this question, allowing Ange to be the victim of our exchange not the perpetrator. *But I was only asking because I was worried about you, Liv!*

'Do you mean Becky?' I said, no whispers.

Ange's mouth sagged open, empty of a response.

'Becky was a friend in a storm, Ange,' called Pete from the front seat.

I picked up Ange's hand and squeezed it. 'We all need one of those, don't we?'

She nodded at this, cautiously; a player knows a player, but she couldn't be certain of the rules to this game.

'Gosh, you must be so nervous!' I said, keeping hold of her hand. The taxi negotiated the first of many hairpin bends and I cast my gaze over Ivy's head to the vertiginous view out the window.

'Why's that?' asked Ange, still cautious.

'Because you're getting married!' I replied as if the answer were obvious. Soon you will be just like me, I was saying, just as vulnerable, joined to someone who could cheat on you, disappoint you, destroy you – just like that.

The taxis dropped us at a gravel car park. The final stretch had to be made on foot – up steep, unmade paths, our sandalled feet crunching against the rough earth, the sun beating its rhythm onto our backs. The old village was not what I'd expected. Ange described it as a 'romantic spot', and it was, to an extent. The landscape was beautiful, with cypresses spearing the sky and shrubs growing wild, lush with berries. The cluster of abandoned buildings had a fairy-tale quality, their roofs missing, vines climbing the walls, ancient brick ovens crumbling in the corner of empty, stone-floored kitchens. But many of these buildings were layered in graffiti. Some were a dumping ground for rubble and litter. In one, flies gathered greedily around a large human shit.

'God, it's so gorgeous up here!' said Beth, breathless from the ascent. This was the company line – everything was gorgeous in Ange's romantic spot; it was wonderful, delightful. Beth ushered Ange and Jason into a pose in front of one of the old, tumbledown buildings, against a wall where someone had spray-painted a heart. Ange echoed the shape of this graffiti with her fingers and thumbs, pressing them against her chest. I turned away. There was something unnerving about the pair of them standing there in front of that sinister cartoon heart, painted in black, the tail of it dripping. I joined Ivy, who was sitting on her haunches, peering into the low gaps of a stone wall, her project book open at her feet.

'Are you looking for the friends of our deadly hotel viper?' I asked.

She gave me an affectionate roll of her eyes.

'Snakes don't have friends,' she informed me.

We made our way to the old market square, to a cluster of tavernas. The restaurant was also not what I had been expecting from Ange; the place was neither glamorous nor chichi, but rustic, even down-at-heel. It had been endorsed by a celebrity chef though. This was why Ange had chosen it – for the bragging rights. Our group jostled into place along a skinny table, nodding hellos to a neighbouring family we recognised from our hotel – a mum and dad, with two almost-adult children. Ange was immediately irritated by their presence.

'What are they doing here?' she hissed at Binnie. To Ange, this was *her* taverna, her secret find. She was under the illusion that all her choices for our holiday and her wedding were startlingly original, that this trip was uniquely curated. But you saw them everywhere – at the restaurant where Ange had proposed, down the alleys in Corfu Town – faces from the hotel, tourists just like us, fetched to the island from leafy little commuter towns to get away from it all. But away from it all with the right people, with familiar types who can be trusted to ask you where your kids go to school and what the house prices are doing in your area. We were locked in the same loops as we always were, walking the same predictable paths as everybody else.

As the perfect punchline to this moment, Clara then appeared in the market square. Alongside her, unexpectedly, was Aunt Mari, decked out in an achingly modern sundress with multi-coloured tiers. By comparison, Clara looked almost shabby, wearing the pretty yellow tea dress she had previously lent to me.

'Isn't that your dress?' said Beth as we said more polite hellos and watched Clara and Aunt Mari take their reserved seats in an adjacent taverna, a move that suggested Ange wasn't as clued up as she thought about the best food in this village.

'I borrowed it,' I said, an answer that did nothing to smooth the furrows of Beth's brow, only deepen them. She was doing the maths – how come I was wearing that dress the morning after returning to the group, the day after dishing the dirt on Clara's family? As far as the girls were concerned, my only remaining connection to Clara was the occasional chauffeuring arrangement made on Ange's behalf.

'You know Ange comes and speaks to me on the sun deck sometimes?' Clara had told me the afternoon we spent plotting in the sports bar.

'When?' I said, stung by this revelation.

'Whenever you're off fetching something from your room, or if you're occupied with Ivy. She always comes with a question, about decorating the car, or timings, or some other spurious thing, but then she'll say, "Oh, I love your swim towels, where are they from?" Or, "Liv says you visit Corfu every year, you must be so knowledgeable about the island." Good grief, that woman knows how to kiss feet.'

'Fuck,' I said, at the audacity of it, at Ange's insatiability. She'd laid claims to Beth, Binnie, Ivy, Pete, and now she wanted Clara too. I imagined Ange finding a way to let Clara know that I'd traded her family secrets to get myself back in with the group. The idea made me queasy; it frightened me.

A waiter arrived at Clara and Aunt Mari's table and the Empress asked loud questions about the menu, which drew our attention. We watched their discussion play out, Binnie distractedly fingering the stitches above her eye, Beth mindlessly hoovering up the contents of her nearest breadbasket, visibly still perplexed by the puzzle of the yellow dress – how could she push me on the issue without using the phrase 'the morning after', without bringing up Binnie's trip to hospital, without triggering Ange?

I seized this moment of group contemplation to lean across Pete to speak to Jason.

'You're not blushing, are you?' I teased. He was – Jason had flushed a bright pink the instant Clara appeared.

He coughed anxiously at my question, as if he might be able to bring up his embarrassment, spit it out.

Ange at the other end of the table latched onto our brief exchange.

'What?' she demanded to know. 'What's going on?'

I caught Pete's eye. He joined in, slapping Jason's back theatrically.

'You all right there, mate,' he said, 'got an aristocratic pube stuck in your throat?'

Jason's boys sprang alert at Pete's use of the word 'pube', grabbing at it, tossing it around between them, sniggering.

'What is this?' said Ange, her voice peaking. 'What are you saying?'

'Nothing, babes,' said Jason, lobster-faced, betraying himself by glancing across to Clara's table, as if checking that he was right, that there really was nothing going on. Clara waved coquettishly, a rippling of her fingers just for him, making Jason whip his head back around lightning fast. Pete and I snorted like teenagers; we cried with laughter.

'Stop it!' said Ange, and I almost felt sorry for her.

After lunch, we walked more of the sloping paths, following the signs for the bees. On one of the high ridges there was a pretty jumble of pastel hives, the sky humming with the insects. True to form, Binnie's boys, George and Henry, flailed and squealed. Dev was charged with managing their hysterics while Binnie, Beth and Ange clustered around a small stall selling honey scrubs and beeswax lip salves. I wandered to the edge of the ridge to take in a view that shimmered in the heat.

Clara and Aunt Mari arrived at the hives not long after us, Aunt Mari stepping carefully across the lumpy terrain in high-wedged shoes. Clara, in her everyday white plimsolls, kept pace patiently at her aunt's side. They struck up conversation with one of the beekeepers and I watched this for a while, from a distance, a tableau reminiscent of a Royal Variety line-up, where the commoner performers get to share words with the attending princess and the Queen. Then I turned my focus onto Ivy, who was exploring the ridge's rocky corners, hopeful of spying an elusive viper.

'Ivy!' I called.

I wasn't worried about her encountering a snake, rather that she would be whacked across the head by Duff or Brady who had found long sticks and begun sparring.

Ivy stood, taking a moment to locate the source of my voice, then the source of my concern. She considered the boys for a moment, thrashing at the air, before wandering off with a sigh, finding a safer spot to hunker down – or so she thought. Aunt Mari had left Clara alone with the beekeeper and was rounding a bank of flowering shrubs, unstable on her platforms. She did not see Ivy crouched low in her path and walked straight into her, almost tumbling to the ground, saving herself by making a grab for Ivy's rising shoulders with those bird-talon claws. I ran to my daughter, to protect her from the Empress's wrath.

'What is the girl doing?' Aunt Mari demanded, switching her steadying grip from Ivy's shoulders to my arm. I looked down at the wattled skin of her hands, the vibrant turquoise of her nails. I was but a convenient railing, a thing of service.

'She's looking for snakes,' I replied squarely.

I cast a glance towards Clara still engaged in conversation with the beekeeper, the man's stance more relaxed now he had got her alone.

'How very strange,' said Aunt Mari, her eyes on Ivy who had, knowing what was good for her, moved away from the outraged old lady. She was continuing her search beneath a fresh patch of under-growth. The Empress's quick judgement made me bristle. Better to be strange, I thought, if this woman was the measure of normal.

I shrugged my arm free from her grip.

'Like mother like daughter,' I said with a taut smile, heading off towards the girls, ready to coo at their unnecessary purchases of lip balms and hand creams.

The wedding rehearsal took place in the manicured gardens of one of the renovated houses of the village, amid neat borders of hydrangea bushes, bursting with pompoms of dusky mauve, on a lawn so fresh and green it might have lain in front of an English country house. We had come all the way up a Greek mountain to find ourselves in Berkshire.

Ange orchestrated the run-through. The celebrant – a hippy-ish blonde expat – swiftly worked out that it was better not to interfere. Ivy, Amelia and Paige were manhandled into a tight arrow formation for their entrance into the garden. At various points during the ceremony, Ange wanted the flower girls to step forward, then back, turn this way, then that. Our daughters were eager to please, but the cues were complicated. One of them was bound to mess up during the wedding proper and be forever labelled the fly in the ointment of Ange's perfect day. My heart sank at the prospect.

When it was my turn, I assumed the correct position on the lawn, ready to give a full recital, knowing that Ange would want to carry out her compliance checks. I had decided to read in the original French so she couldn't understand a word and would have no clue on how to critique me. She also wouldn't know that I'd gone rogue with some solid-gold Jules Laforgue misery – 'Sad, Sad', a poem so gloomy he'd had to name it twice. It was my personal response to Ange's bridal dictatorship, her Facebook letters and her fucking concertina files – four verses on the futility of life, the way we're all doomed to experience the same vices, grief, boredom and sickness, before we ultimately find ourselves pushing up daisies.

'*"Je contemple mon feu"*,' I began. '*"J'étouffe un bâillement…"*'
I contemplate my fire; I stifle a yawn…
'And skip to the end!' directed Ange.

I was dismissed and I didn't argue. The heat at altitude seemed intensified. Standing out on that open lawn for just a short while had left me drenched in sweat. A return to the taverna on the market square appealed – that was where Pete, Kenny and Dev were, sipping cold beers, killing time playing Uno with Dev's boys, all of them currently surplus to Ange's requirements – but I knew I shouldn't stray far. I took one of the curling paths down to a lower ridge, positioning myself in a gasp of shade beneath an ancient fig tree, a spot where I could still observe the rehearsal going on in the garden above and hear any calls for my immediate attendance. That was where Clara found me, my back against the tree's sinewy trunk as I plucked at the neck of my cheap eBay sundress, fanning a breeze onto my chest.

'So, am I allowed to just talk to you?' she said, sidling over. 'Like this? In plain sight?' It was a flirtatious approach and I loved it. In Clara's company, I always felt subversive, capable of anything.

'Nice work with Jason at lunch,' I said. 'Ange was in bits.'

She smiled, pinching the hem of the yellow dress and bobbing a curtsey. 'Sadly, I haven't managed to get close enough to do anything more,' she said. 'The Empress has cramped my style somewhat.'

'Yes! What is she doing here?' I expected some light mocking of the woman, a denouncement of her choice in footwear, followed by a deconstruction of our tense exchange by the hives.

'I asked her to come, of course.'

'Oh,' I said.

'Well, I wasn't going to sit there and have lunch all by myself, was I?'

On the garden stage above, Ange was now manhandling her own children, arranging Jason's trio of best men into a neat line alongside their dad. The Connors boys were not cooperating; they were a Newton's cradle of shoulder-barging.

'So, where's Aunt Mari now?' I asked Clara.

'With the car. We're going to head back down the mountain.' She nodded at the scene above. 'I don't think I'm going to get any more useful access to lover boy today.'

I shook my head. She was right.

'Drive carefully,' I said playfully, ominously.

'Those roads are quite something, aren't they?' she replied, giving a menacing twitch of her eyebrows. 'You look down and the cliff edge is right there, falling away to nothing.'

Above us, Ange's patience was worn to a single thread. She was raising her voice, though not quite loud enough for us to discern the cause. Beth was nodding frantically, obediently, appeasingly. The flower girls wore worried smiles.

'There's nothing but tree trunks that might break your back,' I said, continuing Clara's observations of that roadside drop, 'and rocks to crush your skull.'

Ivy had wilted in the heat, exhausted by the rehearsal, and was sitting down on the lawn, thumbing through her project book. Amelia nudged at my daughter with her foot, a prompt that she should stand again, and quickly, before Ange was to see.

'Yes,' murmured Clara, and I wasn't sure if this was in response to me and the dangers that awaited anyone who swerved from the road, or if she was agreeing with Amelia, quietly urging Ivy to listen to her friend, to get up.

It was too late.

The Newton's cradle of Connors boys collapsed into a pile on the grass and Ange, turning away from them in exasperation, found Ivy sitting cross-legged on the ground.

'You. Need. To. Pay. Attention!' Ange screamed it, wrenching Ivy onto her feet with some considerable force. Ivy was taken by surprise, left shaking, close to tears. On her arm – red welts, visible even from where we were standing on the tier below.

Clara's hand flew to her mouth. 'Oh, god!'

'That's it!' I cried, inflamed, tearing past her.

I will do it this time, I thought, as I marched up that slope to the garden, I will grab Ange's arm and I will bite down, draw blood. I will kill that fucking woman for what she has done to me, to all of us!

I stopped dead, all of my thunder suddenly gone.

'Liv?' called Clara, her voice dispelling this momentary trance.

I turned on the path, slowly retracing my steps, returning to the dark shade of the fig tree, to Clara. There was no fury when I spoke, only a calm kind of certainty. I met her eye.

'This is how we'll do it,' I said. 'This is how we'll get that car to crash.'

5.

The morning of the wedding, I woke at five. The first thing I saw: our outfits hanging on the front of the wardrobe doors, shells of our future selves.

A cream polka-dot midi dress for me, from Clara's suitcase.

A smart lemon shirt and beige cargo pants for Pete, borrowed from Dev.

A grey tulle flower-girl dress for Ivy, chosen by Ange.

I walked straight past them, to the fold-out bed in the lounge and kitchenette, and gently shook awake Ivy.

'Let's go,' I said.

We dressed quickly in shorts and t-shirts, slipping silently out of the door. The air held the whisper of a chill as we took the steps down to the deserted lawn. The pool was a pane of glass; the bar shuttered.

The previous night I had sat there with Beth, Binnie and Ange. Ivy and the other kids were tucked up in bed, under the care of hotel babysitters. The boys, showered and fragrant, took themselves off to the sports bar in the bay, a suitably tacky venue in which to celebrate Jason's final night as a free man. We girls indulged in some tackiness too: Binnie produced a packet of penis-shaped straws, Beth had made a flower crown for Ange with devil's horns and an L-plate. As Ange adjusted that crown atop her meticulously hot-tongued hair, I thought of Ivy's instructions on the raised deck when we'd tried to spot a poisonous viper – *just look for the horns.*

The girls' evening outfits had grown increasingly shorter and frillier as the holiday advanced, the sun regressing their tastes, and for Ange's hen night, tasselled seams rode high against my friends' middle-aged thighs. I, inversely, was growing up, becoming subdued. That night, I wore a long skirt made of something pretending to be silk, the swing tags tucked into the back of my underwear away from Ange's reach. My basic vest was one I might normally have worn to bed. I hadn't bothered with make-up. The sun had changed the colour of my face, making my features seem different, not my own, and therefore easier to like and to leave as they were. The damp kinkiness of my hair felt like something to embrace not obliterate with a hairdryer.

'You look very chic,' Beth said, choosing her words carefully, 'so simple.'

It was a blanking of the canvas, I think. *What would I wear if I had absolute freedom to choose? Who the hell are we if we decide that none of this matters?* The possibilities excited me. I'd begun to visualise a life with no dress codes, no competitive acquiring of things, no overwrought social events where attendance felt compulsory. Beth and Binnie were there, in these imaginings of mine; they too would be released from the spell, at liberty to resume their original human forms. All this, of course, relied on us returning home to a life without Ange.

As we lined up our first round of hen-night drinks at a table overlooking the stretch of lawn that sloped down towards the sea, Clara entered stage left, traversing the grass before us, making for the path that led away from the hotel complex. She looked quietly stunning in a black slip dress and a slick of red lipstick.

'Wow,' said Binnie, saving me the job of calling our attention to her. 'Where's she off to, I wonder?'

'For drinks in the bay, probably,' I said. 'She does that sometimes, to escape her family – gets glammed up, heads out, sees who she can find to party with.'

I left it there. The sound of the lapping sea filled the gap. The tight flat line of Ange's mouth and the deep furrow between her eyes told me that she was picturing the rest – who Clara might bump into, what would happen when she did.

Ange had decreed, as the boys headed off, that she and Jason were not to see each other again before the wedding. Kenny was reluctantly bunking up with Jason and his boys, so that Ange could sleep in Beth's apartment that night. How long, I wondered, before she broke her self-imposed rule, conjuring some phony reason for us to head into the bay so we might spy on Jason? Then it occurred to me – Ange had put that rule in place precisely to save herself from witnessing the bad behaviour that Jason was sure to engage in on his last night as a free man.

I'd told Clara there was little point in her going out to look for him. Ange wouldn't shift from the pool bar, wouldn't be there as witness.

'And anyway,' I said with a flourish, 'I don't want Ange to call the wedding off now. I just want her to get in that car. I've decided.'

'Let me do a little flypast then,' said Clara. 'Just for fun. All dressed up. I'll make it look like I'm off to be naughty with Jason.' She left a brilliant pause. 'Just to make sure Ange is feeling *truly* miserable at the moment that car hits the bottom of the valley.'

The way we talked about the crash had shifted. It wasn't a revenge fantasy anymore, it was *fait accompli,* something Clara and I were powerless to forestall, and I felt surprisingly lighter for this change of tone, no guilt to carry.

There was a quiz. What hen night would be complete without one? We lined up our second round of drinks and Beth extracted a folded question sheet from her sequined clutch.

'So... How much do you know about Jason?' she said by way of introduction, her voice wily.

Ange squawked, delighted, but the earlier sighting of Clara had loaded the question – *how much do you* really *know?* Ange eyed me nervously as the quiz progressed. What question might I have inserted to taunt her? *Name the attractive hotel resident who makes the father of your children blush. Extra points for knowing the reason why.* I believe Ange spent the whole game waiting for it. The tension was exquisite. If Clara and I succeeded in nothing else, we had unmoored Ange, left an indelible stain upon her wedding. I felt powerful as I sipped my cold white wine and watched Ange suck up cocktail after cocktail through a penis straw, desperate to drink away her anxiety. She munched cherries open-mouthed and stabbed the decorative umbrellas into her flower crown, feigning a wild abandon she was too wired to achieve authentically. When the distinctive, opening guitar riffs to the song 'Venus' burst from the pool-bar speakers, Ange leapt to her feet, ordering that the music be turned up. She would do anything to distract herself from the uneasy feelings – and that included gyrating her hips in front of the other, unimpressed, poolside drinkers, anointing herself as the song's titular goddess on the mountain top.

I wasn't really drunk enough to dance. I'd been deliberately spilling great slugs of my wine onto the lawn whenever the girls weren't looking. The following day required a clear head – the clearest. But I let my newfound feelings of power carry me onto Ange's makeshift dancefloor. I bounced across that patio, belting out the lyrics, rolling my fists playfully and not so playfully in Ange's face. I was ecstatic, genuinely, because I knew that soon this would all be over.

It was rich then, after I had committed to such enthusiastic dancing, for Ange to rest her head on my shoulder, late into the night when Beth and Binnie were at the bar fetching the last round of drinks, and for her to say: 'You know, Liv, if you weren't so closed-off, it would make you much easier to like.'

Her words were slurred but the delivery of this smuggled-in insult was trademark – she was just being helpful, offering her well-intentioned advice. I returned the gesture.

'And if you weren't such a fucking bitch,' I replied, just as sweet, 'I wouldn't have to push you off a cliff.'

She lifted her head from my shoulder, eyes wide. Mascara clumped her lashes, black speckles travelled down her cheeks. Her pupils skipped left and right trying to hold my gaze. I had her attention – more intensely than ever before, and maybe for the last time. Her advice was spot-on; opening myself up, dropping my mask, it had worked. I was mesmerising.

She broke our stand-off with a peal of laughter. It was a joke, Ange decided, we were just joking. I laughed along. Beth and Binnie demanded to know what was so funny when they returned from the bar.

'Nothing,' said Ange.

'Everything,' I said, in agreement not contradiction, my conscience clear, because you couldn't say I hadn't warned her.

By five-thirty, the morning of the wedding, we were on the deserted coast road in the Sunbeam Alpine, hair whipping our faces, Clara driving, Ivy sitting cross-legged on the thin back seat. This was the farewell trip we'd planned, yet still I sought reassurance the whole way there.

'Aunt Mari knows we're doing this?'

'Yes,' said Clara.

'And we are allowed to be there?'

'Yes! I told you, I own the horses!'

'You own them? How?'

'Well, Daddy does, some of them.'

I didn't raise a challenge to that, but I couldn't see how it was possible to own animals that you only saw for a few days each year. Wasn't there was more to it than stable rent and stumping up for feed?

We pulled into a scruffy yard off an unmade lane. A tall, lean boy just out of his teens, in a washed-out t-shirt, emerged from one of the barns to greet us. With his help, Clara selected and saddled two horses and a pony. My doubts dispersed immediately; those horses did belong to Clara, whether Daddy was paying for them or not. As she led each animal into the paddock, she communed with it, slinging an arm across its withers, resting her cheek against its neck, speaking softly. It was something to behold.

Ivy's pony was dark and elegant. My horse was a dappled white with a shaggy forelock. Clara chose a rebellious colt, one that needed patience and a short rein, else it steered its own course, grazing on every overhanging branch. Clara had been cured, she said, by a horse just like him in rehab in California.

'The same place I learnt Reiki with Priya,' she added.

I didn't remind Clara that she had called it a 'holistic retreat' the first time around. It wasn't exactly a lie, I suppose; rehab too, no doubt, teaches a person that they are more than the sum of their parts. She elaborated on that time as we rode, speaking candidly. Aunt Mari had sent her there, where the therapy involved grooming the horses, mucking them out and feeding them, all the while observing their unpredictable natures and anticipating their impulses – the same thing she needed to do to herself in order to be well.

'And I'm getting there,' she said. 'Slowly. I drink too much, I smoke. And I can still be a little impulsive.' She grinned. 'But compared to who I used to be, you could call it a transformation.'

Our route took us through a village where stray cats licked themselves clean beneath empty washing lines in the early-morning calm. From there, a woodland trail dropped down to the beach. As the sun pierced the horizon, casting everything in a radioactive light, we made tracks across the untouched sand.

Clara unsaddled the horses and we stripped to the swimsuits beneath our shorts and t-shirts, then we led the animals into the waves, up to our waists. You had to grasp at the mane and use the sea's buoyancy to swing a leg onto the horse's bare back – Clara coached us – and once mounted, we rode towards the battlements of a monastery at the far end of the beach, Ivy at the head of our procession.

'Look at her,' I said. A low covering of clouds gathered ceremoniously above my daughter as she rode in perfect harmony with her animal. The vast amber sea was all hers to command. 'She's a warrior,' I said.

'We all are,' replied Clara. 'This is who we're supposed to be.'

I knew what she meant. With my thighs tight against the fine needle coat of my horse, its muscles working hard beneath, driving against the drag of the water, my body adopted the same arrogant, rolling action. We were woman and beast as one.

Clara guided us back to shore, to our dry clothes and to a breakfast of fruit that we ate while sitting out on the rocks. Ivy tended to the horses, guiding melon skins and chunks of apple between their rippling lips, before heading off to skirt the tideline for shells. We watched her in contented silence, and I wondered how to start a conversation about the day ahead.

So, I might have said, *we're really going to do it, then?*

Hell, yes! would have been Clara's reply. *Let's finish this!*

Or else she would have laughed, said, *I wish! But of course not!*

There was deep comfort in this ambiguity. My innocence remained intact. But it was a trick. For it to work, there needed to be not two women inside the box, but a single hypothetical cat – a cat that was both alive and dead. In one universe, I meet Pete and we have Ivy, and in another we miss each other entirely on that train platform twenty years ago. Just like there is a universe where Ange polluted every aspect of my dazzling friendships with Beth and Binnie, and another where Beth never met Ange, never invited her into our fold. That morning, a universe spiralled ahead of us in which Clara helped me to remove the shard of glass from the sole of my foot, and another in which the shard remained, and I learnt to live with the pain. I didn't need to make the choice; it would all happen anyway. So, I kept quiet. Everything that happened on that beach, everything that was said, would endure – I understood that. The scene was so perfect: a stretch of sand to ourselves, the horses scuffing idly beneath the trees, the sun rising hot and fat. Those kinds of moments don't fade, they remain. I sense the possibility of the day. I hear the hush of the sea and the whipping cry of a gull. I feel the cosmos in balance.

When we got back, the hotel was waking up. A woman moved about the raised deck laying towels on the sunbeds with the best views, staking her claim, marking her territory – an everyday act of fear. We made a swift visit to the breakfast buffet where Ivy loaded a plate with mini chocolate croissants to take back to our room. There was packing to do. Our group was catching a flight home the following day.

'We won't have time to do any packing tonight,' I explained to Clara, as we took the steps up to our apartments, 'it'll be too late by the time we get back from the wedding reception.'

Clara looked at me uncertainly. I must have sounded so pragmatic in that moment. I found a smile, a means to signal that I was only speaking that way because Ivy was there. 'No doubt we'll be celebrating long and hard tonight,' I added, with a wink.

I gave Ivy the key card and sent her on ahead. As we watched her go, balancing her plate of croissants, Clara said, 'Do you think you stop yourself from really loving people to avoid the grief you'll feel when they inevitably leave?'

'No,' I said too quickly. The shot had whistled past my ear, caught me off guard. 'I mean, maybe,' I said, correcting my defensiveness. 'I mean, I haven't really thought about it.'

'Alex died,' she said.

'What? Oh, god, Clara, why didn't you say?'

She looked me in the eye. 'Because I killed him.'

I laughed. Clara didn't.

'Are you being serious?' I asked.

She nodded.

'But...' I couldn't land upon the right question to ask. 'But you loved him,' I said.

'What greater reason can there be than that?' she replied sadly, gnomically. It reminded me of the way she'd told me that her mother was dead that first night we spent together in Corfu Town.

I should have pushed for more – *Yes, but why? And how?* – but Clara launched herself at me, clasping me tightly, and my overriding feeling in that embrace was not alarm at what she'd revealed nor a need for answers, but a desire to reassure her. *If only you knew how bad a person I was inside*, I might have said, *then you wouldn't feel so ashamed*. She had chosen to tell me the truth about Alex then, there, as we prepared for the day ahead, to demonstrate yet again how alike we were, how aligned we were.

'I have so loved being with you,' were the words that made it to my lips.

She extricated herself from our hug, gripping me firmly by the shoulders. 'Why are you speaking in the past tense?' she said.

'Sorry.' I grinned. 'I keep forgetting that you're not going to be in that car when it swerves off the road.'

She took a playful swipe at me, before wrapping me in her arms once more. The crook of her neck smelt musky and salty from our morning ride on the beach.

'I am so pleased we found each other,' I said. 'Present tense.'

'And just think of the adventures yet to come,' said Clara. 'Future tense.'

We took a deep breath in unison, then parted.

'Let's do this,' she said.

Or maybe I said that to her.

Two beribboned people carriers arrived to take us from the hotel to the foot of the mountain. One was for the men – for Jason and his best boys, sweating in their suits, along with Kenny, Dev and Pete – and another was for Beth, Binnie and me, plus the remaining kids.

A photographer, a wiry Englishman with a disobedient wisp of hair, captured Jason's departure, skipping from foot to foot as he snapped, beckoning to Brady, Beacon and Duff to look his way, receiving gurning faces and flipped middle fingers in return.

I watched all this from the sidelines, with Ivy, George and Henry, my gaze twitching to the shared patio across the lawn, impatient for Beth and Binnie to appear. A gathering of hotel staff had congregated on the steps of reception. They waved and applauded as the boys were driven away, then turned their expectant stares onto me. The photographer fixed me in his crosshairs, requesting a smile. It was the kind of moment Ange might have engineered to capture me in my guilt.

When Beth and Binnie eventually surfaced, they came running, in coordinated silk separates, hands clutched to their corkscrew fascinators, heels sinking into the grass. Amelia and Paige gambolled in their wake in pale pewter tulle.

'I thought you weren't coming!' I cried.

They were sour-faced.

'What's up?' I asked.

Beth shooed our children towards the gathering of hotel staff – a diversionary tactic. The women crouched and clucked, hands reaching, urging the girls to show off their dresses. The photographer followed, snapping Ivy, Amelia and Paige as they twirled.

We huddled close. Beth used an Accident and Emergency voice. 'Ange says there's no way she's getting into that car.'

This should have been cause for celebration – Clara and I had thrown a spanner into the works of Ange's pantomime wedding, and it had found its target – but my immediate response to Beth's report was to panic.

'She has to get in that car,' I said, 'that's the plan! That's what we decided!'

The girls didn't blink at the ring of alarm in my voice. It was how we'd been trained to react to Ange's every tantrum, as if it were a matter of life or death.

'Oh, god, she's going to call the whole thing off, isn't she?' said Binnie, the fire of panic catching light in her too. 'She's been in a state all morning.'

'You know why, don't you?' said Beth, stoking the flames.

Binnie chewed at her thumbnail, nodding.

I shrugged.

'Because she thinks there's something going on between Jason and Clara!' Beth was breathless with it.

'No way,' I replied, resisting a sudden urge to smile.

Beth and Binnie stared at me, as if I alone knew the way out of this crisis.

'Well,' I said, nodding towards the far side of the lawn, 'we could just ask her?'

Beth and Binnie turned to see what I was seeing: Clara running down the stone steps of her apartment block, dressed in the white vintage Yves Saint Laurent suit. Beneath the deep V of the jacket, she wore nothing except a thin black ribbon tied around her throat. The three of us were open-mouthed at the sight of her striding across the lawn like a 1970s Bianca Jagger.

'Isn't it marvellous?' said Clara, arriving at our side. She tugged at her oversized lapels and struck a pose, as if the suit were a silly Halloween costume, not something so devastatingly sexy.

'You need to put a top on,' snapped Binnie.

Clara coughed out a laugh.

'Ange has the jitters,' I said, by way of an apology for Binnie's directness.

'It's a bit more than the jitters,' said Beth.

I waited for one of them to explain, but they both looked at their feet.

'Ange thinks you're shagging Jason,' I said with a sigh.

'Oh!' said Clara. Her fingers went to the bare skin of her clavicle, a tentative gesture that said, *Who, me?* She looked to Beth and Binnie in turn, eyes wide and innocent, as if they should be rejecting this ridiculous notion on her behalf. When they didn't, she did it herself, by tipping back her head and laughing loudly.

'See?' I said. 'It's complete nonsense.'

'So, I'm thinking,' said Binnie, stern-faced, unmoved by Clara's denial, 'we should just try to hustle Ange into the people carrier with us, get her up the mountain like that.'

'Is there room?' asked Clara coolly. She took in our number, children and all, then craned for a look inside our waiting vehicle, its sliding side-door open, the restless driver perched against the bonnet, smoking.

'She was in a foetal position on the bed when I left,' continued Binnie urgently, as if Clara hadn't spoken. 'She was demanding that I fetch her some camomile tea for her nerves.'

'Couldn't you just stick a bit of vodka in her orange juice?' I said.

Binnie ignored this too, ploughing on. 'Except the hotel doesn't have any camomile tea. I checked. I checked with, like, three different waitresses. I mean, I could walk to the supermarket in the bay, but look at the time! And look how I'm already sweating through this fucking top!' I thought she might cry.

'We go now?' called the driver, stubbing out his cigarette on the ground, interpreting Binnie's raised voice as a call to action. The women on the hotel steps ushered Ivy, Amelia and Paige towards the people carrier. George and Henry ran over too, eager for the best seats. The photographer sprang alive, taking pictures of the children as they clambered aboard.

'No, kids, wait!' yelled Beth, a futile cry. 'Oh, this is a disaster!' she wailed.

'I have camomile tea,' said Clara quietly.

'What?' said Beth.

I caught Clara's eye – and understood immediately. What a gift Ange had handed to us with this, her latest petty demand. A woman who could sink two bottles of Pinot Grigio of an evening would require something much more sedative than camomile tea to settle those pre-wedding nerves.

'Oh, yes!' I said. 'Clara brought some tea with her from home. I had some. It was delicious.'

'Are you serious?' said Binnie, her face threatening to brighten.

'It's loose-leaf,' Clara said, 'and one hundred per cent organic.'

This is how I imagined it would go: Clara would step through the patio doors of the apartment, a sunlit vision in white. *You know there is absolutely nothing going on between Jason and me*, she would say, forthright from the get-go. Ange would scramble from her foetal position, which she had maintained in anticipation of Beth and Binnie returning to her room, never expecting for one moment that they would send beautiful, imperious Clara in their place, someone who would not respond meekly to Ange's outrageous whims. As Clara brewed tea, Ange would put the finishing touches to her hair and make-up before sweeping the remnants of her poor, uncertain bride act beneath the bed. Out would come her childish voice, high and naïve. *I never suggested there was anything going on between Jason and you! Why would I ever believe that?* Then as they made their way across the lawn, en route to the Sunbeam Alpine, Ange would slip seamlessly into some foot-kissing. *Oh my god, I adore your suit, Clara*, she'd fawn. *Where on earth did you find it?*

The men broke from backslapping Jason to cheer our late arrival at the car park at the base of the village.

'Yeah, all right, all right,' said Binnie, in no mood for banter. She gathered up her slinky skirt as she stepped from the vehicle, placing her heels down tentatively on the uneven gravel.

'Just like you to make a grand entrance,' said Pete, greeting me with a kiss.

I pulled back. Had I told him that Ange liked to accuse me of that, or was this a teasing observation of his own? Was it true?

'What's up?' he asked. 'Are you nervous about your reading?'

I had forgotten all about the reading until Beth mentioned it in the people carrier, instantly putting it out of my mind once more, my focus shifting to the twists and turns of the mountain road, the points where the barriers were absent, where the banks of myrtle and gnarly olive broke, offering a place to stop and admire the view, the drop.

'*Je contemple mon feu!*' said Pete with a flourish, the opening line to my poem, the only bit he knew.

I contemplate my fire.

'Yes,' I said. 'All ready to go.' I patted my shoulder bag. Inside were the words to the poem written out on a sheet of hotel note-paper. Except – a stab of thought – were they in my bag or had I left them on the dresser?

'What's wrong?' Pete said.

'Nothing,' I replied. Because it was nothing. I knew most of the poem off by heart; I could make up the rest. Who would notice?

Would we even get that far if Ange refused to get into the Sunbeam Alpine?

Would we get that far even if she did?

My breath shortened at the thought of the car making that tragic trajectory from the cliff edge.

'Are you *sure* you're okay?' asked Pete.

'Yes!' I snapped. 'Stop fussing!' Then, 'Sorry. Maybe I am a bit nervous after all.'

Beth shooed the boys away and they set off on their climb up the dusty path, past the ruins, to the garden on high.

'Here we go then!' said Dev to Jason, delivering another back-slap, before chivvying along George and Henry

'You could still make a run for it, you know!' I heard Kenny say.

As they turned the corner, it struck me.

'But Jason won't see,' I said to Binnie. 'He won't see Ange turn up in the car.'

'Yeah, he can't, can he?' she replied, like it was obvious. 'It's bad luck for the groom to see the bride before she walks down the aisle.'

'Right,' I said.

Ange had insisted that the car was a surprise for Jason; she wanted to impress him with her arrival. But as it was, only us girls – plus a small scattering of tourists – would see the Sunbeam Alpine bank that final corner. Beth, the skilled warm-up artist, had already pounced, briefing any loitering strangers on the wedding, enlisting them in a round of applause for Ange.

The car was never anything to do with Jason – of course it wasn't. It was just another means for Ange to exert control, to get a thing that she wanted, to have me do her bidding. She would no doubt make the most of her time alone with my new friend, find some way to poison Clara's mind against me. The two of them arriving together as confidantes, as comrades, would be a grand entrance to crush all grand entrances that had gone before. I hoped with all my might that Ange never made it up the mountain. I pictured it, the car's trajectory, the crash, then – *Snap!* – the photographer, recently arrived, captured me in these dark thoughts.

'Shouldn't you be up there with the boys,' I said, turning on him, 'getting photos of Jason looking all anxious or something?'

'No!' cried Binnie, tiptoeing swiftly across the gravel to stand between us. 'You need to stay here and get pictures of the car arriving.' As an afterthought, she added, for my benefit maybe, 'For Jason to see. After.'

We waited.

The sun made slices of sweat bleed into the silk of Beth's and Binnie's coordinated separates. It wilted the flowers in the girls' headdresses. After twenty minutes of forbearance, I ushered Ivy, Amelia and Paige into a patch of shade beneath an olive tree.

'No sitting down!' hollered Beth, halting the girls mid-squat, 'those dresses show up every mark.'

I steered them instead towards the café adjacent to the car park – a place they could sit and not get dirty, not faint from heatstroke.

'But you must keep your eye on us,' said Binnie, grudging about this move. 'And you must pay up front, be ready to stand the moment I wave to say the car is coming.'

I nodded, watching Binnie trot back to her lookout spot with Beth. The pair of them shared a packet of tissues, blotting at their foreheads, noses and chins, eager to look perfect for the arrival of their queen. I'll get them back, I thought to myself, the old versions of Beth and Binnie, the ones I loved so much, before they became an extension of Ange, a vector for her neuroses, monkeys to her witch. After today, I thought, it could all be different.

We took a sheltered table, spread with a red-and-white checked cloth. I bought Cokes for the girls and a large glass of wine for myself – something to take the edge off. There was no agreed end point to this plot I'd been brewing with Clara, I was beginning to realise, no way of knowing it was done – no way of knowing *what* had been done. Would the day round off with a definitive bang, or was I to hunker down for the drawn-out uneasiness of a whimper?

As distraction, I quizzed Ivy, Amelia and Paige – what had been their favourite thing from our three weeks on the island? They debated the question with undue seriousness, Amelia nominating herself as spokesperson, selecting as their highlight the kids' club trip to the beach, the day of Ange's proposal, where they had bounced on giant, inflatable platforms tethered out to sea. It was the only thing they'd done alone, without us adults; of course they chose that.

'Why is Ange taking so long?' asked Ivy, puncturing our chatter, seeing it for what it was, a means to deflect.

I checked my watch: we'd been waiting almost an hour.

'It's traditional for a bride to be late,' I told Ivy.

She stared at me, then at my empty glass of wine.

Almost an hour wasn't fashionably late. Ivy wasn't stupid. But did almost an hour mean dead?

Dead.

Conjuring that word, there, then, made me dizzy. The finality of it. I exhaled, long and deep, focusing on my lap, the pattern of dots on Clara's dress, anything to push aside the image of a mangled Sunbeam Alpine lying smoking in the cleft of a ravine.

That wasn't going to happen, I reassured myself. Ange was still sulking in her room. She had been planning this jilting right from the start – that's what was going on here. Clara and I had only helped her along. Because wouldn't that be absolute classic Ange, to have us all get dressed to the nines, trek halfway up a mountain, only for her to cancel the ceremony, the whole thing an elaborate ruse to prove her point – marriage is a superficial display, love is what's real?

This version of events did nothing calm me; it only made me angrier. I was supposed to triumph over Ange, pay her back, not be a pawn in yet more of her intolerable, manipulative bullshit. Clara will have done it, I told myself, really done it. Because why else would she have confessed to killing Alex at the moment we parted that morning? She wanted me to know what she was capable of. She had killed someone she loved; killing Ange, after that, would be easy, simple.

'Do you think I should text her?' said Beth, suddenly at my ear, making me jump. Her make-up had melted into the creases around her eyes, forming unattractive rivulets of beige. 'Or do you think us texting would make Ange cross?'

'Y-yes,' I croaked.

'Yes, I should text or—'

'No. Yes, I think Ange would be cross.'

Beth stood, nodding, convinced – Ange *would* be cross. She would call it nagging or nannying, something similarly unkind. She would punish Beth for her concern. She would… if she weren't already lying in the fireball remains of a car, the red of her blood deepening the colour of that wine-bottle dress. The image thrilled me, and it terrified me, that I could be craving something so wicked.

'Right! More drinks!' I announced, trying to keep things bright for Ivy, Amelia and Paige. They were down to just the ice in the bottom of their glasses. I signalled a waiter.

That was when Duff came scuffing along the path. His shoes, which had been a polished, shiny black when we left the hotel, were now grey with dust. His fringe flopped over one eye.

'Dad said to ask what's happening?' he grunted, making it clear that he had no personal interest in the answer. He slung himself down into a chair. Paige, who was sitting nearest, scooted closer to Ivy.

'Mummy's just running a little bit late,' said Beth with a robot smile.

The boy winced at the word *Mummy* – he was too old for that.

'You know what, Beth,' I said, 'maybe you should text.'

If Ange was jilting Jason, if that was what this day was all about, then why drag things out? Let us progress to the next depressing phase as quickly as possible. We'd descend the mountain to find Ange holding court in her apartment, all of us doomed to play supporting characters in the emotional one-woman show that continued from there.

The new round of drinks was placed in front of us, my twenty-euro note was turned into change. Beth scuttled away to compose a message and I washed down my nauseous combination of bloodlust and fear with more wine. The photographer, who was leaning against one of the wooden posts of the café terrace, that wisp of hair pasted to his forehead, lifted his camera to his eye as I lifted my glass to my lips. I shook my head at him – *you just dare* – and he let the camera hang from his neck once more, too hot and weary to insist.

'Wait,' I said to him. 'Did you see the bride get in the car before you left?'

He said that he had. 'They were going to go for a bit of a drive around the block, so to speak. Lovely car that, isn't it? Michael Caine drives a version in the film—'

I cut him off. 'You're absolutely sure you saw them leave?'

The photographer leant over me, bringing with him the peppery stench of body odour. On the camera's small screen he flicked through the images he'd already taken: Ange posing against the bonnet of the Sunbeam Alpine in her wine-bottle dress, attempting sultry but not quite committing to it. Ange sitting in the passenger seat, her nose buried in her rose bouquet. Then came some close-ups of Clara behind the wheel, chin high, her confident model eye connecting with the lens. Finally, a shot of the Sunbeam Alpine exiting through the hotel gates.

Acid stung my throat; my breath quickened again. The photographer had arrived at the base of the village not that long after us.

That meant Clara and Ange had been 'driving around the block' for well over an hour.

Beth returned to the table.

'Should we be looking at those photos,' she said, 'before Ange does, I mean?'

'Did you text?' I asked.

She nodded solemnly. 'No answer.'

Ange was not someone who did not reply when she had some burning personal drama to impart. It was done. It had to be. My thoughts swung to Clara. Was she okay? Suddenly, it was *her* body I was picturing in the wreckage, blood staining her bright white suit. The image, vivid and frightening, crowded out all the other images from before.

'I think,' I said, 'that someone should—'

'Oh my god!' cried Binnie.

We snatched our heads around. She was standing in the look-out spot in the car park, shielding her eyes from the sun, peering down at the hills below. 'Did you hear that?' she asked.

'Hear what?' I stood too quickly, jolting the photographer, my chair tipping backwards and banging onto the concrete floor.

'Watch it!' he said.

'Hear what?' I yelled it this time.

'Like a long rumble,' said Binnie.

'A rumble like what?' I was doing everything I could not to sound frantic.

'How many glasses of wine have you had, Liv?' asked Beth.

'It sounded like thunder,' said Binnie. 'Do you think a storm is coming?'

'Oh, no!' wailed Beth. 'A storm would be the absolute worst thing that could happen right now.'

I barked out something approximating a laugh, then I walked away from the café, unable to bear it any longer.

'Where are you going?' Beth called after me, and I felt the echo of that night when I'd fled the restaurant at the bay. I wasn't afraid of meeting a snake this time, though, because I knew the snake was me.

'I'm going to go and find them,' I told her.

It was good to hit tarmac, to be moving, to be playing an active part in this now.

Whatever this was.

The soles of my ballet flats were thin and slid on the descent. I felt every stone beneath my feet, each one a small punishment.

A vehicle approached, making its climb to the ruins, slowing as it passed me. I saw my reflection in the glass of the driver's window – a wide-eyed woman alone, wearing her finest, skirting the verge of a mountain road in 30-degree heat. My hair clung wetly to my neck. I gave the driver and his passengers a smile that said, *I'm fine, everything's fine, this is completely normal.* But my head was spinning – from the exertion, from the two glasses of wine, from the growing dread of what I was about to find.

Clara was dead.

That was the image stuck in my mind, taunting me. Because wouldn't it be absolute classic Ange for her to evade all attempts on her life, only for Clara to plummet from the cliff edge instead? The pulsing drone of the insects in the undergrowth became the whine of Ange's fake concern: *I'm sorry but I don't think I'll ever forget the sound of that crash.*

I would not let this day be all about her. Not like that. I picked up my pace. I was running, breathless, desperate. I couldn't tell you now how long it took. Seconds became minutes, minutes became hours, and as soon as I spied a flash of white between the trees on an outward curve of the road, time stuttered back to full speed; it went too fast.

A small track split away, dense prickly bushes growing on both sides. I slithered down that precarious slope, falling, swearing, finding at the bottom a small platform, a lookout, and standing on it – Clara, her back to me, the tails of her white jacket kicking gently in the breeze, mistress of all she surveyed. Below her was the vast, wooded valley. Beyond that, a pearly glimpse of the Ionian Sea.

'Oh, thank god!' I barrelled into her, hugging her on impact, almost knocking her from that ledge and carrying us both to our dramatic end. 'I'm so relieved you're okay.'

'Of course I'm okay!' Clara was amused by this show of emotion – she was confused. 'Whyever would I not be?'

'Because, because…' My voice rose, frantic still from all the terrible scenes I'd played on a loop in my mind. Clara stopped me with a finger to her lips. She gestured behind me.

I turned to see – the Sunbeam Alpine, intact.

And in the passenger seat, slumped low, asleep, Ange.

'Oh my god,' I said.

I edged closer to the car, my insides plummeting.

Clara spoke with delight. 'She's zonked! Totally off with the fairies!'

Ange's mouth was wide open, tongue lolling, her expression bovine. The skin on her forehead, cheeks and décolletage was so sunburnt it was almost as red as her wine-bottle dress. One of her bra-less breasts was attempting to lurch free.

'If only that photographer were here now,' said Clara. She mimicked his speech, 'Shall we try something sultry, Angela? Or maybe something a bit, I dunno, romantic?' She laughed, a tinkling cascade of glee.

I couldn't find the requisite feeling to join in.

'Don't worry,' Clara said, tuning into my distress. 'It can affect some people like this. And I did make it especially strong. Ange had none of the swirling lights; just went straight to blackout.' Clara came to stand beside me. She bumped her shoulder amiably against mine. 'She'll be back to her usual self in no time.'

'And then what?'

Clara's smile wavered. 'What do you mean?'

Ange had begun to snore. A silvery trail of saliva at the corner of her mouth was turning crusty in the sun. It was pleasing to see

246

her like that, degraded, humiliated. It was edifying, yes, but it was temporary. Soon Ange would wake up, go back to her usual self, and then...

'She's going to know we did this to her,' I said.

'Well, yes,' replied Clara. 'Wasn't that the idea?'

'But she mustn't,' I said, my terror reaching a new peak. 'She can't know that we did this, because Beth and Binnie will take her side and then they won't want to be friends with me anymore.'

'Oh, Liv,' said Clara, reaching out and stroking my arm, 'I don't know why you want to be friends with those two women anyway. Time after time they have chosen this monster over you and—'

I snatched my arm away. 'Why would you say that?'

'Because you deserve better, Liv.' Clara gave me a look so pitying that I had the urge to punch her, to scratch her face.

'You said you were going to do it,' I said by way of retaliation.

Clara was disorientated. 'Said I was going to do what?'

My hand glided through the air. I whistled the car's trajectory, finishing with a sibilant, 'Crash!'

Clara laughed, halting when she saw that I was deadly serious. 'You really thought I was going to do that?'

'Yes.'

'But why would I—'

'Because she's a monster, like you said. And because you're my friend. Like you said!'

'Your friend, sure.' Clara took a step back. 'But someone I just met. Someone I met on holiday and...' She spoke as if being taped, as if she needed to put her distance from me on record. 'You do know that was a game, right?' she said. 'When we talked about revenge, you knew that wasn't real? Please tell me you didn't believe in all of that?'

I slowly shook my head at her, hot tears spilling, stinging my sunburnt cheeks. *Do you think you stop yourself from really loving people to avoid the grief you'll feel when they inevitably leave?* No, I'd said when Clara asked me that question. It was the truth. I never did stop myself. I fell for Gabi, for Beth and Binnie, for Ange, for Clara, all in the same way, two-footed, destined from the start to be disappointed.

247

'But you killed Alex,' I said in the voice of a child, one overlooked and neglected, 'and you loved him – so how hard can this be?'

'I killed him with heroin!' Clara shouted it, like I was stupid, like it was infuriating to her that she must spell it out. 'I was using, I got Alex hooked on it and then it killed him. That's why Uncle Philip can't stand to have me around anymore.'

I let this sink in.

'So… you lied,' I said.

'What?' She looked appalled.

'You told me that you killed him just to show off.'

Clara took another step back, several. She raised her palms – a gesture of innocence, of reasonableness, of the boundary she was drawing between us. 'I get it, Liv, you're upset. And I'm also going to suggest that you're a little bit drunk, and that is not the best combination for—'

'I can hear you.'

We both shrieked, skittering away from the car.

Ange had woken up. Her eyes were open, the irises rolled back. She attempted to lift her head, but the effort was too much. Her chin fell hard against her chest, her teeth champing together with a sound that made me flinch.

'I can hear you,' Ange groaned again, 'you, you, you, you…'

Clara and I froze, our attention trained on her muttering lips, poised for Ange's next movement. The cicadas in the undergrowth provided a persistent, see-sawing note of tension, as if what needed to happen next was ever in question.

'Help me lift her,' I said. I was playing an active part in this now. And I knew what *this* was. I made for the car.

Clara didn't move. 'Lift her where?'

'Into the driver's seat.'

'No!' came Clara's definite reply. She understood where I was going; I was picking up the pieces of the plot we'd agreed beneath the ancient fig tree. 'I won't,' she said, 'and you mustn't either. I won't let you.'

Yet she made no attempt to stop me. She stayed rooted behind that invisible boundary she'd drawn between us. I opened the driver-side door and, kneeling on the seat, leant over to get a purchase on Ange, sliding my hands beneath her damp armpits. This physical contact revived her once more.

'What are you doing?' Ange slurred, her eyes gluey, drool dripping from her chin.

She was heavy in her stupor, slippery with sweat.

I yelled to Clara, 'Go round to the other side and give her a shove.'

'Please, Liv, come on,' Clara begged. 'Let's just talk this through.'

There was no time for that. The others would arrive soon. Pete would be sent down to the car park after Duff. Beth would tell him where I'd gone. They couldn't find us like this. I heaved Ange's uncooperative weight, grunting with the exertion, managing to shift her halfway across the soft armrest between the two front seats. I paused, gasping for breath, for a renewal of energy. Ange was on her side, knees jammed up against the gear stick. She gargled a curse, a threat to kill me, but she was powerless to fight back; her limbs were like lead.

'I'm telling you, you don't want this hanging over you,' said Clara.

'It won't hang over me,' I spat back, 'because it will look like an accident, and no one will ever know. And then I can go home to my friends. My real friends, not someone I just met on holiday.'

The insult didn't touch her.

'But *you* will know,' she said. 'You will know you did it. That's what will haunt you.'

'I can live with that,' I replied. I could. I knew who I was now – I was an animal following its natural instincts. I grabbed hold of Ange once more and, with a roar of effort, dragged her into the driver seat, the wine-bottle dress snagging on the gear stick, tearing loudly. I fastened the seatbelt across her chest to keep her in place, to fit the story.

'My dress,' moaned Ange, her concerns petty even in this moment, 'my dress, my dress.'

I stood and faced Clara. Tears were coursing down her freckled cheeks now. The ribbon around her neck had slipped free from its bow, the knot askew. She was reduced, nothing but a lost dog, an orphaned pup.

'Where are the keys?' I said.

She shook her head with a whimper. I grasped her by the shoulders, putting my face close to hers.

'There is no going back from this,' I told her, enunciating every word, making it very clear. 'You drugged her and then you kidnapped her for, what, nearly two hours? She's heard everything we said. You think Ange is just going to laugh that off? You think we won't both be arrested? Locked up?'

Clara's body shuddered with sobs.

Ange gave a wretched cry of rebellion from the driver's seat of the car. She'd regained some kind of movement in her arms and was pawing pathetically at her seatbelt, at the door handle.

'The keys!' I yelled.

Clara drooped in my grip, feigning collapse – and I took advantage. I snatched at her jacket, thrusting my hand into the pocket that hung heavier than the other, taking what I needed. She found her fight then, lunging for me, trying to get back what I'd stolen. We scuffled in the dirt, Clara's hands clamped over mine, her nails sharp in her effort to prise open my grip on the keys.

'Stop,' I said, 'there's no time for this!'

But she didn't stop, she wouldn't let go and I was furious with her – for pretending, for lying, for not doing what she said she would, for not being my friend. I placed my mouth on the soft exposed skin of her wrist and I bit down.

Clara screamed as she leapt away.

'So, you were driving up the mountain when Ange insisted you pull over so she could have a go behind the wheel,' I said, making my voice firm, steady.

'What?' said Clara, clutching her wrist, keeping her distance.

'Come on,' I said, 'this bit's familiar, you helped me come up with it.'

'No.'

'Yes,' I countered, reaching past Ange, who was hanging heavy against her seatbelt once more, exhausted by her pitiful attempts at escape. I thrust the key into the ignition and turned back to Clara, spoke quickly. 'You were unsure about letting Ange drive because she seemed a bit giddy, but you just put that down to it being her wedding day. You never realised in a million years she'd actually taken something!' I gave that line some suggested emotion – astonishment. Clara was an actress, I'd seen it from the start, I knew she could pull this off.

'This isn't right, Liv,' Clara pleaded. 'You know that.'

'Anyway, you got out of the car and Ange shuffled across to the driver side. But before you could get in—' I leant down and started the engine. It needed to be running; this needed to look real. The growl of the car summoned more curses from Ange – oaths that morphed into pleas. 'No, no,' she mumbled, 'no, no, no.'

I shut out the sound. I refused to feel sorry for her. I finished the story.

'And maybe Ange only meant it as a momentary joke, maybe she wasn't really going to leave you all alone on this lookout, but she misjudged the gears, chose forward instead of reverse, and—'

We both knew the ending.

'I won't say any of that!' said Clara with renewed vigour. She launched herself at me one final time, flinging her arms around my waist, pulling me backwards, away from the car. 'Please! Just think of Ivy!' she wailed.

'Always,' was my level reply. 'And you must think of Aunt Mari and your family, their trust, your recovery.'

Clara let go – a surrender. She sank to her haunches, her head in her hands. I bent over the driver's door and reached for the handbrake. Unlike Clara, I hadn't forgotten where it was. Ange's head lolled against the steering wheel, one eye open, the pupil dilated. What did she see in that moment, I wonder – parasite or host, victim or perpetrator, predator or prey?

All it takes is one big breath, a second of courage. I released the brake, took a strong grip on the door frame and shoved that car forward with the last vestiges of my rage. I watched the trees swallow the Sunbeam Alpine, as easily as the sea might absorb a joyful body leaping from a jetty.

I waited for the satisfying *crash*.

6.

When we were sorting through boxes in preparation for our move to the coast, I found Ivy's project book from Corfu. On the last page was a felt-tip drawing of a snake curled into a perfect circle, its tail inside its own mouth. According to Ivy's neat, joined-up handwriting below, this was an ouroboros, an ancient Egyptian symbol used to represent the cyclical nature of reincarnation. She had copied out some words on the subject, describing how a soul never dies, it just moves on, transmigrating into another body, another creature, over and over, until one day, the soul is so enlightened by this journey, it transcends.

Beneath that, were her last words in the book.

Nose-horned vipers sometimes eat other Nose-horned vipers.

I was pinioned by this line, gripped by the need to know exactly when Ivy had written it. Was it before or after? Was she some kind of soothsayer who had seen it all coming, or was this Ivy's piercing commentary on the terrible actions of the adults in her life on that fateful day? I couldn't come up with a way to broach the topic that wouldn't provoke suspicion or more questions from my inquisitive, intuitive daughter. So, in the end, I threw the book away. I told myself Ivy was probably just writing about snakes.

The first debrief after the holiday happened around Beth's kitchen island, the surface of which was a black, glittery marble, not varnished wood. The same but different.

'I'm sorry but I don't know how I am able to exist day-to-day right now,' she said, as an apology for not properly chilling the wine. 'I'll be doing something totally normal, and then I'll think, oh, I must ask Ange about that, and then I'm useless, done for.'

She started crying. Binnie joined in. I pushed out my bottom lip as I stroked Beth's back, all the while thinking, *You don't need to do this anymore, girls, she isn't watching, she isn't here to check.*

But, in a sense, she was.

This epiphany arrived with the handful of wedding photos, sent over as digital files with the photographer's deepest sympathies.

Binnie clutched our hands in a kind of group prayer before lifting the lid on her laptop.

'Big breath, girlies,' she said.

We pored over those photos for hours, Beth and Binnie crooning admiration for Ange in every picture, even the awful ones where she had her eyes half shut. This murmured worship continued for the pictures of the three of us waiting in the car park beneath the old village.

'We were so innocent then,' said Binnie, 'no clue what was about to hit us.'

'And how perfect you looked in that polka-dot dress, Liv,' said Beth.

I had thought it perfect too, at the time, but in the pictures I clearly looked frumpy. Ange would have had the balls to point this out. *I'm sorry but I'm just not sure about a dress with an empire line; there's something very ageing about that sort of fit, isn't there?* Her baby voice would have kicked in then, shielding her from all charges of being a bitch. *Oh, I'm not saying Liv looks old!! I'm not saying that. I'm just saying I wouldn't choose that fit for myself.*

Ange wasn't dead. She lived on in us stronger than ever. I was compelled to conjure up her every caustic comment, and Beth and Binnie were bound to display their everlasting devotion. It didn't matter that Ange wasn't there anymore. And at the same time, it did. With just Beth and Binnie for company, the people they had become, the people they resolutely were now, I was bored. When Beth's next invitation to meet around her kitchen island arrived, I replied: *I have to work. Sorry.* The ticks appeared against my message, turned blue, and that was that. I tried not to dwell too much on how easy it had been – how easy it would always have been – just to walk away.

I still work in a coffee shop, part-time, for now. Pete and I kid ourselves that our move to the coast was a clean break, a fresh start, but it's remarkable how often I'll serve someone whose face is familiar from that leafy little commuter town we once called home. They come here on holiday, for a break from it all, to a place that's different but not too different. We really are locked in the same loops, walking the same predictable paths. Sometimes I'll see it flicker across their eyes, a suggestion that they recognise me too, and I wonder if they are annoyed to have travelled half-way across the country only to find me steaming the milk for their lattes. Did they think their trip was startlingly original, uniquely curated? I also wonder how precisely these people remember me. Sometimes, I hope that they will ask: *Weren't you friends with that woman who had the terrible accident on her wedding day in Corfu?* It would gift me the opportunity to say her name again, out loud, feel the seditious shape of it in my mouth. *What, Ange?*

They would relay to me everything they'd heard on the local grapevine about her tragic death, all the mawkish details from that *Mail Online* article about how she was such a wonderful mother and partner, such a wonderful friend. It would take everything I had not to set them straight.

She was actually a fucking bitch, I'd say, *that's why I had to push her off that cliff.*

But no one has asked, yet.

Mostly what I imagine in idle moments between customers, as I wipe down the espresso machine, buffing my reflection to a shine in the stainless steel, is how things might have been different.

Because there was no satisfying *crash*. Not in my universe.

In another version of this cosmos, the Sunbeam Alpine draws a graceful curve around the last bend, pulling into the car park below the old village with its engine purring. The tourists applaud and Ange smiles, waving like the Queen.

I picture Clara, the chauffeur, springing from the driver's seat to run gallantly around to the passenger door to open it, one hand tucked behind her back in a display of subservience. Ange steps out, stunning in her wine-bottle dress, curtseying for her audience as the photographer dances and clicks.

When we begin our ascent to the garden, that's when Ange's smile fades.

'For fuck's sake,' she rages, now that we are out of earshot of the applauding tourists. 'I can barely walk in this dress – and look at the state of my fucking hair! It's totally wrecked.' Ange makes it noisily clear that Clara's terrible driving is to blame, not the very physics of travelling in an open-top car.

I turn to Clara and say, 'I think you can go now. You've served your purpose.'

She double-takes. Am I being serious? I nod, getting my rejection in first. Though really, I am being generous; I am giving Clara the chance to walk away, bright white in that suit, unsullied.

Beth and Binnie, meanwhile, scramble for tail combs and hair grips, prodding at Ange's hair, grooming her like monkeys. I stand aside because I know the alpha well. Her rage is not yet spent.

'Get off me!' Ange spits, and she bats the girls away, catching Beth as she does – only slightly; it's a little nothing, hardly worth mentioning, but Beth's neck bears a bloody scratch, and it is not apologised for. Ange switches her focus then to the sweaty creases at the front of her dress, attacking them with sharp flicks with the back of her hand.

'Ugh, look at me,' she groans, 'I'm melting.'

At this point, I like to fast forward to the ceremony on the impossibly green lawn at the top of the village. In this version of events, in this universe, we make it there. I do my reading in French – not the morose Jules Laforgue poem, but a sensual piece by Victor Hugo. Our small, intimate congregation is rapt as I talk of lips pressed to full cups and of the sweet perfume of passion. When I get to the part about never growing old, about a flower within the soul that will never bloom, a tear rolls down my cheek. A tear rolls down Ange's cheek too. We are in sync. The charm she wears around her neck glints, blinding me momentarily, but still, I see it, stirring in the grass. It is grey and scaly. I know it by the horn at the end of its nose.

'Don't move,' I hiss, breaking from my poem. Ange freezes, the congregation too. They swallow their gasps for fear of spooking the creature.

I coach Ange to look at me, to remain still, to take deep breaths, as the viper winds its slow path past her open-toed shoes. It tests the air with its tongue, then it slips beneath the pompom-laden branches of a hydrangea bush.

There is no *crash* in this universe either, but there is satisfaction.

'You saved me,' Ange says, her attention on me, only me.

And it is like the sun, the warmth of her, that light.

ACKNOWLEDGEMENTS

Thank you to Louise for convincing me that this was the story I needed to tell; to Thom and Philippa for reading and commenting on early iterations of the manuscript; and to Lilidh, Grace, Alison and the whole Bloomsbury team for their confident editorial steer. Knowing what (and who) to cut, and when, is a skill you don't stop learning.

A NOTE ON THE AUTHOR

JULIE MAYHEW is the author of the critically acclaimed 2019 thriller *Impossible Causes* and four Carnegie-nominated novels for young adults, including *The Big Lie*, which won the Sidewise Award for Alternate History. She has written both drama and short stories for BBC Radio 4, and now also writes and directs for the screen.

A NOTE ON THE TYPE

The text of this book is set in Linotype Sabon, a typeface named after the type founder, Jacques Sabon. It was designed by Jan Tschichold and jointly developed by Linotype, Monotype and Stempel in response to a need for a typeface to be available in identical form for mechanical hot metal composition and hand composition using foundry type.

Tschichold based his design for Sabon roman on a font engraved by Garamond, and Sabon italic on a font by Granjon. It was first used in 1966 and has proved an enduring modern classic.